CIRCLE OF LIES

PAUL J. TEAGUE

PROLOGUE

1984: Sandy Beaches Holiday Camp

The knock at the door came just after midnight. It was too late for a social call, even at a holiday camp which barely slept at night.

Jenna had been expecting it all day. She still couldn't believe what she'd done. It was already more than twenty-four hours ago, yet the nervous exhaustion that had set in was every bit as intense as when she'd watched the life slipping away from him.

Had he really gone? It didn't seem real. She'd covered him in rubble, concealing the body, expecting him to leap up and grab her by her throat at any moment. If he did, he'd break it like a twig; his hands were so powerful. She'd felt those same hands caressing her body, touching her gently with affection and desire in the early stages of their relationship. But it had soon become clear that Bruce Craven was the kind of man a woman should avoid.

Jenna had spent the day like a stunned bull, waiting for

the final act of slaughter, knowing it would be coming soon, but not sure when. It was an adrenaline-fuelled cocktail of fear, relief and exhilaration. She'd escaped him at last, but at what cost to herself? Was the danger of being found out, the risk of prison, any better than living with his dark, oppressive presence? She'd dug her own hole with Bruce and happily jumped into it. She'd even begun to pull the mud in on herself, right up to neck height.

But when the opportunity presented itself, she decided to fight back and dig her way out; she believed she'd killed him. She'd tried to put an end to the violent bully who'd trapped her in an abusive relationship. And in doing so, the three of them had created a circle of lies and deceit. Only she knew what had truly happened. Only she had watched the entire tragedy playing out. Yet somehow—incredibly—Bruce had handed in his resignation and supposedly walked out of the holiday camp. How could that be?

She'd spent much of the day considering treachery. She could blame it on Will; she could pin it on Charlotte. If the police came, asking questions, she could deflect all the blame. Nobody saw what she saw. They had all killed Bruce Craven; all three of them had played their part. Charlotte struck him with a stone, Will strangled him with his bare hands, and she just finished the job they'd bungled. He was a formidable man; he took some killing. He must be dead.

There was another knock at the door: impatient, more aggressive. Was this the police? Was her time up? Had they found Bruce's body in the foundations of the paddling pool, hauling it out of the newly poured concrete before it had time to set? Was he really alive and had he reported them all to the police? Maybe somebody saw what she did.

Perhaps they weren't the only ones wandering through Sandy Beaches Holiday Camp in the dead of night.

Jenna had run through the scenarios several times. It was easiest to blame it on Will. He wouldn't let Charlotte take the blame for her part in Bruce's assault. She'd done it in self-defence, after all. Bruce was trying to rape her on the beach. Any woman would have done the same thing if the opportunity had presented itself.

As for Will, he'd gone to see if Bruce needed help but, like the feral animal he was, Bruce had attacked him. She'd been terrified as she watched Bruce's pursuit of Will from her hiding place behind the gorse bush. The power and speed of the man was enough to paralyse anybody with fear. There was no doubt about it; it had been self-defence for Will, too.

So, if she removed herself from the equation, her two friends would be charged with manslaughter at the very worst. They'd likely get off without a sentence, particularly if they told the court the truth about what had happened. And if Bruce was still alive? Who knew how he'd take his revenge?

As Jenna had searched her soul that day, she found that when push came to shove, she was lacking in the moral fibre that her parents had tried to instil in her. After all, in the eyes of the law, she was what Charlotte and Will were not. Jenna Phillips was a murderer. At least, she'd intended to murder Bruce.

She hadn't finished off Bruce Craven in self-defence. She'd taken that last, agonised breath from him because she hated the man. She could no longer face the rough way he forced himself on her in bed, and the constant, erosive comments about her appearance and her behaviour, knowing that she simply did not have the courage to walk away. Bruce Craven had to be stopped. Jenna could see no other way out.

Yes, she would happily throw her friends under the bus to avoid prison, if it came to that. The thought of the police coming to question her, taking her down to the station for fingerprints and those terrible prisoner photos that she'd seen on the TV and in the papers; the fear and shame of it all consumed her.

In the twenty-four hours or so since she thought Bruce Craven had drawn his last breath, Jenna had learned some harsh truths about herself. She was a coward, treacherous, preferring to see her friends suffer rather than have to go through the process of facing justice for Bruce Craven's attack. If this was the police at the door, she'd deny everything and point the finger at her friends.

There was a third knock. Someone was leaning against the door, trying to force it open. She'd have to answer it now; if she didn't, it sounded like they were coming in anyway. Would the police behave like that?

She looked at the LED alarm clock at the side of the bed. It was Bruce's. Ten minutes past midnight. Bruce had supposedly left a letter with the admin department saying he was quitting his job at the holiday camp without notice. Jenna hadn't a clue how that had happened or who'd written that note. There was no way Bruce Craven was alive when she left him in the foundations of that pool and, even if by some twist of fate he'd survived, he hadn't come back to his room to collect his things.

Jenna walked up to the door and twisted the small handle on the Yale lock. Before she'd even completed the motion, two men burst into the room. One of them pushed his hand against her neck and propelled her over to the bed, lifting her up from the floor momentarily and throwing her down onto the mattress.

The other checked that they hadn't been seen, quietly closed the door, then locked it. He stood in front of the entrance, blocking it with his massive frame.

Jenna drew breath to scream. The first man sat on the bed, his substantial weight compressing the mattress so that she rolled towards him. He put his finger to his mouth and indicated that she should be quiet.

From a sheath attached to his belt, he removed a large knife with serrations at the tip; the type a hunter might be seen with in an American movie. Slow and deliberate in his movements, he gently pressed the knifepoint into her groin, then ran it up to her stomach, moving to her neck, then bringing it level with her eyes.

'Such pretty eyes,' he said.

Jenna was motionless on the bed. With only three words, she knew they were more dangerous than Bruce.

'Where is Bruce Craven?' the man asked. His voice was steady and regulated, approaching the intimidation of Jenna in much the same way as she'd place a cup of tea in front of one of her customers in the dining hall. To him, it was all in a day's work.

He placed his free hand on her thigh and moved it towards her groin, working underneath her nightshirt so he was in direct contact with her flesh. His skin was smooth, but his hands were fat and threatening. She flinched.

'Where's Bruce Craven?' he asked again.

Jenna tried to speak, but her throat was dry and taut; the words wouldn't come.

The man moved his hand up a little further. Jenna tensed again, fearful for what was coming.

'I don't know,' she managed to say.

'Where's Bruce Craven?' the man said again, as if this was the extent of his vocabulary.

His hand was now gently massaging just below her groin, the knife perilously close to her right eye.

'No, please,' Jenna pleaded. 'I don't know. We argued last night. He never came back to the room. I've been waiting for him all day. Everybody says he left the holiday camp and went back home. Ask the people in the admin block. He left a letter. He never came back, I promise.'

'Who saw what happened?' the second man asked. His voice was deep and gravelly; she'd never heard one like it before. It was as if he'd had some kind of throat problem in the past.

'Nobody, I swear. We argued in the pub last night and he stormed out. I thought I'd find him here, but he wasn't in the room when I got back. I assumed he'd stayed in a friend's room, maybe even gone with another woman. I waited all night. When I went to work this morning, everybody was talking about it. Bruce Craven just quit. He went back home. It's a pretty shitty place to work; we just assumed he'd thrown the towel in. That's it, that's all I know.'

In the few minutes of the exchange, her nightshirt had become sodden with sweat.

The man with the abrasive voice moved closer to Jenna. She stayed on the bed, not daring to move for fear of the knife.

'If you see Bruce Craven, tell him we're looking for him. We're not finished with him yet. And if I find out you're lying... have you ever been with two men before? That look on your face tells me no. Well, we'll be back if we find you're lying to us. And next time we might even bring a friend. It'd be a shame not to make the most of a nice girl like you. Especially before we remove your skin and throw it in the waste paper basket.'

Jenna closed her eyes tight shut, like she used to when she was five years old, to repel the bogey man in the dark. She kept them closed for ten minutes after they'd left her room. She had never known fear like it in her life. But it was a fear that would find her once again, many years later.

CHAPTER ONE

Day One: Tuesday

There was an effusive round of applause as Barry McMillan finished his question-and-answer session at the Midland Hotel. He'd pulled a large crowd; as the homecoming hero, it was only to be expected.

Charlotte was a recent convert to his novels, having lived in Morecambe for almost a year. The residents always spoke of Barry McMillan with pride, as the local boy made good. He'd risen from the boy who used to get his short stories published in magazines to the man who'd snared a big-time publisher with his compelling historical fiction based in that part of Lancashire.

Charlotte liked the books because they were bodice-rippers. The historical dimensions were purely secondary to her. Judging from the size of the largely female audience, she wasn't alone. She suspected Barry McMillan's female-friendly and highly erotic love scenes were the real source of his literary success, not the historical accuracy or sharp definition of the local landscape, as the dreary man who'd introduced him had claimed.

Even better, Charlotte had exclusive access. For some unknown reason, the author had chosen to stay in her guest house for the night, rather than availing himself of the luxury and elegance of the Midland Hotel, the art deco jewel in the crown along Morecambe's sea front.

Charlotte and Will were making their business work, beginning to feel like a part of Morecambe's furniture. When she attended events like this one, spotting people that she knew well or at least recognised, it made her believe that their life was now firmly secured in the resort. Olli was settled at school and had a lovely girlfriend. Will wasn't so happy in his job, but he was getting by and bringing in his share of the cash. And she had escaped from teaching and found a rhythm at the guest house which suited her. Isla had played an important part in that.

'Fancy a Prosecco, Isla?' Charlotte asked. 'My treat; it's the least I can do, considering you saved those sausages from burning tonight. I'm sorry, I was completely distracted. I got carried away talking to our friend over there.'

'I can't blame you,' Isla smiled. 'Did you read the boudoir scene in his latest book? It made me blush. I didn't dare mention it to George; I wouldn't want to make him feel inadequate.'

Charlotte burst out laughing. 'I'm saving the new book for the weekend, when I can sneak some time on my own. I'll make sure Will is elsewhere when I get to that bit. I swear he can detect my face flushing from a hundred metres when I'm reading the naughty bits!'

Charlotte stood up and made her way along to the end

of the row to reach the bar. There was a long queue already, but the bar staff had poured the Prosecco in readiness for the rush, and were serving as swiftly as was humanly possible.

'Good to see you here, Charlotte. How are you?'

She recognised the voice straight away. It was Nigel Davies, from the local newspaper. He wasn't a friend, as such. But after what had happened at the holiday camp, she felt like they were bound by something more than just a casual acquaintance.

'Are you here for work or for pleasure?' Charlotte said with a smile.

'I'm not sure I ever go anywhere entirely for pleasurable purposes,' Nigel replied. He'd foregone a Prosecco and opted for a soft drink instead. Charlotte paid the barmaid and picked up a glass in each hand.

'I always seem to pick up some titbit of information when I come to events like this' Nigel said. 'However, it is primarily for pleasure. Barry McMillan is a bit of a local hero to all of us, I suppose. He gives off a hint of possibility that we might all make it one day. And secretly, I'd quite like to write a book.'

'It won't be a bodice-ripper like Barry's, will it?' Charlotte teased.

'I doubt it,' Nigel replied, his cheeks colouring a little. 'I'm more likely to write crime or real-life stories, I think. I'll leave the adoring female audience to Mr McMillan.'

They exchanged smiles and Charlotte made her way back to Isla. The majority of the seats had cleared now, and Barry McMillan was surrounded by fans seeking an autographed copy of his latest book and a selfie with the great man.

'Must be nice, mustn't it?' Isla asked as she took her glass from Charlotte. 'To know that whatever you do, there'll always be people who appreciate it and adore you. I wonder what the real Barry McMillan is like. I'll bet he's had to fight his way to the top of the tree. It won't all be sweetness and light, I'm sure.'

Charlotte looked at Isla, surprised to hear her speaking that way.

'Well, I know it's not the same, but that's the way Will and I feel about you and George. It's been almost six months, and we couldn't have got the guest house running so well without you. I'm so grateful for everything you've done for us. And look at George: handyman, occasional barman, kitchen help and general good egg. We couldn't be happier. Thank you, Isla. Here's to us!'

They chinked glasses, and Charlotte took a large gulp of Prosecco.

'I'm certain this stuff makes me feel light-headed the moment my mouth comes in contact with it, but this is a nice one. I'll have to see if I can get a couple of bottles for our lounge bar from the cash and carry.'

The evening passed slowly after the main interview on stage, and the line for autographs seemed to take forever to die down. Isla had left some time ago, Nigel looked like he'd made his escape, and the crowds were dwindling, if persistent. By the time Barry McMillan was finally ready to leave, she'd drunk three glasses of fizz. She was beginning to regret having agreed to wait for him so he could escort her back to the guest house. A combination of alcohol and a long day changing the bedding in all the rooms had worn her out, and she was ready for bed.

Although she wanted to pounce on Barry and guide him out the moment he'd signed his last book, she gave him a wide berth, allowing him to go through some pleasantries with the organisers and hotel staff first. Somebody had left a copy of Barry's book on one of the chairs, so she absent-mindedly began to flick through the pages, scanning for the scene which Isla had mentioned earlier.

When she looked up, Barry had gone. She placed the book back as she'd found it and looked around the room. As she stood up, she realised Barry had gone outside; she could see him through the windows of the dining area. He was on his phone, obviously shouting at somebody. He'd been cool, calm and collected since the moment he checked into the guest house. Charlotte wondered what could possibly perturb a man in his position.

Then she thought of the attitude and outbursts they'd had from Lucia over the past few weeks. Barry was probably suffering at the hands of hormone-fuelled teenagers, just like any other parent. Being an author didn't give him a *Get out of jail free* card.

White-faced and agitated, Barry stepped back inside. There were only a few people left in the room, most of them waiting staff, so he homed in on Charlotte immediately. The worried look changed to a professional smile, and he strode up to her, apologising for keeping her back so long.

'It's no problem. I'm just pleased that your event went so well.'

Barry McMillan seemed distracted as they walked along the illuminated promenade back to the guest house, accompanied only by the sound of the waves swishing gently on the sand and the cries of seagulls nesting on nearby roofs. Charlotte attempted several conversational topics, but each time Barry let the embers fade and die.

He was probably exhausted, keen for some quiet time. It was the same for her when they were hosting a wedding or birthday party. It was great fun at the time, but once the room was clear of guests, she just wanted to crash.

As they walked through the front doorway of the guest house, Charlotte could see that Olli had got caught with a late arrival. Barry made his excuses and headed up the stairs to his room, and Charlotte moved into work mode, keen to release Olli who had probably been disturbed from his studies. Not that it took much to distract him.

'Hello, Mr Norris, I assume?' she asked. Charlotte gave Olli a small nod, and he wished the customer well and ran up the stairs back to the family accommodation.

Mr Norris explained at great length how his train had been delayed due to either a cow on the line or an excess of leaves; he hadn't managed to determine which. Charlotte let him speak, then encouraged him up the stairs, eager to see him to his room and then lock up for the night.

'You're lucky,' she said quietly, aware that many of the guests would already be asleep. 'You're staying next to Morecambe's famous author, Barry McMillan.'

'The history guy?' Mr Norris replied. Charlotte nodded.

'I'm a big fan. His attention to historical detail and local authenticity is astounding. I'll look forward to catching his attention.'

From the few words Charlotte had caught as she flicked through the book whilst killing time at the Midland Hotel, she was looking forward to enjoying the other aspects of Barry's writing. She walked ahead of Mr Norris, opened up his room with her pass key and showed him inside. Once she'd given him the tour—TV, WiFi, breakfast timings and checkout time—she moved towards the door, eager to get away.

There was a thud from the room next door.

'Did you hear that?' Charlotte asked, looking at Mr Norris. 'It sounded like something heavy being dropped.'

'I didn't hear it,' Mr Norris said. He listened. 'No, I can't hear anything.'

'Well, have a good sleep, and we'll see you at breakfast tomorrow.'

She closed the door, stepping out onto the landing. She could hear something in Barry McMillan's room, a movement, but not footsteps. There was a creaking too, like woodwork under duress. Just as she started to move towards the stairs, there was a grunt that made her creep up to the door and listen. She didn't want to disturb him; for all she knew he was watching pornography, and he had every right to his privacy, after all. But something made her linger.

Charlotte tapped at the door quietly.

'Mr McMillan. Are you still awake? Is everything okay?'

She could hear Mr Norris busying himself in the room next door.

'Mr McMillan, it's Charlotte. Are you okay in there?'

Still no reply. She began to walk away, ever mindful of the importance of online reviews. All she needed was a one-star review from a famous author revealing that he couldn't even take a midnight toilet visit at the guest house without the SAS busting the door down to find out what he was up to. Yet something made her stay.

She waited another five minutes, perfectly still outside his door. Then she tapped one last time.

'Mr McMillan, it's Charlotte. I'm coming into your room to check you're okay. I'm opening up your door now...'

She inserted her pass key and opened up the door. The main lights were off, but with the curtains still open, the room was lit by the glare from the street lamps along the road. She sensed him before she realised what had happened.

Barry McMillan was hanging from a curtain cord looped around the structural beam which ran across his room. His body was perfectly still, except for a small twitch in his right foot.

CHAPTER TWO

The moment she realised what had happened, Charlotte switched on the main light and cried for help. McMillan must have stood on a wooden chair to raise himself to a reasonable height, then kicked it away from underneath him. Charlotte picked up the chair, stood on it and tried to take his weight, but it was impossible for her to lift him or do anything that might reduce the tightness of the ligature.

'Will! Olli! Help me!'

She was so desperate to get help that it didn't even occur to her that she didn't want Olli to see this, until it was too late. Will and Olli came running down the stairs, Olli in his boxers and T-shirt, and Will in pyjama bottoms. Between them, they tried to take McMillan's feet and lift him up so that his body weight couldn't pull down onto the noose. After a couple of minutes, they gave up.

'It's useless,' Will said, 'He's dead, he has to be.'

Several guests had gathered at the door, some of them backing off immediately when they saw what had happened, and a couple of more hardy souls standing and watching, offering words of advice from the sidelines.

'Do we have any doctors or medical people in?' Charlotte asked. It sounded corny asking that question, like someone had just had a heart attack on a plane, but she had to ask it.

'I've called an ambulance,' one of the female guests said.

'Will one of you please help us cut him down?' Will said impatiently. 'Get a kitchen knife or something. We can't hold him up here much longer.'

Eventually, McMillan was cut down and lowered to the floor. The ambulance team arrived first, followed by the police. There was apparently some small chance that he might make it, probably with brain damage, but the fall that Charlotte had heard through the wall was heavy and final; it looked like it had broken his neck. The only consolation, if there was one, was that he hadn't been thrashing around fighting for his final breaths while Charlotte had been listening through the door, wondering if an intervention might result in a poor online review.

The emergency services performed their jobs with calm efficiency while Charlotte, Will and Olli retreated to the downstairs lounge, ready to face the barrage of questions from the police.

A woman arrived, clearly holding the respect of the officers the moment she walked into the guest house. After exchanging words with two of them, she headed directly for Charlotte.

'Charlotte Grayson?' she asked.

Charlotte nodded. She knew this woman already. She'd been in charge at the holiday camp, after the security guard had been attacked.

Charlotte was still trying to process what she'd just seen. For some reason, it hadn't shocked her. She was trembling, and her heart was beating fast, but she wasn't as startled as she felt she ought to be. She simply couldn't figure out why a man like McMillan, having just experienced all that adoration, could possibly go straight back to his room and hang himself; it made no sense. If anything, her overwhelming feeling was one of sadness. She'd spent much of the evening with the man, yet hadn't an inkling that he intended to end his life.

'I'm DCI Kate Summers,' the lady said, extending her hand. 'I think we've met once before?'

She was pleasant, though clearly a no-nonsense sort of person. The partly washed away splashes of brightly coloured paint on her hands gave the game away. Charlotte knew the signs, as any mother would. She was a working woman who'd managed to get home in time to squeeze in some painting with her kids before they went to bed. And now, before she'd had the opportunity to clean up properly and settle down for the night, she'd got a call-out to their guest house. Talk about the stuff of nightmares.

'So, walk me through it,' DCI Summers said.

Charlotte took her through what had happened, step-by-step. Something in her felt daring, as if she was playing with fire, imagining the DCI was questioning her about the disappearance of Bruce Craven. What if his body had been found while they were digging out the foundations on the site of the old holiday camp? Would she feel as calm then?

She knew she wouldn't, but as she spoke to DCI Summers, Charlotte imagined that she was in the interview room, resisting the question and giving nothing away.

Only this interview was easy. She was guilt-free and had nothing to hide. Barry McMillan, for whatever reason, had decided to end his life that night. It was tragic, definitely an inconvenience to the business, and it had shaken her a little. But all in all, Charlotte was doing better than expected. Perhaps she was finally getting over the events of the past months: the mystery threats, the kidnapping of Lucia, the fear of being attacked by Jenna's horrible boyfriend.

DCI Summers didn't dwell long on her questioning of Charlotte, and there was no suggestion of foul play. The police seemed puzzled by the question of motive. DCI Summers moved around the building, checking McMillan's room, asking questions of the officers in attendance and getting a sense of what had happened. Eventually, she started to make signals that she was about to leave.

'Just one thing,' she said to Charlotte as she headed for the door. 'Did you see him use a phone?'

'What, a landline or a mobile phone?'

'A mobile phone,' DCI Summers replied.

'I can't remember... oh, yes, he did, at the Midland Hotel. I saw him calling someone outside while I was waiting for him.'

'He couldn't have left it anywhere, could he? You don't have a safe or anything like that?'

'No, it should be in his room. Or in his pocket maybe?'

'We've looked, and we can't find anything,' DCI Summers replied. 'It's unusual that he wasn't carrying a phone.'

At that moment, a face appeared at the glass in the front door.

'Late night arrival?' DCI Summers asked.

Charlotte hadn't even thought about Lucia's whereabouts in among all the drama. But now here she was, on a school night, arriving back home at almost one o'clock in the morning. As she came in, Charlotte saw she was heavily made up and wearing a very revealing, short dress. That most definitely had not been a topic for discussion at the breakfast table that morning.

CHAPTER THREE

Day Two: Wednesday

Breakfast was tense the next day, as the guests held hushed conversations, stunned and shocked by what had happened the night before. What would make a man so celebrated and successful do something terrible like that?

Will had left the local radio station playing in the background, and every time the news programme returned to the topic in a news bulletin or interview, the lounge would fall silent as the guests listened to hear the latest update. There was a sense of crisis in the guest house, as if they'd all gone through something terrible together.

Not for the first time, Charlotte was grateful for Isla's calm efficiency in the kitchen. In the cold light of a new day, she discovered that she had been shaken by the events of the previous night. She was so exhausted by her late night and early start that she was functioning on auto-pilot, going through the motions but not really taking things in. Having supported a man's dead body while her husband cut him down seemed more important to her than getting Mrs Hartley's poached eggs not too soft and not too hard.

All she could think of was Barry McMillan's bloated face and bulging eyes. If anybody thought hanging was a peaceful way to kill yourself, Charlotte now knew otherwise. It was troubling how he'd managed to get to that dark place in such a short time; he hadn't given any impression of a man who was contemplating suicide. But she didn't even know what that would look like.

'Thanks for coming in to help, George; you have the knack of knowing when to step in,' Charlotte said as she came into the kitchen, balancing a pile of carefully stacked plates which had been wiped clean of their full English breakfasts.

'No problem. Isla and I are always up at the crack of dawn. Besides, Una likes her early walk along the promenade, and it's always so lovely looking out across the bay at that time of day. I heard it on the radio on the five o'clock news, and I suspected things might be a little tense around here.'

It was not just the suicide that had caused Charlotte to be distracted; there was another showdown brewing with Lucia. What had she been thinking of, sneaking out like that and coming back home so late at night? She hadn't had the energy for a row about it there and then. Besides, the guests were up and alert, and it wouldn't have been the best time. But Charlotte was furious.

If there was one downside to running a guest house with teenagers in the house, it was that she was frequently distracted by guests and the usual routines. And with people coming and going at all times of night, it made it easier for Lucia to avoid detection if she stayed out a little later than she should.

After a shaky start, her daughter seemed to have settled in school and found some new friends. Now it was looking like she'd picked up some bad influences. Charlotte was walking that precarious tightrope of trying to give her daughter more freedom as a young adult while looking through the rose-tinted glasses of a parent who still remembered in glorious Technicolour her first day at primary school.

'Go upstairs and have breakfast with your family,' George said, shaking her out of her distracted state. 'Isla and I have got this. We'll serve the late diners and clear everything up.'

Charlotte gave him a peck on the cheek and thanked Isla for her help. Nobody could beat her poached eggs, anyway. She did something that made them come out perfect every time. Charlotte could only dream of Isla's prowess in the kitchen.

She removed her pinafore, now splashed with fried egg, and threw it into the washing bin. Then she checked in with the guests and made her exit, walking up the flights of stairs towards their family accommodation on the top level.

The sight of the police tape across the door of Barry McMillan's room gave her a jolt as she stepped up onto the landing. DCI Summers had reassured her that they probably wouldn't need to access the room again as there were no suspicious circumstances to Barry's death, but until they'd located his phone and accounted for his last movements, they'd need to keep their options open. With it being a Wednesday, they had flexibility with the allocation of the rooms, so she and Will had already worked out that it wouldn't be a problem until Friday.

Charlotte took a breath before she walked into the family accommodation on the top floor. She could hear Will and Olli chatting; Will was always more relaxed with the kids and never seemed to worry as much as she did. She wished she shared his laid-back attitude.

'Hey, Mum,' Olli said as she walked in and joined them at the breakfast table.

'No sign of Lucia?' Charlotte asked.

'Haven't you see her?' Will replied. 'She left for school early this morning. Didn't she say goodbye?'

'No, she didn't,' Charlotte said, the anger of the previous night beginning to rise again. 'Did she say anything to you?'

'Just that she'd got talking at her friend's house and she'd lost track of time.'

'What, dressed like that?' Charlotte interrupted. 'She looked like she'd just rolled in from a night club.'

'She said she was just dressing up to see what her friends thought of her new gear. We have to let her off the leash, Charlotte; she's not long turned seventeen. If we keep restricting her every movement, she'll grow to resent us.'

'You know why I'm like this!' Charlotte shouted at him, more aggressively than she meant to. 'She was abducted, for God's sake. Whatever you say about her being an adult, nobody should have to live with that experience at her age.'

'She told us she didn't need to speak to the psychologist,' Will said, his voice calm and reasonable.

It wasn't the first time they'd had this conversation. But Charlotte just couldn't shake off the fear that Lucia might disappear again; what had happened to her was every mother's nightmare.

'I blame it on her taking that job in the arcade; she's mixing with boys from the town there, rather than her school chums. We should have insisted she only work here.'

'We can't do that to her,' Will protested. 'She's allowed

to get a job of her own choosing and make her own friends. Besides, she lives in the guest house, and she's entitled to want to get out of here from time to time.'

There was a cautious tap at the door. They looked at each other and Olli jumped up.

'I've gotta go. I said I'd meet Willow at half-past eight and I'll be late if I don't hurry.'

Will got up and answered the door. Charlotte recognised the voice immediately; it was Nigel Davies.

'Good morning Charlotte,' Nigel said as he entered the family kitchen, led by Will.

'I've got to be on my way too,' Will said. 'I need to speak to you this evening, about that thing at the university we discussed.'

He gave Charlotte a kiss and was on his way, chatting to Olli as they made their way down the stairs.

'I'm sorry to call in on you so early in the morning,' Nigel began, settling into a chair at Charlotte's invitation. 'It's just that I was in the office early this morning to start writing up this news story and... sorry, I should ask how you are first, I suppose?'

'Better than I should be, but still a bit stunned,' Charlotte replied. 'You saw Barry last night. Did he look like a man who was about to go back to his room and hang himself?'

'No, he didn't,' Nigel said. 'How are the kids? Did they see anything?'

For the first time, Charlotte saw how fortuitous it had been that Lucia was out late; she'd avoided having to see the body. She'd been so busy focusing on the negatives of the situation, that she'd neglected to see the silver lining. It would have been much worse if Lucia had had to help with Barry McMillan's corpse. Olli appeared to be none the worse for it; besides, she'd always considered her son to be more mature and resilient. For some reason, she never worried about him as much. She resolved to check in with Olli after school and give Lucia an easier time over her late night. As it turned out, it had probably been for the best.

'The kids are fine. Lucia missed it, and Olli seems to have taken it in his stride. Have you got any more information about Barry's death?' Charlotte asked.

She knew that Nigel Davies often found out interesting information a long time before everybody else in the town. It was one of the privileges of working for a respected news organisation; people told him things. She'd enjoyed the buzz of joining him at the scene of the assault on the night watchman at the Sandy Beaches Holiday Camp, and in her idle moments she'd begun to speculate about what being a local reporter might be like. As a former teacher, that career path had never even occurred to her. But getting to know Nigel had piqued her interest.

'I wanted to show you this,' Nigel said. He had a photocopy of a newspaper clipping in his hand. It was black and white, and from the old-fashioned fonts Charlotte could tell that it wasn't recent. She took the sheet of paper from Nigel and studied it.

It showed a photograph of five men sitting around a circular table. The cutting was from the local newspaper but was dated 2006, well before Nigel's time. The headline read *Morecambe Stars On The Rise*. The only striking thing about it was that a thick, black marker pen had been used to place a cross through one of the men.

'What's this?' Charlotte asked, not entirely sure why he'd handed it to her.

'Look closely at the man with the black cross through him. Recognise him?'

Charlotte looked hard at the cutting. At first, it wasn't clear enough to be certain, but the tiny caption below the photograph confirmed her suspicions. It was Barry McMillan, thirteen years younger, with a full head of hair and a stylish, well-cropped beard.

'It's Barry,' she said, looking up. 'But what's this about?'

'I was first in the office this morning,' Nigel told her. 'This was posted through the letterbox, addressed to me. As you can see, it's from 2006, and that's a much younger Barry McMillan in happier times. He'd just landed a huge international book deal, and this was a feature on the great and the good in Morecambe.'

'I'm sorry if I'm being a bit slow, but so what?' Charlotte said, a little impatient for Nigel to get to his point. 'Did you put this cross through Barry?'

'That's just it; I didn't,' Nigel replied. 'That's how it was delivered. But look closely at the background to the picture. If you scan the text, you'll also find it in there.'

Charlotte was beginning to feel like she was back at school, trying to coax an answer out of a pupil who wasn't getting it. Only she was the pupil who was being slow.

'I'm sorry. Nigel, you'll have to tell me. I can see it's a picture of Barry, but what's the big deal?'

'There were two things that caught my attention,' he began. 'First of all, why would someone send a picture like that to me?'

'Charlotte suspected he wasn't looking for an answer to his question, but she gave one anyway.

'Maybe they just wanted to let you know there was an old photo of Barry that you could use in your newspaper report?'

'Perhaps, but I don't think so,' Nigel said. 'I'm surprised you haven't noticed it yet.'

'What, Nigel? Noticed what? Why don't you just tell me?'

She knew she was being intolerant, but she'd had a lot to deal with; he needed to spit it out.

'That photograph was taken in this guest house, Charlotte. It was taken in this very building where your guests are currently eating their breakfasts. I recognised it from the fireplace. I'd remember it anywhere. Somebody is trying to tell us something. I think there's a reason Barry McMillan booked into this guest house and I reckon it has something to do with why he decided to hang himself.'

CHAPTER FOUR

Charlotte couldn't wait for the guests to clear the lounge, so she could get into the room and compare the photograph with the genuine article. Nigel had been most insistent that the newspaper cutting was a tip-off of some sort, but he hadn't a clue what it was telling him.

'Do you mind if we send our photographer Chris around to take a few external pictures of the guest house?' he asked before leaving. 'Normally, we don't make a big thing of suicides, but in this case, we have to report it. Besides, I think there may be more to this than meets the eye. What did you say the name of the officer was who spoke to you last night?'

'It was DCI Summers, the lady we met when the security guard was attacked at Sandy Beaches Holiday Camp. I like her. I bet she doesn't take any shit from her subordinates, but she's nice. Very thorough, I'd say. Are you going to let her know?'

'That's good if it's DCI Summers,' Nigel replied. 'I'll have to tell her, this is something which might suggest there's more to it than a straight suicide. And didn't you say his phone had gone AWOL? You get a sixth sense for this sort of thing when you're a journalist, and I'm going to stick my neck out and guess he had money worries or something like that. There's nothing we can report on just yet, but I reckon there's more to this.'

After Nigel left, Charlotte checked out the last of the guests and briefed her two maids not to go into the room Barry McMillan had been using. One of the small luxuries of the guest house being fully operational was that they could now afford to pay a couple of additional staff members to take care of the morning drudgery, leaving Charlotte more time in a management role.

It suited her, providing a wonderful freedom between the hours of 10 o'clock and 4 o'clock when the rest of the world was out at work. The maids were Polish, two young women who'd come to the UK to study and pay their way through University. They were diligent and thorough, spoke better English than many of the locals and the work suited them perfectly. Charlotte couldn't believe her luck.

By half-past-ten Chris, the photographer from the paper, had taken his pictures, and she was clear for the rest of the day. Charlotte knew exactly what she was going to do next.

She was used to walking around the town; from where they lived on the promenade, it was easy to walk along the sea front and head for the town centre. Besides, she'd become addicted to the sight of the bay, whatever the weather, and it remained a treat for her to walk along it.

Ever since things had settled down over the matter with Bruce Craven, she'd begun to see that it had been a good plan moving from Bristol to Morecambe. It had given them all a fresh start, and she was feeling much better in herself. Her confidence had returned; she no longer felt as fragile as when she'd suffered her breakdown in the classroom. The panic attacks were a thing of the past, and if she sensed that one might be on its way, she knew how to calm herself. With the memory of Bruce Craven now properly buried, she was beginning to trust that things might be taking a turn for the better.

As Charlotte walked along the front, she realised that she could now admit something to herself that once upon a time she would never have dared to articulate. There was a time, not so long ago, when she too might have considered ending her life like Barry McMillan had done. When her teaching career was imploding, and she believed herself to be losing her mind, she'd inhabited that dark wasteland; there were definitely two days on which she came very close to taking her life.

But when it came to it, it had been easy to shake herself out of it on both occasions. She was never a genuine suicide risk, even if she'd gone there in her mind. The first time, Will had sent her an old photograph of them as a young couple that he'd found tucked into one of his diaries. She'd forgotten all about it and seeing the photo again brought her such joy that it rescued her temporarily from that dark place. On the second occasion, Lucia had given her a hug and a kiss. She never did that. Had she sensed her low mood? Perhaps, but it was enough to prevent her self-destructive thoughts that day.

Now, as she walked along the promenade, past the toddlers being pushed in their pushchairs, the joggers, the dog-walkers, the bird-watchers and the tourists, she felt a sense of joy and elation. In some bizarre way, Barry McMillan's death had helped her to mark a milestone in her own life. There was no way she would ever do what he had done. She saw it clearly in that moment, and she was pleased to be alive. It hadn't always been the case over the past few years, but now she could say it with confidence. The old Charlotte was back, and she and Will were doing okay again.

It didn't take her long to make it to the library, and she knew exactly who she needed to speak to. Nigel had allowed her to take a photograph of the cutting on her smartphone and she was going to show it to her local historian contact, Jon Rogers. He liked to lurk behind the scenes, so she had to check in at the main reception desk and ask if he was around. It wasn't long before he emerged from wherever he went to hide from the public, to escort Charlotte into the archives area.

'Do you recognise me?' Charlotte asked when he shook her hand.

'Yes, I do recognise you. It's funny; I was only thinking about you the other day. How long ago was it that you came to see me? Six months?'

'Yes,' Charlotte replied, 'probably about that. It's gone so fast. What made you think about me after all that time? I'm Charlotte, by the way. I expect your colleague told you that already? I run the Lakes View Guest House at the Town Hall end of the promenade.'

'Yes, she did. Hello, Charlotte. You came to mind because somebody was asking similar questions to you. About that chap, what was his name? Bruce Cranfield?'

'Craven,' Charlotte answered immediately, her tone cold and clipped.

'Yes, that's the chap! She was researching her family history. Reckoned she'd read about what happened at the holiday camp in the national newspaper. She'd come to a dead end trying to trace Bruce to the holiday camp, and there was no record of him after he left there. What a strange coincidence that you should turn up so soon after she got in contact.'

Charlotte could feel the blood draining from her face. It felt like the grim reaper had come to take away all the joy she'd felt not ten minutes previously.

'Who was it?' she asked. 'Who was looking for him?'

'She was some obscure relation, a half-sister, I think. Either way, she was very interested when I told her about that photograph of the new paddling pool being opened. Is that what you've come about today?'

Charlotte was rigid with fear. Everything she thought they'd put behind them had reared up like the fury of a dragon about to incinerate its prey. Who the hell was this person? As far as she knew, Bruce Craven had no family. Why wouldn't the man just stay dead?

Charlotte shook herself out of her trance.

'It's a different subject, actually,' she began. She pulled out her smartphone from her jeans pocket, navigating to the picture of the press cutting.

'Can you locate me a better copy of this?' she asked.

'Now, that photograph takes me back,' Jon said, taking the phone from her hand and studying it closely. 'It's 2006 or thereabouts, off the top of my head. We'll have that stored on microfiche. I'll be able to get you a better copy. I can remember it appearing in the newspaper. We were all much younger back then; I had more hair than Barry in those days, and I didn't have to wear these glasses. I knew Barry in school as a child. It's so sad that he took his life; I heard about it on the local radio this morning.'

He handed the phone back to her. 'I've always wanted to be a writer, but I never followed through with it. As a younger man I looked at that photo with a burning sense of jealousy about how well he'd done. It turns out I needn't have been envious; clearly all was not well in his life, or he would not have ended it like he did.'

Charlotte realised she'd never felt that sense of belonging or home, because she'd never lived anywhere long enough. Perhaps the move to Morecambe might be different.

Jon invited her to get to a coffee from the staff kitchen and then led her to the microfiche machines. Using his honed skills and encyclopaedic knowledge of the archive, it wasn't long before he'd not only isolated the clipping but also managed to lay his hands on another newspaper feature that he was eager to show her. He wouldn't be drawn on what it was until he could place it in her hands.

'I didn't realise that you owned the Lakes View Guest House, and I certainly didn't put two and two together until you showed me that photograph. Take a seat. I think you'll be surprised by what I'm about to tell you.'

For a man who looked like he should be caked by the dust from ancient artefacts, Jon Rogers had an uncanny ability to surprise. His monotone delivery and bland persona concealed hidden talents: this man knew how to draw a white rabbit out of a hat.

'Here's the photocopy of that first cutting you showed me, without the big, black cross through poor old Barry McMillan. Your cutting was a bit clipped, too. As you can see, there's a little more detail on this copy.'

Charlotte took the sheet of paper from him, keen to study it. Nigel's copy had been of terrible quality, but Jon had managed to print out a much sharper version.

'This is excellent, thanks. What else did you say you had for me?'

'Well, when you told me you owned the Lakes View, it rang bells immediately. This is one of the curses of living in a town for so many years. I remember all this stuff.'

He handed over a second photocopy to Charlotte, who devoured it like she might set upon a burger after a day without food. Jon summarised it for her as she read.

'You probably don't even know this, as you're so new to the town. But shortly after that photograph was taken in your establishment, the owner ended up in prison. He kidnapped a minor and held her in an attic room in your guest house. Rex Emery was his name. It was a huge news story at the time. In fact, he's been in prison for so many years that he must be out by now.'

CHAPTER FIVE

The day couldn't end soon enough for Charlotte. As she passed the newspaper offices on her way back from the library, she dropped off a copy of the cutting for Nigel Davies. He was delighted to receive it, acting like a man relieved to have an interruption from generating the lead story for that week's edition of the newspaper.

'You see this?' he said, looking closely at the image. 'There's something in it that was cut off the original clipping.'

Charlotte leaned over. She'd never been invited upstairs to enter the heart of the news operation. It was far busier and noisier than an office workspace.

'What is it?' she asked.

'Well, this picture was taken by a photographer from this newspaper. I've got a student from the local college digging out the details for me as we speak. We should have a colour copy of it somewhere, but it's more likely to be in storage now. We keep all the paperwork in a facility on the White Lund Industrial Estate, so it may be a devil to find. Anyhow, think about how this would have been set up. The photographer is standing behind the camera. But look; there's somebody standing at his side. You can see their sleeve.'

Charlotte studied the area of the photograph he was pointing to.

'Oh yes. I just ignored that. I didn't know what it was.'

'Now, take a look to the side of this guy's head. There's a mirror there. You can just make out somebody's face.'

'You've got better eyesight than I have,' Charlotte replied, after squinting at the image for a couple of seconds. 'Are you sure that's what it is?'

'Yes. The photographer should have known better. It's a bit of a rookie error catching a reflection in the mirror. Anyhow, it's not his reflection; it's the reflection of the person standing at his side; you can see from the angle the picture has been taken.'

Charlotte wasn't entirely convinced but decided to take his word for it.

'What does that tell you?' she asked, none the wiser.

'It tells me that at least seven people were in that room; the five men at the table, the photographer and whoever it was standing next to him. I can trace the photographer from the number on the image. We always have a reference number in case the people in the photograph want to buy a copy; it's one of the ways the newspaper makes money.'

'But why does it even matter?' Charlotte asked. Not for the first time that day, she was exasperated by Nigel's slow release of information.

'I spoke to DCI Summers today,' he continued. 'She's asked me not to report it yet, but there are some suspicious circumstances surrounding Barry McMillan's death. They've already ascertained that there were no financial problems in his life, and his marriage doesn't appear to have been showing any cracks; his widow was distraught by all accounts. But his phone is still missing, and they've managed to see from his records that a call was placed to it just after his author event last night. It was an anonymous call, just after eleven o'clock.

'I saw him take it,' Charlotte exclaimed. 'I was watching him through the window at the Midland Hotel. I told the police he had his phone then. That was the last time I noticed it. I don't know what happened after that. How come the police shared all that with you?'

'It seems DCI Summers likes to keep the information flowing. She was very grateful that I told her about the cutting being posted through the letterbox, so she asked me to stay in close touch. I think she feels the same as me; there's more to this than meets the eye; we just can't put our finger on it yet.'

Charlotte contemplated keeping the second cutting to herself. She wasn't sure how to process the new information about Rex Emery. No wonder the guest house had taken a long time to sell, tarnished with a historical kidnapping story. The agent hadn't thought to mention that to her and Will when they bought it; but the incident was over a decade ago, so why would they?

She opted to follow DCI Summers' lead and told Nigel everything. It was like a red rag to a bull. He could barely contain his excitement. He all but dismissed her there and then, eager to make some calls and see what he could unearth from his contacts.

Charlotte left the newspaper office intrigued but uncertain; as far as she could tell, Barry McMillan's death was tragic, untimely and unexpected. But then, wasn't every suicide? She stopped off at her favourite coffee shop on the sea front. It always made her think of Jenna. She'd be seeing her the next day. It was the least she could do for her former friend. She'd come to see her as a victim, in spite of the terrible things she and her boyfriend had done to her daughter. She felt guilty too, that Jenna's life had turned out so badly. At least visiting times at the prison were later in the day, so she didn't have to catch the early train. She hated seeing somebody she knew in that horrible place, but she was lucky: at the end of visiting time, she could walk through the gates, but Jenna couldn't.

She'd been furious with her old friend at the time, but the collusion between her, Will and George meant that they were bound together forever, drawn into the same sordid mess of deceptions.

And now here was somebody coming out of the blue to look for Bruce Craven. They'd have to stay sharp and keep their stories straight, or they'd all be joining Jenna in prison.

Isla had clocked on early that afternoon, giving Charlotte an opportunity to talk to her. She was busying herself in the kitchen when Charlotte got back.

'Hi Isla, everything okay? Our first check-in is between five and six o'clock. We're quiet tonight, unless any new bookings have come in.'

'I decided I'd come in early and make a start, after all the fuss last night. I thought you'd probably have fallen behind, after all the disturbances. The police have been. They're finished with the room. They left some details of specialist cleaners who can sort it out before you get any more guests in there. I've left the note by the reception desk.'

'Did you know Rex Emery?' Charlotte asked. She couldn't wait any longer. She just wanted to cut to the chase.

It was only momentary, but she saw Isla flinch, and the

potato she was peeling rolled out of her hand and onto the kitchen floor. She recovered herself quickly.

'Silly me, I'm sure I'm getting arthritis. Rex Emery, did you say? The name rings a bell, but I can't quite place it. Why do you ask?'

Charlotte watched as Isla picked up the potato, threw it into the bin, then began to peel a new one, turning her back as she spoke.

'Well, apparently, he used to own this guest house. And from our previous conversations, you must have known him; you would have been working for him in 2006.'

CHAPTER SIX

Charlotte listened while Isla tried to explain away her apparent lapse in memory.

'I'd been experiencing some personal difficulties at the time and had spent some time away from the guest house. I was in a bit of state back then. Yes, I did work with Rex, I'm getting forgetful in my old age.'

Charlotte considered Isla to be as sharp as a tack when it came to her mental faculties. She resolved to find out more, uncomfortable about doubting Isla but convinced that something about her account of events didn't quite work.

It wasn't that long since she'd left the newspaper office, but Nigel Davies phoned her soon after, excited and keen to call round.

'The girl who was abducted and held in your guest house lives locally, in the West End. I've got to go up there and speak to her. Do you want to come?'

Charlotte hesitated a moment. These events were bringing the police back into the orbit of their family; one wrong move, a single misstep, and the truth about what they'd done might come into the open. But she felt the same compulsion as Nigel, wanting to stay ahead of events. The kids and Will hadn't landed back home yet, and a trip to the West End wouldn't take more than half an hour, she reckoned.

'Are you all right holding the fort?' she asked Isla.

'Yes, no problem, I'm on top of everything here. Go on, do whatever you have to do.'

Had Charlotte been a little less forgiving, she would have been inclined to think that Isla was pleased to be rid of her.

'Can you pick me up?' Charlotte asked Nigel.

'I'm walking to the car park now. Be with you in five,' he replied, ending the call.

Charlotte was eager to share the news with Will, but if they struck gold with this visit, she'd have an even better story to tell him when they were all back home again. They'd have to tread carefully and coordinate their information. If the police started sniffing around the guest house in connection with the Barry McMillan suicide, the heat would be turned up on them.

It took Nigel no time to get to the guest house. Charlotte was looking out for him from the lounge window.

'That was fast,' she said, climbing into the passenger seat. 'How did you find that information?'

'The reporter who worked the case still lives locally. He's retired now, but he was happy to chat on the phone. He says there were a lot of unanswered questions. As far as he's concerned, it's an open case. The police thought differently.'

Nigel turned the car at the Town Hall and drove back along the promenade, towards the West End. They were heading for bedsit Morecambe, the most startling indication of the town's struggles for survival. There, once-grand Victorian houses had been carved up into units, now housing the unemployed and low-waged. In days gone by this would have been a part of Morecambe's crowning glory. Now, it had become a source of income for investors and landlords who could pack tenants in where once families had thrived.

Nigel pulled up down a side street, checking that they were free to park without the risk of getting a ticket.

'We're about to do some door-stepping,' Nigel said as he reached back to take his notebook and pen from the back seat. 'Sometimes it can get a bit tense, so be prepared. She may not want to speak to us, so hang back a bit. I've developed a thick skin over the years; I'll take the hit if she's rude.'

They got out of the car and Charlotte surveyed the street. The houses would have made ideal guest houses in the days before EasyJet and the like made foreign travel more accessible. Now there were rusting bicycles chained to corroding gates, wheelie bins with large, white numerals painted on their sides and recycling bins packed to the brim with empty lager cans and beer bottles. Residents sat smoking on the front steps, banished from their residences by health and safety regulations, transferring the waves of cigarette and vaping smoke to the street instead.

'Which one?' Charlotte asked, turning to Nigel.

'Number 35, just on the other side of the road,' he replied.

They crossed the road and walked up the four steps to the front door. The houses on this street were three storeys high, though many landlords had done loft conversions. To the right-hand side of the door was a cluster of doorbells and a speaker. Most of the cards bearing flat numbers were weathered and grubby, the ink smudged by the damp.

'She's in Flat 3. Her name is Piper Lawrence,' Nigel said as he searched for the relevant button. Piper's was clearly written, as if she was keen to ensure that visitors found the right place when they called. Nigel pressed the buzzer and waited. There was no reply. He tried again. Nothing.

There was the sound of heavy stomping then the door opened and a man rushed out. Nigel stepped into the hallway before the door closed again.

As they went inside, Charlotte's foot clipped a large pile of abandoned post and leaflets, missives to long-gone residents who would never read their contents.

Nigel scanned the numbers on the doors along the hall.

'Weird numbering,' he said. 'She must be upstairs.'

The staircase was steep and high; at one time, it would have been impressive and commanding. Now it was fitted with a well-worn, brown carpet which had seen better days. The wooden rail was greasy from the hundreds of hands which had passed along, forgotten by the cleaners.

They made their way up the stairs until they reached Flat 3 on the second landing.

'How many people are packed in here?' Charlotte asked, not expecting an answer.

Without warning, the door to Flat 3 opened, and a man dashed out, ignoring Charlotte and Nigel as he passed them and ran down the stairs.

'I'll be reporting you to the agency!' came a female voice from within the flat. She sounded tired and exasperated.

'That's our lady,' Nigel said, heading towards the open

door. Piper Lawrence walked onto the landing, dressed only in a light gown, her hair dishevelled. She looked at them in surprise.

'We don't have a booking, do we? Were you ringing the buzzer? You need to book through the agency.'

'I'm Nigel Davies, from the local paper,' he said, holding out his hand. 'And this is my... er, colleague, Charlotte Grayson. Are you Piper Lawrence?'

Charlotte sensed Piper's defences being raised.

'If you haven't come through the agency, I can't help you,' she said, moving towards her front door.

'I own the guest house where you were held captive all those years ago,' Charlotte said gently. 'We're just trying to find out what happened there. I didn't know anything about it when we bought the place. We're not here to cause any trouble; I just want to understand what happened there.'

Piper stopped for a moment, thinking it through.

'If it wasn't for your guest house, I wouldn't be here doing what I'm doing now. Those bastards took my youth away from me. I'll never forgive them for that!'

She darted into her flat, but Nigel moved fast to get to her before the door was slammed shut in their faces.

'We only want to ask one or two questions, Piper. I'm not writing anything in the newspaper. It's just that Rex Emery is due for release—if he's not out of prison already—and we just wanted to investigate the background to the story. Can we come in?'

He fumbled in his pocket for a business card, found one in his wallet and passed it to her. As she reached out to take it, her gown fell open slightly; she was naked underneath it. Nigel looked away while she pulled it closed once again, seemingly without embarrassment.

'Okay, just for five minutes, though. When the buzzer goes, we're done.'

Charlotte and Nigel looked at each other, then stepped into the flat. It was a one-room arrangement with a double bed, settee, TV and kitchen all sharing the same space. The bathroom seemed to be separate, at least. Soft music was playing on a CD player, and the ill-fitting, gaudy curtains were drawn. The sheets on the bed were rumpled, and some lingerie had been discarded on the floor.

'One moment,' Piper said, disappearing into what Charlotte assumed was the bathroom.

'Is she a prostitute?' Charlotte whispered to Nigel.

'More likely an escort,' Nigel said, just as quietly. 'She keeps referring to the agency.'

A few minutes later, Piper stepped out of the bathroom. She had discarded the robe and was wearing a one-piece black dress. Her hair had been combed, and she looked fresh and groomed.

'Excuse me while I tidy up,' she said, setting about the bed and straightening the sheets.

'Can we just ask a couple of questions?' Nigel asked. Charlotte let him take the lead, feeling a little out of her depth.

'Shoot,' Piper replied, removing the discarded lingerie from the floor and placing it in a linen basket.

'What do you know about Rex Emery?' Nigel asked.

'Not a lot,' she replied. 'Only that he was innocent. He was stitched up good and proper, a fall guy. He didn't deserve to spend that time in jail. But the police didn't care. They just wanted to blame somebody and move on. It was a cover-up, but I've long since stopped worrying about it. It's water under the bridge. They got away with it, the bastards, and people like me and Rex Emery just have to pick up the pieces.'

'What happened in the guest house?' Charlotte asked. 'Why were you held there?'

Piper was now lighting a scented candle. She moved over towards the CD player and changed the music to something more old-fashioned.

'They rented that room at the top of the building, the one with the attic room, and held me there, gagged and tied up. Rex Emery didn't even know. He thought it was just a regular booking. I was there for five days. Two of them did some horrible things...'

She stopped. Charlotte didn't want to push her, knowing they'd taken her back to a dark place, even though it was so long ago.

'Who took you, Piper? And why? What did your parents do?'

'Don't mention my parents!' she turned around, fire in her eyes. 'I never even knew my dad and my mum... the stupid bitch just caved. She didn't dare speak up. I was too young at the time and I couldn't speak for myself. She did nothing to protect me. I never want to see her again.'

'Who did this, Piper? If it wasn't Rex Emery, who abducted you and did what they did?'

Charlotte spoke as gently as she could. She couldn't believe this had happened in the guest house. The top rooms were now their family living space, and the attic that Piper referred to was Olli's bedroom.

Piper turned and looked at both of them.

'I'll never say publicly who was responsible, because even now they'll kill me if I do. They have people everywhere. I'd rather live like this, out of the way, than see those people again. They were horrible and violent, and it terrifies me just thinking about it. I can never say who it was, for fear of word getting back to them. Besides, I have no proof anyway. What good is the word of a cheap escort compared to theirs? But I hate every single one of them and the day they die a slow death from cancer will be the happiest day of my life.'

CHAPTER SEVEN

Nigel and Charlotte passed Piper's next client on the stairs. He must have been over sixty and reeked of cigarette smoke. Piper had escorted them to the door the moment the buzzer sounded, the sound of Ella Fitzgerald playing in the flat as they left.

'I feel terrible for her,' Charlotte said. 'Isn't there anything we can do?'

'I'm not sure what we could do,' Nigel replied. 'She's obviously still scared of someone, but wouldn't you be, if you'd been threatened?'

Charlotte thought about the dreams she still had, where Bruce Craven had a knife to her daughter's throat. She knew he was dead and couldn't get to her from his concrete grave, yet he still had power over her.

'I can't believe all that happened in our home,' she said, avoiding his question. 'All those echoes from the past... I'm not sure I dare tell Olli what happened there. If it was Lucia's room, she'd freak out.'

As they reached the bottom of the staircase, a tall, athletic woman came out of the first flat along the ground floor hallway. She hadn't seen Charlotte and Nigel and made directly for the pile of post on the floor. She began to sift through it, then turned as she heard their footsteps. She smiled, but it was empty, more out of obligation than desire.

'Do you know Piper Lawrence?' Charlotte asked, surprising herself at being so forthright. 'The lady in Flat 3. Is she all right?'

Piper was troubling Charlotte. She knew that prostitution was a thing, and she'd read about escort agencies, but she'd never put a real person next to the news story or magazine article. It had unsettled her. What made it better for Piper to see an endless procession of clients in her own home rather than getting a regular job? She couldn't square it in her own mind.

'Yes, she is a friend of mine,' the lady replied. She had an eastern European accent. Charlotte guessed that she was Polish. 'Is she okay? Why do you ask?'

'We just met her, and I'm a little concerned about her,' Nigel added. 'I'm Nigel Davies from the local newspaper, by the way.' He fumbled for a business card but was unable to find one. 'Sorry, I gave my last card to Piper.'

'I know your name. I see it in the newspaper. I read it to improve my English. My name is Agnieszka. Agnieszka Kowalski. Are you friends of Piper? I am worried about her too. She gets visits from a man with a horrible voice who is not a client of hers.'

For the first time, Charlotte noticed that Agnieszka was dressed unusually for that time of day. She wore high-heels and a tight dress. She looked like she was going somewhere.

'Piper and I work for the same agency, Morecambe Babe Escort Services. They keep us safe. We check in with them on the phone. They make sure we are not found in the bottom of a ditch, is that how you say it?'

'It's really none of our business,' Charlotte replied, uncomfortable with the topic of conversation. Agnieszka was an intelligent, beautiful woman; why wasn't she at the university studying or in some professional field?

'I see you looking at the way I am dressed,' Agnieszka continued. 'It is just a job for us; we can earn some good money. I do it while I am saving up to study.'

Charlotte hoped that she wasn't coming over as judgemental. It was the last thing she wanted.

'I'm concerned about Piper,' Charlotte said, sensing that Nigel was allowing her to take the lead. 'Is she safe?'

'I am worried for my friend too, but she insists that I no worry,' Agnieszka replied.

'What do you know about her?' Nigel asked. 'Are you good friends?'

'Piper helps me to join the agency when I arrive here, so we become friends. She—how do you say it—shows me the ropes. We talk and chat. I like her, but I am worried for her. This man come to her flat, sometimes with friend. They are not clients, I don't think. There is shouting, and I hear her crying. When I knock at her door, she tells me she is okay. I don't think everything is okay with her.'

Charlotte felt her stomach knotting; she knew this scenario well.

'Has she told you about her life?' Nigel asked.

'Yes, she tell me about the horrible things that have happened to her. Sometimes she cry. I comfort her, but her wounds are deep—'

She stopped as Charlotte's phone sounded. It was a Facebook message. She ignored it, wanting Agnieszka to continue.

'Go on,' she said softly.

'She is very angry that her mother does not look after

her. I don't know how you say it here... she was in the care?'

'In care?' Nigel suggested. 'Was she in care? It's when somebody else looks after children, the council or social services.'

'Yes, she was in care,' Agnieszka confirmed. 'When she was only sixteen years of age. She have to leave when she is eighteen. She cannot get a job or look after herself properly. She says her mother abandoned her when she needed her most. She does not know her mother now. She says she hates her. I do not think she hates her. I think she needs her. She never knew her father, but she takes his name to spite her mother. There is much anger there.'

'Do you know the name of her mum?' Charlotte asked. 'Is she local?'

'Yes, she lives somewhere in Morecambe, but I do not know her name. She say it once to me as an accident, but I forget it now. It was long time ago.'

'Have you reported your concerns about this man to the police?' Nigel asked.

For the first time, Charlotte noticed Agnieszka tense.

'What is it?' Charlotte asked. 'Is there something wrong?'

'I cannot go to police,' she replied. 'I do not want to be on the radar. Things are changing in your country. We are not so welcome here now. I do not have the right to reside here. It's why I work for the agency. I am invisible here. I do not want to go back to Poland, so I stay quiet, and I avoid your tax.'

'We won't say anything, we promise,' Charlotte said, looking at Nigel for some reassurance that he wouldn't go on some moral crusade to get Agnieszka expelled from the country. The look of concern on his face suggested that he shared her worries for this woman.

'I'm going to write down my number of a piece of paper,' Nigel said. 'It's the telephone number for the newspaper. If you're ever concerned about Piper's welfare—or your own, come to that—give me a call. I promise you I won't say anything to the police. I'm worried that Piper may be getting visits from a man called Rex Emery, the man who was imprisoned for abducting her when she was a child—'

'But she said he wasn't responsible,' Charlotte interrupted.

'Yes, but whoever it is, Agnieszka says he's upsetting her. I'm going to find out a bit more about this Rex Emery fellow. I want to know if he's out of prison yet. It's been thirteen years or so since he was imprisoned. He must have been up for parole during that time. It's unlikely they threw away the key as nobody was killed.'

Agnieszka took the piece of paper and examined it.

'Thank you. I will call you if I worry. I will try to talk to Piper again and make sure she is safe. I do worry about her though. Something has changed about her in the last weeks. She is more scared. I can see it in her face.'

Charlotte's phone cheeped again, and this time she stood to the side in the hallway. She'd learned long ago that a single message was usually fine, but two in swift succession meant that somebody was after her. It was Will, and he'd sent two messages via Facebook messenger, their preferred way to stay in touch during the day.

The first message was simple. *Where are you? Isla said you rushed out.*

The second made Charlotte's stomach knot a little tighter.

We need to talk about Lucia. Just found out she gave up her arcade job three weeks ago. So where is she getting her money?

CHAPTER EIGHT

Day Three: Thursday

Charlotte was beginning to feel that things were running out of control. Everything had been going smoothly for a short time, but now the bumps in the road were back.

She and Will had agreed not to tackle Lucia until they'd had time to talk. Besides, Charlotte needed to fill him in on the fallout from Barry McMillan's death. While Will had been at work, she'd been busy chasing leads and making connections.

'We need to agree our strategy for tackling Lucia,' Will said. 'She's still not home. All the time we thought she was working at the arcade, it turns out she quit some time back.'

'How did you find out?' Charlotte asked.

'Olli let it slip,' Will replied. 'We were chatting after school. By the way, I have an interview for that university job I applied for. Things are looking good.'

Charlotte skimmed by Will's job news, preferring to focus on the kids before they got deflected. She knew Will was keen to move on, but he'd already had a couple of knock-backs, and she wasn't holding her breath.

'Should we tell Olli about what happened in his room? The thought of that poor girl being held captive in there is terrifying. I think it'll unnerve him.'

'He's a tough kid, Charlotte. If we present it right, he'll be fine. It was years ago. Anything could have happened in this house. It must be full of echoes from the past. Besides, don't you think Barry McMillan is a slightly more pressing issue?'

'I'm worried, Will. It just feels like the vultures are circling. I know this Barry McMillan thing is not connected with what we did at the holiday camp. But it's unsettling me. The less we have to do with the police, the better.'

'That reminds me, are you still seeing Jenna tomorrow? Nothing's changed?'

'No change; I'm on the train at ten-thirty. I can't wait to be frisked and searched. I don't know how Jenna puts up with it.'

The next morning, despite what they'd agreed the night before, it was all Charlotte could do to keep from yelling at Lucia when she joined them for breakfast. Instead, she arranged for them to chat that evening.

'We need to talk, Lucia,' she said, taking a breath before she broached the issue. They all knew they'd been skirting around the matter and now it was time to grasp the bull by the horns.

'What's there to talk about?' Lucia replied defiantly. 'I think finding a man hanged in one of the rooms is more pressing than me coming in a bit late one night.'

Will looked at Charlotte with a furrowed brow as he took a bite of toast. She gave him a small nod, confirming that she'd do her best to behave.

'Let's not get into that right now. We've all got places to be. But please make sure you're around at eight o'clock. Me and your dad want to sit down with you and talk.'

'I'll be at the arcade at eight o'clock.'

'Lucia,' said Will, calm and reasonable. 'We spoke about this last night. Eight o'clock please, no excuses.'

Lucia stood up from the table, letting her cereal spoon drop into her bowl. She stomped over to her school bag, picked it up, and stormed out of the room. Charlotte sighed.

'You did right to tackle it,' Will said. He'd kept his silence while Charlotte spoke, always less tempestuous than her. 'She's fallen in with a different group at school. Even I find it difficult to have a normal conversation with her these days. I'm worried about her. She seemed to settle down after the abduction, but now it's like all those pent-up feelings are just waiting to get out.'

'You can say that again.' Charlotte answered. 'I can't work out if it's just normal teenage attitude or if something really is up. She's been lying to us, that's for sure, and I want to know why.'

While Olli and Will were getting ready for the day ahead, Charlotte finished her breakfast and made her way downstairs to join Isla. George had tagged along too that morning. She was always grateful when he did. It gave her more time to see the family before they went their separate ways.

Isla was in the kitchen, washing the dishes from breakfast. George was in the dining room, chatting to a couple of guests who were just about to return to their rooms.

'You cleared the dining room early today,' Charlotte said after the couple had left, keen to catch George while he was alone.

'Yes, they're all going to see that kite display on the

beach this morning. I can't remember the last time we were empty in here before nine o'clock.'

Charlotte pulled up a chair at the table, pushing aside the plate in front of her which was empty except for a piece of bacon rind and a half-eaten tomato.

'Can I have a private word, George?'

'Of course,' he replied, sitting down at the opposite chair. 'This sounds intriguing.'

'I just wanted to have a chat about all the police activity and attention we've had here this week. After what happened at the holiday camp, I'm getting a bit jittery. I need to be certain that we all agree on our story. I'd hate to get caught out while we're casually talking to the police about Barry's death.'

'You're right to raise it,' George confirmed. 'I've got other reasons to steer clear of the cops. It's a long time ago now. I'd be surprised if there's even a record of it anywhere. But I'm an old man now. I want to put it all behind me.'

'Does Isla know you had a run-in with the police in the past?' Charlotte asked. That was her primary worry. Their deceit had to remain confined to the immediate circle as far as she was concerned, and Isla needed to know as little as possible.

'No, I haven't told her. I haven't gone into much detail about my old life. We're at the wrong time of life for that, Charlotte. What's happened before isn't important any more. We just want to enjoy the time we have left.'

He gave a rueful smile. 'Jenna knows she needs to keep quiet, especially now she has a criminal record. She'll be in no hurry to spend more time in Fletcher Prison, believe me.'

Charlotte could second that, the prison was a terrible place to be incarcerated.

'Jenna's boyfriend, Pat Harris, knew nothing about

Bruce Craven,' George continued. 'He was just the idiot who took care of the abduction. If I ever get my hands on the little shit, I'd like to set about him with a baseball bat after hurting my Isla like that.'

He paused and looked out of the window for a few moments.

'Anyhow, he's out of harm's way, he can't hurt us. That leaves you and Will, and you won't be saying anything, will you?'

Charlotte thought it over. He was right. Nobody else knew. Unless one of them tripped up, they were safe. But there was another matter she wanted to discuss with him, and she was nervous to raise it.

'Can I ask you something about Isla?' she ventured.

'Go on,' George replied, with a wary expression.

'What do you know about her family? She never talks about them. I don't even know anything about her first husband.'

'She's cagey about it all,' George agreed. 'And I don't push her. Some of the memories from our past are best left behind. Besides, I more than make up for it talking about my Una. Isla's very good, the way she tolerates it. Some women can get very jealous about previous wives, my friends tell me.'

'So does she never talk about her first husband? What about her kids? I don't even know how many she had.'

Charlotte knew she was pushing her luck. Isla was being evasive, whereas most people wouldn't shut up when speaking about their families.

'Has it never struck you as strange, that she doesn't talk about things as openly as you? Surely it's the most natural thing on earth to chat about the happy times in your life.'

George looked unusually serious.

'What you have to remember, Charlotte my dear, is that not everybody has experienced as good a life as you and me. Sure, we've had our difficulties, but we're still here, fighting and surviving. As you get older, you'll realise your good fortune. Isla seems happy living in the present. She's contented now, and she looks forward to the future. Why would I push her about the past if she doesn't want to make a big deal of it?'

Charlotte sat in silence for a moment, thinking over what he'd said. He was right. Not everybody wanted to dwell in the past. So what was it in Isla's life that had made her lie about not knowing Rex Emery?

CHAPTER NINE

Charlotte almost missed her train. Since Olli had gone to school, she had been very tempted to go into his bedroom and take a look at the roof space where Piper had been held captive. She'd barely registered it before, throwing some boxes in there when they first moved in and never going anywhere near it since. Piper's story was bothering her. There was a mix of defiance and sadness in her that she'd never seen in a woman before, and she couldn't help but be troubled by her situation.

In the end, she resisted the temptation, deciding to walk to the station at the last minute. The train was about to pull away as she arrived, so she was forced into the indignity of having to run for it. She just made it through the sliding doors of the small shuttle train before it pulled away, arriving red-faced and exhausted. She was so out of shape; she'd need to do something about that.

Fletcher Prison was a couple of hours away on the train. Like most railway routes in the UK, if there was a complicated or a simple way of getting there, the train companies had opted for the complicated way. It was more of an endurance test than a journey. She had changes at Lancaster and Manchester Airport, of all places, and had to tolerate two regional trains in the process, an experience akin to being on a cattle truck. If it wasn't for Jenna, she'd have steered clear.

Out of breath and embarrassed by the red face she knew she had, Charlotte took a seat on the train. If there was one small advantage in setting off from Morecambe, it was that it was normally quiet and empty at that time of day. She sat down, took some deep breaths and thanked her lucky stars she'd made it.

When she and Jenna had met again after so many years, Jenna was a changed woman. Of course, they were all younger, more carefree and less troubled when they were eighteen years old and working at the holiday camp. They'd gone to Sandy Beaches Holiday Camp as best friends, but left as former friends at best; at worst, they were estranged.

Had she let Jenna down? That was the thought troubling Charlotte as she began the journey to the prison. When she and Will had got together, she'd all but abandoned her friend, pushing her to the sidelines. It was one of the reasons Charlotte made the visit to Cheshire once a month. In spite of the botched kidnap attempt and blackmail that Jenna had tried to pull on them, she still felt that she owed her former friend something.

Jenna had the hard look of a woman whose life had been tough. And now she was in prison, and as far as Charlotte could tell, nobody was visiting her. It was upsetting. Although she and Jenna were a million miles away from the relationship they'd once had, she felt the obligation of past connections. She had no intention of abandoning Jenna.

As the connecting train left Lancaster, Charlotte received a call on her mobile phone, enough of a rarity for her to feel anxious. She was still old-fashioned enough not to conduct her business in the middle of a train, so she walked to the end of the carriage to take the call with a degree of privacy.

'Hi, Charlotte. It's Nigel Davies.'

'Hi Nigel, you're the last person I expected to hear from.'

'Have you heard the news on the local radio today?'

He sounded like he was bursting to tell her something.

'No, I was a bit caught up this morning. What's happened?'

'I knew before I heard it. The newspaper cutting was posted to me again this morning, with a new person crossed out in black. Somebody else is dead.'

'Who? What happened?' Charlotte asked.

'The police are all over it now. DCI Summers was a bit dismissive the first time I told her about the cutting. But I think they'll come round to your guest house again, now they suspect that picture is linked to Barry McMillan's death. It's all beginning to look a bit suspicious now.'

Charlotte was struggling to keep up.

'Hang on a moment, slow down. Who's dead?'

'Can you picture the photo of those men around the table in your guest house? Barry McMillan was in the middle. Do you recall the thickset man on the left? That's a local builder called Fred Walker. Well, he used to be a local builder; he runs a huge construction company now. He was found this morning in a box at the Winter Gardens, strangled by a cord from the theatre curtains. It's a terrible way to die.'

'So, what does that mean?' Charlotte asked, struggling to work out the implications of the death as she tried to make out Nigel's voice over the crackling line.

'It means that those men are connected in some way. It means that someone is trying to tell me something by sending me that cutting. They want me to dig into this story. There's something there, I'm certain of it. And wait until I tell you the next thing I've discovered.'

Charlotte was catching up now. Those men were involved in something, and it took place at her guest house. A girl had been held hostage there and a former owner—Rex Emery—was in prison for it. She could sense storm clouds gathering, and she wasn't happy about it; all of this made them vulnerable. It could reveal the truth about what happened back in the eighties.

Nigel didn't wait for the prompt.

'The police have put the other men in that picture on a high state of alert. But here's the thing; one of them is dead already.'

'Well, I'd expect that,' Charlotte said. 'They must be getting on a bit, they'll be nearing retirement, won't they?'

'This was another suicide, a while back,' Nigel continued. 'Only it was a gruesome one. It was a senior police officer, a man called Harvey Turnbull. He was decapitated. He put his head on the rails of the big dipper at Adventure Kingdom. It took it clean off, according to the old news cutting I managed to dig up.'

The violence of it took her aback. First Barry McMillan and now Fred Walker. She thought about the horror of it, being slowly suffocated by a cord pulled around his neck. And before all this, there was Harvey Turnbull.

She could hardly believe it. Who would kill themselves in that way, so violent and bloody? A police officer, too. And all of them had been in her guest house thirteen years ago.

'I don't know what to say,' Charlotte replied. 'This is almost too much to take in.'

'It means Barry's death was no fluke. These men are linked in some way, going back at least thirteen years, if not more. And it looks like someone is trying to finish them all off.'

'Does DCI Summers have any theories?' Charlotte asked, a sense of fear rising in her. This was too close to home, threatening and unsettling.

'No, I was slightly ahead of her on this one. But listen, I've managed to fix up an interview with Harvey Turnbull's wife this evening. Do you want to come?'

'I'm not sure if I can. I'm on a train to Cheshire at the moment...'

'I told her you would be coming. I'm sorry. I thought you'd want to, with that photo being taken in the guest house. She wasn't going to speak to me until I mentioned you. Apparently, she and Harvey used to eat at your place a lot in the nineties. It had a restaurant in the lounge back then; it was quite a destination, apparently.'

'What time?' Charlotte asked, pulling the train timetable from her pocket.

'Half-past seven at the Midland Hotel?' Nigel suggested.

'Can you pick me up from the station? The guest house is covered for staffing already, so I can make it. Are you writing a news story on it?'

'Not yet, but I reckon I will be soon. Something was going on between those men in that photo, Charlotte. And now, thirteen years later, someone appears to want them dead. And it all links up with your guest house in some way. There's something up, and I want to find out what it is.'

CHAPTER TEN

Fletcher Prison made Charlotte shiver. God forbid she should ever end up in a place like that. She could barely believe that her friend was incarcerated there. Jenna was no criminal. Sure, she'd been an accomplice in a kidnapping, but she wasn't violent or psychotic; she'd just been desperate.

The site was surrounded by high fencing topped with razor wire. It reminded Charlotte of a military barracks, much like their own college had been before it had expanded massively. She couldn't imagine what it must be like for Jenna. At least as a visitor she could leave at the end of the day.

Charlotte was subjected to the usual round of scans, searches and pat-downs. Everything about the process made her feel she had something to hide. It was a bleak experience; the officers checking her for weapons or contraband were hardened and unfriendly.

She sat in the visiting room, waiting for Jenna to arrive. Considering it was a women's prison, there was a distinct lack of male visitors. They'd probably long since made themselves scarce, moving on to the next poor soul to make their lives hell.

As the inmates began to pour into the visiting room, the supervising guards visibly tensed. Many of them had tattoos and short hair, and most had haunted looks in their eyes, hardened by life's blows. There was an absence of smiles in the room, despite it being visiting time. Young children cried around her, no doubt confused by seeing their mothers when they couldn't come home. Charlotte thought that there had to be a better way.

Jenna entered the visiting area, her eyes empty of emotion. It made Charlotte want to cry. Had she and Will done this to her? In her less forgiving moments, she wondered if they'd all have been better telling the truth. But Will would get cross with her, claiming Jenna had brought it upon herself. She'd deceived and threatened Charlotte. She'd seen a blackmail opportunity when they arrived back in Morecambe and had been merciless in taking it.

'Her prison sentence is nothing to do with Bruce Craven. You need to remember that,' he'd say to her. But Charlotte knew different; it was all connected in some way to Bruce Craven.

Jenna sat opposite Charlotte at the small, grey table. It had been heavily vandalised with offensive words and images scribbled in pen and even some names carved into the grubby, plastic covering. In the centre of the table, directly between them, were the words *Fuck the pigs* etched deeply.

Jenna sat down, as blank as if she was sedated. The spark of life had gone.

Charlotte never knew what to say. 'How are you?' she ventured. But all she really wanted to do was to hug her friend, apologise for how she'd abandoned her and then walk her out of that place.

'Fine,' Jenna replied, tersely. 'I've got a parole hearing coming up. Pat was found guilty on some other charges from way back. It could play in my favour as a first-time offender.'

'I brought you a couple of books,' Charlotte said. 'They've been checked. You're fine to take them.'

She took them out of her bag and slid them across the table. She'd learned on her first visit to Fletcher Prison not to bring anything with pockets and compartments. She'd once arrived with a plain supermarket bag containing her belongings. Even that was seen as a potential risk to suicidal inmates. The prison had a reputation for it. Charlotte had found an old documentary on the subject on YouTube, which had made her shudder.

The three books sat on the table. They'd been checked already for concealed compartments, drugs, weapons, mobile phones or whatever else visitors tried to smuggle into the place. Jenna reached out to examine one of the books. As she did so, her long sleeve moved up her arm, revealing a bandage around her wrist.

'Jesus, Jenna. What's that?'

As Charlotte blurted the words out loud, the guards tensed instinctively, expecting some trouble to break out. She held her hand up to indicate that all was well.

Self-conscious, Jenna pulled her sleeve back down and withdrew her arm.

'It's nothing,' she replied.

'Jenna, it doesn't look like nothing. What happened?'

'I don't want to talk about it,' she replied.

Charlotte let it drop for the moment, but she knew that

surgical dressings around the wrist area were seldom a positive sign.

They exchanged monosyllabic pleasantries for ten minutes, until one of the inmates kicked off and had to be restrained by the guards. It came from nowhere, a desolate, harrowing scream as if she'd been told something terrible.

'She should be in a psychiatric unit,' Jenna said, as the woman was escorted from the visiting room. 'But there are no places available for her, so they keep her here. She's on a constant suicide watch; they can't believe how she finds ways to kill herself. Ligatures, sharp implements, drugs; you name it, she manages to lay her hands on it. She's actually a very nice woman when she's on her meds and calm. Her estranged husband raped her, killed their kids, then shot himself. Is there any wonder the poor woman is a basket case?'

It was the most she'd heard Jenna speak for months. There was a controlled anger in her voice, as if she wanted to scream out loud, but had to wait until the right time to do it.

'I'm sorry, Jenna...'

'What are you sorry for?'

'I'm just sorry. That you're in here, that your life has come to this. And about Bruce Craven. I should have warned you about him back then. I'm sorry about us and our friendship. I abandoned you for Will. It was a shitty thing to do.'

They sat in silence for a few minutes, the hubbub of chatter now restored in the room after the recent incident.

A tear rolled down Jenna's cheek.

'What is it, Jenna?' Charlotte asked, reaching out to touch her friend. A guard tensed to the right of her; they didn't like sudden moves in this place. Charlotte retracted her hand, placing it onto her lap. She didn't want to cause any trouble for Jenna.

'It's nothing bad, I promise,' Jenna replied. 'Just a low moment in my cell. I don't know what came over me.'

'You didn't try to commit suicide, did you? Oh Jenna, please tell me you're not going to do that?'

'No, I promise I won't. It was just... I don't know what it was. A cry for help, I think. It's just so lonely in here, Charlotte. I'm surrounded by people all day, yet I've never felt so alone. I crave closeness. It's all I can think about. I feel ridiculous.'

Slowly, Charlotte reached her hand across the table so as not to startle the guard who was now watching them closely. She gave Jenna's arm a gentle squeeze.

'What is it, Jenna?' she asked. 'Look, if you can't talk to me, who can you talk to? I promise I'll do what I can to help.'

'You have to show strength in here. You can't let them see you're weak,' Jenna replied.

'Please don't keep it to yourself.'

'I have to tell you, Charlotte. I don't want to bring him back into your life, but you need to know. You might be in danger.'

The knotted feeling in Charlotte's stomach was back. It had been lingering all week, ever since she'd found Barry McMillan hanging from the beam in his room at the guest house. She'd put it down to delayed shock.

'There was something I never told you about Bruce...'

'There were plenty of things none of us talked about.'

'No, this is important, Charlotte.'

Charlotte sat in silence, sensing that she was about to be told something that would rock her life once again. If only she could press a pause button.

Jenna cleared her throat, then began to speak with some difficulty. 'After that night with Bruce, I was terrified, wondering if someone had seen what happened. But as the day passed, and we heard that Bruce had left the holiday camp, I saw I was in the clear.'

'That's how we all felt, Jenna. The man was a monster. We all did what we had to do.'

'But some men came round looking for Bruce. They were horrible, threatening to do terrible things to me.'

'Who, Jenna? What men? Was this at the holiday camp?'

'Jenna nodded, her eyes now red, her cheeks wet with tears.

'They were looking for him, Charlotte. Somebody was looking for Bruce. He was involved with something, and they wanted to know where he was.'

'Did you tell them?' Charlotte asked, desperate for her to get to the point now.

'No, they threatened me, then left me alone.'

'So that's it then, isn't it? I mean, it must have been terrifying for you, but that's all in the past. Isn't it?'

'I thought it was too, Charlotte. But they've started to threaten me again. There's a woman in this prison who keeps intimidating me. She must be connected with them in some way, because she keeps asking me what happened to Bruce Craven. Somebody very powerful and dangerous wants to know what happened to him, Charlotte.'

CHAPTER ELEVEN

Charlotte began the return journey in a trance. Once again, the demons of her past were being swept up by a strong wave, ready to come crashing at her feet. Why wouldn't Bruce Craven stay buried?

Piece by piece, she'd extracted the information from Jenna. How the men had visited her the night after Bruce was killed. How scared she'd been for her life, afraid to tell anybody about it, terrified they'd come back for months afterwards.

She, Jenna and Will were all victims of that man, and now he was pulling them back into his shit. What the hell had he been up to back then that was still so important now? It was over three decades ago. It seemed unbelievable that whatever he'd been involved in could still be making ripples so many years after. They were all kids back then, yet he was continuing to haunt their lives. Charlotte wanted to scream.

It was hard to leave Jenna at Fletcher Prison. She'd finally admitted that the wound on her wrist was due to self-harming, but she didn't know what had driven her to it. In her frustration, fear and helplessness, it had seemed to be the only thing that would alleviate the situation.

'Should I tell the guards? Can I contact the governor?' Charlotte had asked.

'No, I have to deal with this in here. If I get the screws involved, I'm a dead woman. I'll be labelled a snitch. I have to try to avoid contact with this woman. If I'm lucky, I'll get parole and be moved to a less secure prison. Please don't interfere with this, Charlotte. It's easy for you on the outside, but it could misfire badly in here.'

Charlotte longed to be back in Morecambe. Every time the train stopped at a small station, she cursed, willing it along the tracks faster. As the train neared Preston, she chanced her luck with Wi-Fi again. Eureka, she had a connection. She wanted to do some research on Fred Walker. She could feel the grim, black clouds gathering overhead, but she couldn't tell when the raindrops might begin to fall on her and her family. If somebody was looking for Bruce after so many years had passed, they had to make a call on her and Will soon, surely?

The connection was slow, and it took an eternity for the web pages to load. Nigel had already published the bare bones of the news story on the paper's website, but there were no names and detail about how he'd died. She knew nothing about legal matters, but she assumed it was the police who'd requested an information blackout because the family hadn't been informed about the death yet.

She searched for information about Fred Walker, but it was such a common name that it was tricky to pin down. By refining her search, she found an article from a building industry magazine with a detailed profile about his life. He was an impressive man, with an incredible rags-to-riches story, not unlike Barry McMillan.

Charlotte skimmed the article, noting the points of interest. He'd started his working life as a brickie after leaving school at fifteen, then set up his own business from a wooden shed in his back yard in 1981, winning his first major infrastructure project in 1983. His rise thereafter had been nothing short of meteoric. If there was a major redevelopment project going on in and around Morecambe—and further afield throughout the north-west—then Fred Walker was likely to be involved in it. No wonder he'd been featured in the article in the local newspaper, along with Barry and the other men sitting with him around that table.

So who wanted them dead?

What was the other name that Nigel had given her? She could only remember the surname. A Google search brought up a single result, a Flashback feature from a more modern edition of the newspaper. Harvey Turnbull was the man behind Rex Emery's arrest.

2006 Flashback: Popular hotelier and restaurateur Rex Emery is charged with abduction and imprisonment. The officer responsible for his arrest, DCI Harvey Turnbull, receives a commendation for his work. In other news, Morecambe hotel refurbishment project begins, and Bon Jovi tribute band wows crowds.

These men were connected, but it was not clear how. And Harvey Turnbull had committed suicide, in a violent and gruesome way. They'd all been in her guest house too. The echoes of whatever they'd done were lingering in the very fabric of the building; if only she could hear them.

It was too much for her to get her head around. As the train pulled away from Preston, Charlotte closed her eyes and tried to figure out what to do next. If Jenna was being bothered about Bruce Craven again, that might potentially come back to her own doorstep. What if Jenna revealed what had happened? They'd discussed that possibility in the jail. Jenna had sworn she wouldn't say anything, yet she had been treacherous about the facts already. If George hadn't seen her finishing off Bruce among the broken bricks and rubble in the paddling pool's foundations, she and Will would have forever believed that they were responsible for his death. As far as that story was concerned, Jenna had previous form.

George could vouch for them. He was their living proof. A surge of heat coursed through her body as she realised how vulnerable they were. If George were to die—and the possibility had to be considered—it would be down to Jenna's word against her and Will. And the body was still there, in the foundations. There was still proof that he'd been killed.

Charlotte looked around at the people in the carriage, imagining they all knew what she had done, looking at her, accusing her. For the first time since they'd rescued Lucia, she realised how exposed they still were. There was nothing to stop Jenna sending those men over to see her and Will. Her children would be in danger.

Eventually, Jenna had told her what the men had done. How they'd touched her and implied that they would rape her. She felt faint even thinking that she might have exposed Lucia and Olli to that level of danger.

Yet, how could she tell the police? She couldn't. It would mean having to admit what they'd done. She was as trapped as Jenna. This was dangerous, even worse than before. Although she'd been scared out of her mind by the threats from Jenna and Pat, she now knew they were false, intended to blackmail her out of money she and Will didn't have. It was a botched and clumsy attempt, scary at the time, but ridiculous in retrospect.

What Jenna was telling her now was truly chilling. What if they came to her house? What if they threatened her children? How far would they go to find out the truth about Bruce Craven?

The only thing that was preventing Charlotte from imploding was the single consolation that she could take from her two hours with Jenna: for whatever reason, the men had not come to visit her and Will. Maybe their information was wrong. Perhaps they didn't know about her link to Bruce.

Her phone sounded. She expected it to be Nigel Davies again, but it was the school, one of the telephone numbers Charlotte dreaded seeing. To her horror, it was Mr Hyland, the man who'd instructed her to stay away from the school premises if she was unable to behave like the other parents.

'Mrs Grayson? It's Mr Hyland from school. I need to speak to you about Olli and Lucia. Are you able to come over?'

Her heart began pounding violently in her chest, as if it were about to break out.

'I'm on a train just outside Lancaster at the moment. I won't be home for some time, I'm afraid. My husband is also tied up at work today. Are you able to tell me about it now? Neither of them are hurt, are they?'

She walked along the train carriage, seeking the relative privacy of the linking corridors. It was unlikely to be good news. She could sense Mr Hyland's apprehension, even at the end of a poor-quality mobile phone line.

'I'm afraid we've had to take the serious action of suspending Lucia from school for one week. She started a fight in the canteen at the end of lunchtime and threw her tray of food at another student…'

'Oh my God, I'm so sorry. Was the other student hurt? What on earth came over her?'

'We had to move her into isolation while she calmed down, Mrs Grayson. It's taken us all afternoon just to be able to speak to her.'

'Did anybody get hurt? Who did she throw the tray at?'

'That's just it, Mrs Grayson. Your daughter threw the tray at your son.'

CHAPTER TWELVE

Nigel Davies was waiting for Charlotte as the train pulled into Morecambe station. She'd used the journey as a guilt trip, allowing her more than an hour to have a debate with herself about which was her greatest priority. Her daughter, who had experienced a meltdown at school? Her son, who had been on the receiving end of Lucia's attack? Or the visit to Harvey Turnbull's widow, which might give some clues to the terrible events involving a group of people who had met in her guest house?

In the end, Nigel Davies got her attention. Despite the embarrassing events at the school, and even though she wanted to tear a strip off Lucia for her appalling attitude of late, the security of the whole family was more important than anything else.

Unfortunately, Will didn't see it like that. Charlotte had had to abandon a Facebook chat conversation with him after it had got heated, with Will misinterpreting what she was saying. She needed him onside, so she rang instead, desperate to bring him up to date on the latest developments in the town and Jenna's news in particular.

'You're spending more time running around with Nigel Davies than attending to the guest house or your own children,' he complained.

'My shift's already being covered by Isla and George. You know they always help out when I visit Jenna, in case the trains are held up. And as for Lucia, she's almost an adult. I shouldn't have to come rushing back home because she can't control her temper with her brother. Besides, we need a good sit down and a proper chat with Lucia; there's obviously something going on at school.'

'Yes, but she's been suspended for a week. Doesn't that give you cause for concern?' Will asked.

The phone signal was perfect, for a change. Charlotte would have been grateful if the train had passed through a tunnel and cut him off unexpectedly.

'Of course it does; it's an embarrassment, another humiliation in front of Mr Hyland. But for all we know, the school could be the source of whatever is going on. Maybe it's for the best that she's away from classes for a week. It'll give us a proper chance for a chat. And as for rushing home, I suspect an evening alone in her bedroom thinking it over will do her the world of good. Besides, I need to talk to you about Barry McMillan. I can't do it here, but I need you to trust me, Will. I'll be back home as soon as I've met up with Lara Turnbull. It's important.'

The best Charlotte could achieve was acquiescence. She'd have to settle for that; he wouldn't stretch to endorsing her actions. As she ended the call, she realised that the issue of Barry McMillan was starting to become a full-time preoccupation, along with the threats Jenna was receiving.

'Good trip?' Nigel asked as she stepped down from the train. 'I'm parked across the road in the free parking.'

It struck Jenna that she wasn't confiding in anyone fully. Nigel, Will, Jenna, George and Isla had all had conversations with her about recent events, yet she hadn't given any one of them the full picture. Not even Will. She resolved to tell him everything when she got home. After all, it was concealing the details of the past that had brought events to a head last time.

Charlotte changed the subject to a more interesting one.

'Any more information about Fred Walker?' she asked Nigel.

'What a news story. The newspaper staff are on overtime, putting together the front page. DCI Summers is holding a press conference about his death at the Winter Gardens tomorrow morning. I'll pick you up if you want to come?'

Charlotte could hear Will's voice in her head. Lucia wouldn't be in school the next day. She ought to make her presence felt.

'What time is it on?' she asked.

'Eleven o'clock,' he replied. 'They're expecting TV, radio and possibly even national newspapers. Walker was on the Times Rich List. Barry McMillan wasn't far from it. DCI Summers is reluctant to link the deaths publicly, but the press has done it already, so she's probably lost control of the story. That's probably why she's holding the press conference, in an attempt to wrestle it back from the media.'

Charlotte had already decided to attend the press conference. Will would be at work by then and would never know that she'd gone. Lucia would still be in bed by the time she got back anyway, since she didn't have to get up for a school day. Her newly made resolution about honesty had fallen at the first hurdle. Charlotte was confident that it was justified, to protect her family, even if not telling Will sat uncomfortably with her conscience.

Within ten minutes they were parked up at the Midland Hotel, sipping their coffees in the dining section while awaiting the arrival of Lara Turnbull. Charlotte surveyed the area, thinking back to Barry McMillan's presentation earlier in the week. They'd been using this same room for his author event, facing out towards the sea, with spectacular views and a prime location.

She pictured him just outside the dining area, on the terrace, taking the phone call. Who was it from? Was that the call that had set in motion the events leading to his death? She wondered if the police had located his phone yet. That would throw more light on the issue, surely?

'Nigel Davies? I'm Lara Turnbull.'

A grey-haired but well-groomed woman, probably in her sixties, was standing by their coffee table. She wore severe glasses and her voice was strong and assured. She dressed conventionally, just like a lady who sat on committees and was heavily involved in her local community.

Nigel stood up to shake her hand. She was the kind of woman that required a firm handshake, nothing of the wet fish variety. He pulled out a chair for her and introduced Charlotte.

Lara Turnbull was straight to business, not even waiting for her order of Earl Grey tea to arrive before she started.

'I take it you're here because of what happened to Fred Walker this morning?'

Nigel was taken aback by her directness but recovered swiftly.

'Yes, we believe that the death of your husband may be linked to Fred Walker.'

'Well, it's about time too. My husband's inquest was

nothing more than a cover-up, Mr Davies. Do you know how he died?'

'No, I don't,' said Nigel.

'There was nothing wrong with my husband on the day he died. I know that people always say that about suicide cases, but Harvey was made of sterner stuff. We met in the military as teenagers. He joined the police in civilian life. Believe me, he was not the type to kill himself.'

Charlotte looked at her. Right or wrong, she was convinced about what she was saying.

'He was decapitated by the wheels on the roller coaster at Adventure Kingdom, did you know that?'

Nigel nodded, and Charlotte wondered how Lara Turnbull was able to carry on, having known such violent tragedy in her life.

'Did you know that he was secured to the wooden sleepers by a length of rope?' she added.

'No, we didn't,' Nigel replied, looking at Charlotte.

'The inquest found that he'd secured himself, probably so he didn't turn back at the last moment and move his head before the roller coaster train came along the track. It happened instantly, Mr Davies; it took his head clean off. I wasn't allowed to view him in his coffin before we buried him; the undertaker said it would be too upsetting.'

Charlotte and Nigel sat in silence, not knowing how to continue the conversation. Lara Turnbull carried on.

'When we moved to Morecambe, we lived in a small, terraced house. As my husband worked his way up the ranks, we managed to move to a semi-detached house. It was our pride and joy, and we thought we were made for life. Then Harvey got into some kind of business with these men.'

Lara Turnbull reached into her formidable handbag

and took out a black-and-white photograph. Charlotte and Nigel looked at each other in surprise as they both realised what she was showing them. It was the five men, pictured around the circular table in the guest house. But it was a slightly different shot, not the one that Nigel had been sent as a newspaper cutting.

'Where did you get this image?' Nigel asked.

'The newspaper photographer sent it to Harvey as a favour. It was one of the photographs which didn't make it into the paper. You can see that somebody's arm is getting in the way on the left-hand side. But Harvey wanted a record of that night. He said it marked a special moment for us.'

'You were about to say something about where you were living?' Charlotte reminded her. She was fascinated by the photograph. As an original print, it was sharp and extremely clear. She couldn't imagine the guest house looking like that.

'Soon after this picture was taken, Harvey and I moved to my present house at Hest Bank. It's a very nice house, with remarkable views and located in a very well-to-do area.'

'Hest Bank is a lovely area,' Charlotte said.

'Indeed, it is, Ms Grayson. Have you ever looked at the police salary scales? A DCI earns a good salary, but not an exceptional one. The way we were living was more akin to how a Chief Constable would live. I wasn't working then—our children were at school—and Harvey would insist it was all due to clever investments and our previous houses growing in equity.'

'It sounds like you were very fortunate, Mrs Turnbull.'

Charlotte was struggling to see what the problem was. She wished some of her own financial affairs had worked out so well.

'That's just it, Ms Grayson. After Harvey died, I found out that all of our investments had come to nothing in the financial crash in the eighties. Yet somehow, perfectly legally, we had managed to buy our very substantial house in cash; there was no mortgage on it, so we were living for free.'

'Do you think this is connected with your husband's death?' Nigel asked. Charlotte thought they worked well as a team, alternating the questions and keeping her talking.

'I have no doubt about it whatsoever, Mr Davies. I believe my husband was involved in something serious at a very high level. Whatever it was, he was well-rewarded for the part he played in it. Something must have turned sour. If he did kill himself, then it was connected with whatever he was involved in. But I do not believe his death was a suicide. I think he was killed because of what he knew. That's why these men are dying now. They were all involved in it. I'm absolutely certain. And I think that before we're done the last two men in that photograph will be dead too.'

CHAPTER THIRTEEN

Olli had a cut on his forehead where a can of coke had struck him as it flew through the air, propelled by an angry swipe from Lucia in the school canteen. Charlotte had hoped the reckoning with their daughter could be postponed until the following day, but Will had other plans.

The conversation with Lara Turnbull had been productive, if terrifying.

'I have to tell DCI Summers about this,' Nigel said after Lara left them. 'I can't believe she let us get the photograph scanned in the hotel office. That was good of them. I took a photo of it and texted it to her. They have to make sure those two remaining men have decent protection. They must be next in line.'

'But Barry McMillan committed suicide,' Charlotte pointed out. 'He wasn't killed. If you believe the coroner, Harvey Turnbull did the same. Maybe they just got in over their heads.'

'If it wasn't for Fred Walker dying the way he did, I'd agree with you. But being strangled in a theatre box? That's a horrific way to die. It was done to make an example of him.'

'Maybe,' Charlotte replied, thinking it through. 'I wish walls could talk. Imagine the tales our guest house could tell.'

Nigel and Charlotte had left the Midland Hotel soon after Lara Turnbull's departure. Charlotte was worn out from her day, and Nigel was keen to get a good night's sleep in anticipation of the next day's press conference. He dropped her off on the road outside the guest house, promising to pick her up again the next day at ten-thirty.

By the time she'd checked that the guests in the lounge were happy and that all was well in the kitchen, Charlotte was eager for an early night. But as she arrived upstairs, she walked in on a court case that was already in progress. Will was sitting at the table, with Olli beside him sporting a sticking plaster on his head. Lucia was opposite them sitting with her arms crossed and a hostile look on her face.

'Ah, your mum's home, let's see if she agrees with me.'

Charlotte wasn't ready for a hijack. She was preoccupied with what Lara Turnbull had told them.

'So, what do you think?' Will asked.

'I think I'd rather discuss this at another time,' Charlotte replied, not in the mood for a family intervention.

'I think we should discuss it now.'

Will was pushing his luck. If he carried on the way he was going, Lucia wouldn't be the only one getting a row that night.

'I'm just too tired to do this now, Will...'

'Then when will we do it?' Will said, more forcefully than usual. 'You seem to be out with Nigel Davies most of the time. I think it's important that we deal with this now.'

He'd made a reasonable point about her going off with

Nigel. She probably owed him some response. Charlotte decided she'd better engage in the process.

'What happened?' she asked Lucia.

Her daughter's body language suggested an answer wasn't going to be forthcoming.

'Olli? How about you start?'

'It was something about nothing, really. I just wanted to talk to Lucia at school, away from home. We're all worried about her—'

'Get stuffed, Olli!'

'Lucia!' Will warned.

'I'd seen her talking to some guy on the way in to school this morning. He had a purple Mohican and a tattoo all around his neck. You might say he stood out a bit...'

'Why can't you just keep your big mouth shut!' Lucia screamed at him. She thumped the table, stormed out of the room and slammed her bedroom door behind her.

'That went well,' Charlotte said. 'I told you to leave it until we'd chatted.'

Will was on her back immediately.

'How many evenings this week have we been saying we need to talk to Lucia? A man died in this guest house at the beginning of the week, and we're treating it like he just checked out as normal. I don't know about you, but I'm feeling pretty goddamn tense about it. And this behaviour from Lucia is not normal. She's been lying to us. She's quit her job at the arcade, she's out late at night and now this. Tell her, Olli.'

Olli looked at Will to make certain he'd got the go-ahead, then turned towards her, as if checking she would be receptive. Charlotte gave a small nod of encouragement.

'This guy I saw her with, he was older than us, in his twenties or maybe even thirties. His Mohican was shaped like a lizard on his head, and the neck tattoo was some kind of dragon or snake or something. He was pierced heavily too. Let's put it this way; he's not a student at the school. Lucia was talking to him like he was a best friend.'

'Does he work at the arcade?' Charlotte asked. 'He's not the sort of person you could miss, by the sound of things.'

'I've never seen him there,' Olli replied. 'Anyhow, I decided to ask her about it away from home, just to see what's going on. I spotted her in the school cafeteria, all alone, so I asked if I could join her.'

'Thanks for looking out for her, Olli,' Will said.

'I pulled up a chair and just talked nonsense to start with. You know, school stuff, music stuff, the usual crap. Then I mentioned casually that I'd seen her with this guy. I asked her who he was.'

'What did she say?' Charlotte asked.

'She just started tearing into me,' Olli continued. 'Talk about being on a short fuse. She just exploded. She told me to butt out of her business and get back to Miss Pretty Pants. That's what she calls Willow now. They used to be best buddies until a few weeks ago. I pushed her on it again, and that's when she stood up, shouted that I was a fucking dickhead, threw her tray at me and ran out of the dining hall. You could have heard a pin drop. Everybody was looking at me. It was so embarrassing.'

'At least she's not the only member of the family to have made a spectacle of herself at the school,' Will said.

'That was uncalled for,' Charlotte protested. 'If you remember, I was trying to do something similar when I accosted that man outside the school gates. My intentions were good, even if the outcome was embarrassing.'

'I'm sorry,' Will said gently. 'I'm just really bothered by

all of this. It's not like Lucia. And this chap with the tattoo, he sounds like he might be trouble.'

'You can't dismiss people because of the way they look,' Olli said.

'I know that Olli, I see enough of it at the college. It's hard for us oldies, you know. Me and your mum have managed to make it to our fifties without having anything pierced, dyed or tattooed. When we were young, people dressed like that were punk rockers, and they were often damned violent as well. This guy is as likely to be the local vicar, but I can't help but be concerned. If he was the local vicar, Lucia wouldn't be behaving like this, would she?'

'I guess not,' Olli admitted.

'How did the school deal with it?' Charlotte asked.

'As well as could be expected,' Olli replied. 'Lucia was hiding in the toilets. The school counsellor went to find her and brought her to see the head teacher. They patched me up in sickbay and then we had an inquest. They couldn't raise you or dad on your mobile phones, so they told Lucia they were going to suspend her for one week. It's a bit more than a week, actually; it's the remainder of this week and all of next week.'

'The letter is over there,' Will said, nodding towards the kitchen counter.

'Are you okay, Olli?' Charlotte asked. 'Did you get hurt?'

'No, I'm fine; it was only a slight knock. You know what school's like. They had to record it all in the accident book, check me for concussion, make sure I'm not allergic to plasters and all the rest of it. They were just covering their arses.'

There was silence as they all considered the events of the day.

'I'm going to head back to my room if that's okay?' Olli said. 'Homework waits for no man!'

He left them in the kitchen and Charlotte pulled up a chair opposite Will.

'What a day!' she said, grateful to sit down. 'I'm ready for bed.'

'We're not done just yet,' Will said, looking up at her. 'I need to speak to you about Nigel Davies. Why do you appear to be happier spending time with him than with your own family at the moment?'

CHAPTER FOURTEEN

Day Four: Friday

Charlotte was feeling guilty when the alarm woke her up on Friday morning. It felt like she was failing everybody. There were fires all around her that needed putting out and she hadn't managed to extinguish any of them. A morning in the kitchen with Isla, serving the guests and chatting about their planned excursions for the day, was just what she needed.

'Thanks for covering for me yesterday, Isla,' she said, as she fastened a clean pinafore. The guest house worked like clockwork most days, enabling her to come and go as she pleased. She was aware Isla was becoming slower and, in spite of her vow to die in the job, it had struck Charlotte that she ought to consider some succession planning. She needed to think about getting that immense manual inside Isla's head transferred to a new and younger member of staff; but where would she find somebody as dependable as her?

'No problem,' Isla replied, managing the hob like a pro, ensuring that the fried eggs were runny, the bacon perfectly grilled and the toast crisp but not burnt, just as the guests preferred it. 'How are we looking for bookings over the weekend?'

'Fairly busy,' said Charlotte. 'Just one room free, otherwise it's a full house. Barry McMillan's room was professionally cleaned yesterday while I was out, so that's also available now.'

It felt like Isla had something on her mind. Charlotte lingered in the kitchen a little longer than she needed to, giving her friend ample opportunity to get it off her chest.

'You know our little chat the other day?' Isla asked, not meeting Charlotte's eyes. She pretended instead to be intent scooping the hot oil from the frying pan over a fried egg. 'This chap wants his egg hard you said, that's right, isn't it?'

'Yes, Mr Levens, he likes his yolk completely hard. Like rubber is how he described it.'

'I didn't mean to be evasive about your questions. It's just that... well, my early days working at this guest house were not all as happy as they are now. I used to come here as a customer too. The downstairs lounge used to be a restaurant; it was very busy back then. The dates get confused sometimes, that's all.'

'I didn't mean to be pushy, Isla. I'm sorry if you felt I was. We've had a lot of pressure on with Barry McMillan's death, and there are other things going on with the family, as I'm sure you already know. Lucia is proving a bit of a handful at the moment. My mind's elsewhere, that's all. I'm sorry.'

'I'm worried about George,' Isla said, out of the blue. 'I

think he's keeping something secret from me. I'm worried that he might be ill.'

'Oh, no, I'm sure he's not,' Charlotte began, then recalled her private conversation with George. Flustered, she couldn't stop herself uttering the next words.

'I'm sure he's okay; he certainly hasn't said anything to me.'

It was another lie. It was getting harder to keep track of them all.

'Please don't keep anything from me, if he's trying to protect me,' Isla said. 'I want to know if there's anything wrong. I never thought I'd find this joy with someone like George so late in life. If it's going to be torn away from me, I want to know. I can't face losing him. I couldn't live with it again.'

Charlotte waited to see if she was going to say any more. Every now and then she would sense a deep sadness in Isla. She saw it at that moment, as she dished up Mr Levens' rubbery egg. She could only speculate as to its cause, but it might be something family-related, most likely a child. She was certain Isla had had at least one child from the references she made to Lucia and Olli. She'd been around children; she knew what they were like.

The phone in the hallway started to ring.

'Can you whisk those out to the lounge, Isla? I'd better take that.'

It was just after nine o'clock. Will and Olli had departed already, and Lucia hadn't shown her face yet. That suited Charlotte. She'd take Lucia out for lunch after the press conference. They could have a proper chat then. She'd follow all the advice in the books; no confrontation, no accusations, just active listening as they referred to it.

Charlotte went to answer the phone.

'Hello, Lakes View Guest House; Charlotte Grayson speaking.'

'Hello, is that Charlotte Grayson as in Will and Charlotte Grayson?'

It was a woman's voice with a strong hint of a north-east accent.

'Yes, that's me. How can I help you?'

'I'm sorry it's short notice, but do you have a room available tonight and Saturday? I may extend beyond that, but I'll decide when I'm there, if that's okay?'

Charlotte consulted the bookings. She could accommodate the booking and, except for Barry McMillan's room, that gave them a full house for the weekend. She'd decide where to put this guest later. She was relieved that they didn't have any events in the lounge that weekend. It was always all hands to the pumps whenever that happened.

'Yes, I can book you in on those dates. If you decide to stay, we've also got a couple of rooms free throughout the week. Whose name shall I book it in?'

'Mrs Bowker. Daisy Bowker.'

Charlotte took down her details, went through the credit card procedures and secured the booking in the online management system.

'Just one last question,' Charlotte said. 'What's your reason for visiting Morecambe? Leisure or business?'

'A bit of both,' Daisy replied. 'I'm researching my family history. I've got a relative whose last known whereabouts were in Morecambe. I want to see if I can track him down.'

Charlotte's interest was piqued.

'Now that sounds interesting,' she said. 'We have a lovely local library and I can recommend the local historian to you; he's excellent. Jon Rogers is his name. He seems to know everything there is to know about Morecambe. I'm not sure if he works Saturdays, mind you.'

'Well actually, I wanted to book in at your guest house for a reason. I read about you and your husband online in a recent article about the guest house. I don't think you've had it very long, have you?'

Charlotte tensed up. This woman had sought them out rather than selecting them at random from a list of search results, as most guests did. She hesitated as she answered, nervous to find out more.

'Yes, we've been here for some time now. What was it that caught your eye? That story has been read by a lot of people. It's amazing how far the local newspaper travels.'

'Well, I saw that you and your husband met at the Sandy Beaches Holiday Camp in the eighties.'

Charlotte's stomach tightened and she started to feel sick.

'Yes... that's right. It's been demolished now; they're building houses on it.'

'So I've read,' Daisy continued. 'It looks like it's a big project, from what I've been able to work out. I'm trying to find somebody connected with the holiday camp, but it's proving to be quite some task.'

Charlotte tried to silence the alarm bells that were sounding inside her head. Thousands of people had passed through the Sandy Beaches Holiday Camp over the years. Some were staff, but most were holiday-makers. She scolded herself for being too jumpy. This woman would come and go; there was nothing to worry about.

'Have you managed to track down the electoral roll or the phone books from the time? They can be useful,' Charlotte suggested.

'Oh yes, I've been through all the usual channels,' Daisy

replied. 'I'm used to doing research like this. Most people are much easier to find, but my half-brother is proving to be the proverbial needle in the haystack. He moved from Jesmond in 1984 and then I lose track of him completely. It's unusual for somebody to slip below the radar like that, particularly in these days of digital records. He even seemed to evade the Poll Tax, and that took some doing.'

Charlotte knew the answer to her question already, but she had to ask it; she had to know. They hadn't even considered the possibility of a marriage breakdown, a broken family and a half-brother or half-sister. That prospect had passed them by completely.

'It sounds like you've got quite a task ahead of you,' Charlotte said, trying as best she could to keep her voice steady. 'Sandy Beaches was such a huge place, it's unlikely that I'd have met him. What was his name, just to be certain?'

'It was Bruce. My half-brother is called Bruce Craven.'

CHAPTER FIFTEEN

It was as much as Charlotte could do not to scream down the phone when Daisy Bowker revealed her identity. She needed to speak to Will, but he'd be at the college, either chatting in the staff room or with his students already. This was getting too close. The woman would be in their home. She could almost feel Bruce Craven's breath against the back of her neck. It was paralysing.

'Are you all right? You look like you've seen a ghost.'

Isla's voice shook Charlotte out of her silence.

'I'm fine, Isla, just another booking. Is George coming to the guest house any time soon? I could do with having a word with him.'

She had to warn Will and George. They needed to get their stories straight. Daisy Bowker had to meet a dead end when she visited Morecambe. If she didn't, who knew what a storm she might create?

'You know George. He'll be in and out, no doubt passing when he takes Una out for her walk. Shall I tell him you need to see him?'

'Yes, please do that,' Charlotte said. 'It would be good if he could pop in before Friday evening.'

Daisy Bowker would arrive at the hotel after four o'clock the next day. She'd want to know all about the holiday camp and their time there. They would have to agree to answer honestly, up to the point where Bruce disappeared that day. And they couldn't say a thing about her brief fling with Bruce. Daisy would never let it go if she discovered that connection. She'd ask all sorts of questions: what was he like, what did he talk about, who were his friends? It would never end. Sooner or later, they'd be exposed.

Daisy Bowker had to hit a brick wall when she visited. If she didn't, it would all blow up in their faces.

Charlotte checked the time. She had over an hour before Nigel Davies came to pick her up. Will had given her a hard time about her new friend the night before. He wasn't suggesting an affair, but he was concerned about the amount of time she was spending with him at the expense of being there for Olli and Lucia.

'They need us to be more available, now they're teenagers,' he said. 'The toddler stage is easy by comparison; the trouble they can get in at their age is far more harmful.'

Charlotte brought him up to date with what Jenna had said. She also explained why she was like a dog with a bone over Barry McMillan and Fred Walker.

'It's all getting too close for comfort, Will. This situation makes us vulnerable. The more we get involved with the police, the more likely it is that one of makes a slip. I'm working with Nigel to protect our family, not to abandon you all.'

In the end, Will got it. She even got an apology from him. He'd felt pangs of jealousy, and he had—only for a moment—wondered if there was anything going on between her and Nigel. There wasn't. Charlotte was certain of that in her own mind. Nor did she think that Nigel was attracted to her. But there was a professional spark there; they worked well together, as colleagues might.

She found the journalistic process absorbing. It was like being in the police, only without the same level of information about suspects and evidence. She enjoyed the increased access that Nigel got as a reporter, and the excitement too.

The guest house brought in the money that they needed, helping her transition from a near-nervous breakdown to being a fully productive member of the family once again. It had spared her from having to return to teaching to help pay the bills. But the investigative work she'd done with Nigel Davies fired her brain, providing a glimmer of something else, possibly a change in direction.

Charlotte cleared the dining room, wiped the tables and checked on Isla. She was chatting to the cleaners who were just clocking on for the day. They helped with the set-up for the evening meals while guests were clearing out of their rooms.

'I'm heading upstairs,' Charlotte said. 'Give me a shout if you need me.'

There was something she wanted to do while Olli was out, without his knowledge. She didn't want to spook the poor kid. He'd had enough to deal with after his run-in with Lucia.

She was pleased to see that Lucia wasn't out of her bed yet. With a day off school, she'd no doubt be in there until midday. Charlotte left a note on the kitchen table asking her daughter to text her if she wanted to meet up for a late lunch in town at one o'clock or thereabouts.

Then, feeling like a burglar, she took a torch from underneath the sink and crept along to Olli's bedroom door. Slowly and as quietly as possible, she pushed down the door handle and stepped inside, closing the door behind her. This was Olli's private sanctuary; she knew better than to go prying around a teenager's bedroom. She moved over to the half-door that led to the roof space.

Placing the torch on the floor, Charlotte knelt on the carpet and opened up the door. They'd thrown her old teaching folders and lesson notes in there when they moved in. She wanted them out of the way, so she wouldn't have to look at them.

Olli ran light on possessions; his life was in the cloud. No more were the books, CDs, LPs and videos of her youth. Most of Olli's possessions were stored on his laptop hard drive, so apart from clothing and school textbooks, his room was sparse.

She'd forgotten what the roof space looked like. She seldom entered Olli's room and barely had cause to think much about that space in the building. She pressed the light switch and was delighted that the bulb still worked. It illuminated the area well enough, but there were still some dark areas in there, for which she'd need the torch.

Charlotte was just about able to stand up straight once she was inside. It was tight with boxes, so she began to move them out into Olli's room, to make space to move around properly. She didn't even know what she was looking for; she just needed to get a sense of what had happened to Piper in that place.

Before long, she'd moved all the boxes out. It felt good to be safely away from the clutches of teaching and able to throw all those things into the tip now. She'd move them into the living room, then get rid of them as soon as possible.

It would feel cathartic throwing them into a skip at the local waste disposal unit. Good riddance.

With the roof-space now empty, except for a few bits and pieces that Olli had saved from his toddler years, Charlotte turned on the torch and began to have a good look around. The joists were boarded over, so there was no trying to avoid putting her foot through the ceiling. The roof felt above her head was dusty, and the red brick wall housing the chimney breast was dulled and home to several cobwebs.

She closed her eyes, trying to imagine what it would be like to be a terrified teenager, restrained and no doubt gagged to ensure her silence. There was no place to wash, just a simple sink in the corner of Olli's room which looked like it had been there for some years. The half-door would have been closed. If her captors were especially cruel, they'd have turned off the lights and left her in darkness. It didn't bear thinking about. The poor girl must have been scared out of her mind.

Lucia had undergone a similar experience, kidnapped by Jenna's useless boyfriend, Pat Harris, tied up and left on her knees in the dried out paddling pool at the derelict holiday camp. She appeared to have recovered well, but perhaps the incident had had a greater impact on her than they'd thought.

Charlotte wanted to reach out and hug her daughter through the wall of the adjoining room. But Lucia just shrugged off any attempts at closeness. They put it down to her being a teenager. Perhaps they did need to spend a little more time with her.

There was a scratching just to the side of Charlotte's head. It shocked her, and she dropped the torch. She recovered quickly; it was just the sound of a bird nesting under the tiles of the roof. It had been right next to her ear.

As she moved to pick up the torch, Charlotte noticed the beam illuminating a dulled carving in the floorboards. She'd missed it before, but she might have been standing on it. She brushed away the coating of dust and debris to get a closer look, moving the beam of the torch so she could make out what the carving said: *Piper Phillips, age 16, 2006.*

It was a simple enough carving, scratched with an old nail or perhaps a fragment of a chipped brick. But Piper had displayed that most human of instincts: even as a prisoner, she had wanted to record that she'd been there, that her life counted for something.

But why Piper Phillips? She knew her as Piper Lawrence. Was that her escorting name, perhaps to protect her real identity from her clients?

Charlotte checked the time on her phone; it was just before ten o'clock. If she moved fast, she'd still be able to get to the press conference in time. She had to speak to Piper, and it couldn't wait. She had to know if it was a coincidence that she shared the same surname as Jenna.

CHAPTER SIXTEEN

Charlotte didn't bother packing anything away in Olli's bedroom. She left everything exactly as it was. Neither did she care about disturbing Lucia any more; this had to be more than just chance.

Leaving the light on in the roof-space and rushing down the flights of stairs two steps at a time, Charlotte listened to be sure that Isla was still around to pick up on any straggler guests, then shot out of the front door without even announcing her departure. This couldn't wait.

She crossed over to the promenade side of the road. It was always faster-moving along that side; the pavements could become congested further up where the B&Bs and hotels were replaced by stores, arcades and coffee shops.

It was cold along the promenade, making her wish she'd brought a coat, but it was reasonably quiet and she could make fast progress. It also meant she could jog along and send Nigel Davies a text message at the same time.

I'll make my own way to the Winter Gardens. See you there at 10.30.

She was out of breath already. She slowed to a fast walk,

the strong wind blowing along the sea front making it difficult to run. She passed the RNLI hut, then the town clock and eventually the Midland Hotel. The West End seemed a long way away on foot, but it was such a nuisance getting the car out of the back alleyway that most days she walked; it was usually quicker.

She passed the bus stop opposite the end of the promenade where she and Will used to catch the last ride back to the Sandy Beaches Holiday Camp. They'd usually been for a scampi and chips at the restaurant close by, which was now closed. For a moment, she thought back on that time with fondness. Then she remembered the danger that it had placed them all in.

When she reached Piper's street, Charlotte couldn't remember the house number. They all looked the same to her, houses of multiple occupancy with clusters of doorbells to the side of their front doors. She wished she'd taken more notice when she'd visited with Nigel.

Charlotte knew roughly where the house was positioned on the street, but had to step up to a couple of front doors to check the names on the doorbells. At last, she found Piper's. She rang the bell but there was no answer. She tried again. It was just past half-past ten. There was no way Piper could have a client in at that time of day, surely?

A man walked up to the door with a dog which looked like it had seen better days. Both dog and owner appeared tired out by life; both needed a haircut, and neither looked like they'd eaten properly in some time.

'Excuse me, luv,' the man said, pushing past.

'Okay if I go in behind you to see my friend?' Charlotte asked.

'Be my guest,' he replied.

Once inside the property, she recalled the layout and

headed up the stairs to Piper's room. She banged at the door.

'Piper! It's Charlotte Grayson. I need to speak to you. Open up!'

She heard voices inside. She hadn't even considered that Piper might have a personal life, a boyfriend or a husband, perhaps. There was a movement at the door. It opened, revealing a middle-aged man, his paunch hanging over a pair of ill-fitting boxer shorts. He was mostly bald, though he was hanging on for dear life to the little hair he still had.

'Sling yer hook, darlin', she's on the clock until eleven.'

He began to shut the door, but Charlotte pushed it open. This couldn't wait. The curtains were closed, and Piper was in bed. A plastic whip and a bottle of lubricant had been placed on the bedside table. She wanted to cry for her; there had to be better ways to make a living.

'Jesus!' Piper said, sitting up in the bed. 'This is my work, you know. You can't just come barging in here whenever you feel like it. If I don't answer the doorbell, it means I've got a client in.'

'I'm sorry, I won't do it again, but I have to speak to you.'

'Can't it wait, luv? Me and Piper here can get a lot done in half an hour. Time is money yer know. I'm back at work for midday.'

Charlotte ignored the man, looking directly at Piper.

'I went into the roof-space where you were held as a teenager...'

'Do you have to?' Piper said, agitated. 'I want to forget all that. It was a long time ago. I need to get back to my client. I have rent to pay, you know.'

'I saw your name carved in the floorboards. Piper Phillips. You're Jenna's daughter, aren't you?'

Piper was silent.

'Am I getting my punishment or not?' the man asked.

'How much are you paying?' Charlotte asked.

'One hundred pounds. So far, I've only had fifty quid's worth.'

'Look, give me five minutes, and I'll be gone. I have to speak to Piper.'

The man mumbled something and went to sit on an armchair by the window. He found his phone and began scrolling through his messages. Charlotte turned back to Piper. She was sitting up in bed now, not bothering to pull the sheets up to her shoulders. Charlotte wondered what it must be like to be so lacking in self-consciousness about your body that you couldn't care less if your top half was naked while you were talking to a stranger who'd just barged into your flat.

'Piper, this is serious. I need to know.'

'I detest the bitch,' Piper said at last. 'She gave me no help after the cops found me. It was like it had never happened.'

Charlotte thought back to Lucia; had they done enough to support her after her trauma?

'So Jenna is your mother?' she asked.

'Yes, but I wish she wasn't. I took my father's name. I wanted to forget my mum. My dad was almost as useless as she was, but at least he'd take me to the pub and let me get drunk out my mind. It's how I blotted it out. I was only sixteen years old.'

For the first time Charlotte heard Piper's voice break, as if decades of pent-up emotions were about to spill over. She wanted to reach out her arms and hug her, desperately sorry for the life she was living.

'Look, Piper, I'm going. I'll book in with the agency for another time, but I expect that last half hour, right?'

Piper nodded at him. The man pulled on his clothes and checked his sparse hair in the mirror. Before he left, he took his wedding ring out of his trouser pocket and slipped it back on his finger.

'See yah!' he said, leaving the flat.

Piper exhaled, evidently relieved he was gone.

'He has bad breath,' she said. 'It's all I can do not to be sick, but he's a regular. I don't even have to have sex with him. He just likes the whip. He has a lovely wife and two teenage kids at home. That man pays my rent every month.'

'You know, I have work at the guest house. I'd be happy to help you with a job if you think it would help?'

'I'm not sure cleaning out rooms and wiping tables would pay as well as this. Some clients are horrible, but I can make good money at it, more than the minimum wage. And I don't have a boss either. I control my hours. I've got the rest of the day free now, until nine o'clock this evening.'

Charlotte would rather make up a hundred guest bedrooms than have to spend an hour with a man like she'd just encountered. He made her flesh creep. How privileged she'd been in her relationships, except for Bruce. She'd had a good marriage with Will. Her life was punctuated with laughter and affection; she'd never stopped to appreciate that.

'Do you know about me and your mother?' Charlotte asked, sitting on the side of the double bed while Piper pulled on a T-shirt.

'I've never heard of you. Me and my mother never hit it off.'

'We were best friends at college. We worked together at Sandy Beaches Holiday Camp...'

Charlotte hesitated; did she know Jenna was in prison?

'What do you know about your mum? Do you know where she is now?'

'I wouldn't even recognise her if I saw her in town,' Piper replied. She spat out the words as if the hardness in her voice was well-practised, a defence mechanism to conceal the pain.

'Did you know she was in prison?' Charlotte said, as gently as she could.

'Doesn't surprise me,' Piper said. 'She used to jump into bed with all sorts of unsuitable men. Guys doing drugs, guys stealing stuff. It made my dad look like an angel.'

'I still see your mother,' Charlotte began, searching for the best way to frame what she was about to say. 'She's had some tough times, you know. She'd love to see you again, I'm sure. Would you be up for it if I suggested it to her? I'd be happy to come along with you if it made it easier. I know how I'd feel if I was estranged from my own daughter like that. It would break my heart.'

'I'm not sure she'd welcome that,' Piper answered, a glimpse of regret in her voice. 'My mum has spent a lifetime trying to hide me from the world. She would never acknowledge me or tell people I existed. What kind of mother would do that?'

Charlotte was quiet as she thought it over. She knew one possible answer to that question. She'd have done the same thing too, in Jenna's situation. The one thing that would force her to keep quiet about Lucia was if she was scared for her daughter's life.

CHAPTER SEVENTEEN

Charlotte was late for the press conference, having spent too much time with Piper. She ended up running along the pavement from the West End to the Winter Gardens, and was so out of breath she could hardly speak to the police officer who stood outside the ornate, wooden doors.

A TV van with a satellite dish had drawn up on the pavement outside. The BBC also had a broadcasting vehicle outside the building. It was creating quite a buzz among the locals.

'I'm sorry, you can't go in until the press conference is done. It's media only.'

That stopped Charlotte dead in her tracks; she wasn't media and the police officer at the door looked like he was accustomed to dealing with lame excuses. Without Nigel Davies, she had no access. There was little point arguing.

She pulled out her phone and sent a text to Nigel.
Sorry, I'm late. Cops won't let me in. Can you help?
She waited a few moments, watching her phone.
Coming.

Seconds later, Nigel appeared outside the Winter Gardens and waved her over.

'It's all right—she's with me,' he said to the police officer. 'She's on a job exchange.'

The officer seemed to know Nigel already and was happy to wave Charlotte in.

'Does that mean you're going to clean the rooms in my guest house as part of the job exchange?' Charlotte whispered.

'Not a chance,' Nigel replied. 'But you won't get in here unless you're press, so a little white lie won't hurt.'

Charlotte had been to look around the Winter Gardens before, and its architecture never failed to impress her. It was a well-preserved relic from a bygone age when the resort was flourishing, and thousands of tourists would flock there throughout the summer. The ornate boxes over-looked the stage area which was closed off by a heavy, velvet curtain. The seating had long since been ripped out, leaving a large, open area with a worn, wooden floor, where the press conference was taking place.

Charlotte had seen it a hundred times on the TV. Two wooden tables had been brought in, a white table cloth placed over them and four chairs positioned behind.

DCI Kate Summers sat in the middle of the table, surrounded by microphones bearing the logos of the various radio and TV stations. They included ITV and BBC; this had become much more than a local story.

To the left of DCI Summers was a man who had the appearance of a performer; he didn't seem to belong there. Sitting close to the right-hand side of DCI Summers, her eyes red raw from crying, was a family member, probably Fred Walker's daughter, judging by her age. A police officer was to her side, her hand on the other woman's arm. Charlotte assumed she was a police liaison officer.

Nigel guided her to a seat. It looked like they were about to get started. She looked up at one of the theatre boxes to her right-hand side and saw the police tape over the lip of the balcony. It chilled her to think Fred Walker had been found there.

'Thank you for attending this press conference today,' DCI Summers began. She was calm and business-like, treating it like a job that had to be done. 'I'm joined by Mr Walker's eldest daughter, Francesca, and Steven Terry, a clairvoyant performer. It was Mr Terry who helped to discover Fred Walker's body. I'm sure you'll join me in passing on our condolences to Ms Walker.'

Francesca Walker began to cry. DCI Summers stopped momentarily and reassured her.

'I would ask members of the press to respect Ms Walker's recent loss of her father in very tragic circumstances. She will be making a short statement but will not be answering any questions today. Mr Terry and I will be happy to field your questions once Ms Walker has delivered her appeal.'

DCI Summers then ran through the factual details of the murder, most of which Nigel had told her already. Fred Walker had not come home the previous night. The police had been informed, and his car had been found parked in a supermarket car park in town.

Steven Terry, who was due to perform at the Winter Gardens for a short run over the weekend, had immediately sensed that something terrible had happened while the theatre manager was giving him a tour of the venue. The clairvoyant had found the body and the police were alerted. That was all they had to work with.

'Who's this Steven Terry guy?' Charlotte whispered as Francesca Walker was readied for her appeal.

'Haven't a clue,' Nigel replied. 'He's one of these clairvoyant acts that constantly tours the country, I think. The posters say he's doing four shows here over the weekend, including a Saturday matinee. I've never met him before. God knows how he *sensed* Fred Walker's body. This clairvoyance business is just a big con act as far as I can tell. Still, it'll help to pack out his shows, I guess.'

'Francesca Walker will now issue an appeal to anybody who might know anything about her father's tragic death,' DCI Summers announced.

Charlotte had seen this before on the TV and always felt for the poor families, wheeled out in front of the media at the worst time possible. Francesca looked like she was struggling to get through it. It felt rawer to Charlotte, being there in person.

'Fred Walker was a much-loved husband and father. My sister, Anna, my brother Gerry and I are distraught at the loss of our role model, our inspiration and the most important person in the world to us—'

Her voice was faltering. DCI Summers gently encouraged her to continue.

'We can't believe that somebody would want to murder our father. He was well-loved locally and respected by everybody who knew him. He built up an incredible business in Morecambe and the north-west of England. Please, if you know anything about his disappearance and subsequent death, contact Morecambe Police. The Crimestoppers line is available if you wish to remain anonymous. Somebody must have seen my father leaving the supermarket car park. Somebody must have noticed something unusual around the Winter Gardens. If you saw anything—anything at all—please contact DCI Summers at Morecambe Police Station. Thank you.'

She'd delivered the words slowly and with pauses and interruptions. If it wasn't for the constant reassurance of the police officer and DCI Summers, Charlotte didn't believe she would have made it to the end. As she spoke her last words, Francesca Walker looked up towards the theatrical box where her father had perished, and became distraught. The police officer escorted her out of the press conference, and the members of the press maintained a respectful silence. The moment she'd left and Steven Terry had switched places to sit directly in front of the microphones, all hell broke loose.

What truth is there in the rumours that Fred Walker had been awarded building contracts in favour of more suitable construction companies?

Was Mr Walker having an affair with his secretary?

DCI Summer dealt with the questions in a calm, measured manner. She'd obviously heard every crass suggestion the press could come up with. She brushed idle conjecture or unsubstantiated rumour aside, admonishing the journalist each time with a reminder that somebody's husband and father had died.

It took just under an hour to wind up proceedings, but for DCI Summers and Steven Terry, the work continued as TV, radio and print journalists took them aside for one-to-one interviews.

'I caught Kate Summers before the press conference began,' Nigel said to Charlotte as they tucked themselves away to the side. Just ahead of them, Steven Terry was being interviewed by a local TV reporter, the shot framed so that the theatre box in which he'd discovered Fred Walker's body was just behind him. Charlotte noticed how he seemed distracted as he was speaking to the journalist, glancing at them now and then.

'Kate Summers admitted they're clueless about who did it. She still thinks Barry McMillan's death was a suicide job. There's no evidence to the contrary, though they still haven't found his phone.'

'I felt sorry for his daughter,' Charlotte said. 'Imagine having to put yourself through that ordeal.'

'Excuse me,' came an unfamiliar voice.

Charlotte looked around. Steven Terry was heading towards them, looking intently at her.

'Hello, I'm Steven Terry,' he said, holding out his hand for her to shake. His voice was confident and commanding; it was obvious he was a performer. Charlotte shook his hand and waited to see what he wanted.

'I hope you don't mind me reaching out to you, but I don't think I've ever seen it so strongly in one person before,' he continued.

Charlotte was taken aback. She wasn't sure what he was talking about.

'Now look, I'm not sure it's appropriate for you to be peddling your clairvoyant stuff—' Nigel began to interrupt.

'It's okay, Nigel, let's hear what he has to say. Go on, Mr Terry.'

'I know you're probably sceptical about what I do; many people are. But I feel compelled to tell you this. I can't see what I see and not share it with you.'

Charlotte felt her nerves jangling, but like a child who's been told not to touch something dangerous, she couldn't help herself.

'What is it, Mr Terry?'

'You are surrounded by danger. I don't know who you are, and you don't know me. But your life is in danger. Those who you love are also at risk. It's to do with a dark episode in your past. The ghosts of your life are coming back to haunt you. And it's the same evil force that claimed Fred Walker's life.'

CHAPTER EIGHTEEN

'That's how people like him make their living,' Nigel said, as Steven Terry was ushered away for his next interview. 'They give you a hint of something sensational. Then they clam up.'

Charlotte couldn't tell Nigel, but the clairvoyant had hit a raw nerve. How had he known about her connection with the case? Maybe he'd already spoken to DCI Summers. She wasn't ready to dismiss what he'd said as quickly as Nigel Davies was.

'I'm not sure we're any further forward,' he said, after surveying the room. 'We have a head start over the other media outlets with this story, and I don't think the police have got any more information than I have. Notice how they haven't mentioned the photograph to the news guys; it'll be explosive when that gets out.'

'When will you run it?' Charlotte asked. 'It can't stay hidden forever.'

'We've agreed not to publish it just yet, but only because DCI Summers raised a safety issue with us over the lives of the other two men. The photograph is the newspaper's copyright, anyway. They have to seek our permission before they can run it. Which keeps us firmly in the driving seat.'

Charlotte was watching Steven Terry. He was caught up in the media frenzy and it didn't look like he'd be free for some time.

'I'm going to go for a coffee next door,' Charlotte said. 'I'm hoping to meet up with Lucia for a bite to eat. Will you let me know if you hear anything else?'

Nigel nodded, took out his notepad, and headed into the clusters of reporters to secure his own story for the newspaper. Charlotte surveyed the old theatre, considering what a macabre place it was for Fred Walker to die. She sat down on one of the chairs that had been set out for the news reporters and texted Lucia. *Fancy meeting up for a panini and coffee? I'm at the coffee shop by the Winter Gardens. Mum x*

She was about to add that it was close to the arcade where Lucia worked, but she erased that bit. This lunch was about building bridges and trying to get a dialogue going with her daughter. To her surprise, she got a text back straight away.

With you in 10. I'm starving. Order me a brie and cranberry panini and an Americano. Lx

That was unexpected. It gave her ten minutes on her own to think, and she was grateful for it. She placed the orders and found a table with a view across to the promenade. Her mind was whirring frantically, trying to work its way through the new information. She didn't know what to do other than to carry on until their untruths were revealed. But what Steven Terry had said shook her; it made it feel like they were in danger.

She would have to warn Will about Bruce Craven's

half-sister. She thought back to the holiday camp. It was too far back in time to recollect what Bruce had said about his family. She knew his parents were dead, killed by carbon monoxide poisoning, but she was as certain as she could be that there was no other family. Besides, when Bruce Craven's name had resurfaced once again after their move back to Morecambe, she'd checked at the library. The newspaper cuttings hadn't mentioned a half-sister.

There was nothing unusual about Bruce's father having a child by another relationship. But for it all to work chronologically, the sister would have to be older than Bruce. That would place her around sixty years old, or even older, Charlotte calculated.

Whenever she imagined Bruce, she recalled him as a young man: strong, powerful and thickset. She wondered how he would have looked more than three decades on, and she shivered at the thought that his half-sister might bear some resemblance to him.

Then there was Jenna and her secret daughter. She'd been cagey with Charlotte when they'd talked about relationships; perhaps she'd had some bad experiences and didn't want to discuss them. It was fair enough. There were things in Charlotte's life that she didn't care to share.

But concealing that Piper was her daughter? Jenna must have known she and Will had purchased that guest house all along. It must have sent a chill through her when she realised it was the place where her daughter had been held a captive. But why hadn't she said anything? Was this part of the intimidation that she'd experienced after Bruce's disappearance from the Sandy Beaches Holiday Camp? Charlotte was desperate to make connections, but she just couldn't see them in the limited information that she'd got.

'Hi, mum!'

Lucia seemed unusually bright and not out of breath.

'That was quick,' Charlotte said, looking at her phone to see how long she'd been in a world of her own, mulling things over.

'I was heading into town anyway,' Lucia replied. 'I might as well make the most of being off school.'

The waitress arrived with their food and drinks, and they sat in silence as she went through the routine of working out who had ordered what.

Charlotte had been thinking about how to tackle Lucia, and against all her parental instincts, she'd decided to go softly with her daughter. If it flared up, Lucia would become even more secretive and then she'd be none the wiser about what was going on in her life.

'Have you and Olli made up now?' she asked, thinking that was probably safe territory to make a start.

'Yes, it's all blown over. He just caught me at the wrong time, you know me and Olli, we fall out then we patch things up.'

'He's only worried about you, you know. We all are.'

Charlotte watched Lucia tense. She reckoned her daughter was viewing this as her own press conference. Tell them what they need to know, but don't give them all the facts. She wanted to reach out and hug her tight, like she used to do when she was a little girl. She knew that if she did, she'd be spurned with a teenage display of mock disgust.

'Look, mum, I'm almost an adult now. I know what I'm doing. You'll have to trust me.'

There were so many questions Charlotte wanted to ask. Who was this guy with the purple Mohican, for a start? Instead, she kept it non-confrontational.

'I know we have to let you off the leash sometime,' she

began, 'But please promise me that if anything is wrong, you'll tell me or your dad. Or Olli. Please don't keep it to yourself. We're here if you need help.'

'I'm fine, Mum, honestly.'

Lucia was devouring the panini like she hadn't eaten for months.

'Will you tell me what happened at the arcade? Why did you leave your job?'

Lucia took longer to chew the mouthful of food that she was working on, making her wait for an answer.

'I just got bored, that's all. Have you any idea what a crappy job it is exchanging notes for coins all day? I just wanted something different.'

'You know there's always work at the guest house. You used to enjoy that, working with your friend.'

'Well, we've fallen out now, so that won't be happening any more,' Lucia replied, taking a big sip of her Americano.

'That's sad. I liked Terri a lot.'

Charlotte paused a moment, nervous about asking the question.

'Where have you been getting your money from?'

Lucia finished her coffee. Charlotte didn't think it was physically possible to polish off that much food and drink so quickly.

'Oh, you know,' Lucia replied, her face reddening.

'That's just it, I don't know,' Charlotte insisted, as much as she dare.

Lucia flared up, as if Charlotte had gone back to a lit firework and there was still unburned gunpowder left in it.

'You've heard of the internet, right? I'm just selling stuff online until I find another job, okay? Old clothes, books, CDs from when I was a kid, that sort of thing. You said you'd trust me. This doesn't feel very much like trust to me!'

'You just seem to have a lot of money at the moment—'

'Look, mum, thanks for lunch, but I think I'm done now. I'll see you later.'

She moved her chair backwards, scraping it on the floor, and stormed out of the shop, leaving Charlotte feeling like an embarrassed, incompetent parent.

'Kids… you just can't win, can you?'

She recognised the deep, confident voice and turned around to confirm it, coming face to face with Steven Terry.

'I thought I'd come in here for a coffee. I was worn out after all those questions. I'm on stage this evening too. What are they like in Morecambe, a friendly lot?'

He seemed much different now, more informal and chatty than the man who'd startled her earlier.

'Yes, the Winter Gardens is a lovely venue. That's when nobody is leaving dead bodies there, of course.'

She stopped abruptly. What a stupid thing to say. 'Oh, I'm so sorry. That was insensitive of me. It must have been terrifying, finding his body like that.'

Why couldn't she have a conversation with anybody without causing offence?

'That's all right. I'm more accustomed to all of this than I'd like to admit. I know DCI Summers of old; I was involved in a very sad case not far from here, in Blackpool. She's a tough cookie, but I'd rather have her on my side than against me. The bad guys don't stand a chance.'

'What is it you do?' Charlotte asked, moving her chair so she could face him directly. He was sitting two tables away. She'd been so intent speaking to Lucia that she hadn't noticed him walking in.

'Officially, I call myself as a clairvoyant, but that doesn't describe what I do very well. I can sense things, in people and in places. It's how I knew Mr Walker was up in that theatrical box. The moment I walked into the Winter Gardens I felt the echoes of his fear, the hatred that lead to his death, and the pain of his final moments.'

'Can you see what happened? Do you know who did it?' Charlotte was genuinely intrigued.

'No, it's hard to explain, it's something I feel, not something I see. I felt it when I saw you. I hope you didn't mind me saying. It's just that sometimes it's so powerful that I have to speak up. I felt it with your daughter just now. That was your daughter?'

'Yes, it was? What did you feel? I'm so worried about her. She just won't speak to us, but I know something is wrong.'

Steven Terry looked at her, studying her face.

'Not everybody wants to hear what I have to tell them. Are you certain you want me to say?'

Charlotte wasn't certain at all, but with so many worrying things going on around her, she felt compelled to listen.

'Go on,' she said. 'I don't really want to hear it, but I think I need to.'

Steven Terry took a deep breath.

'Your family is being torn apart by secrets. You are gripped by the past, and it will not let you go. Your daughter is carrying secrets too, though I think you know that already. These secrets are about to surface. But if you keep them to yourself, if they don't come out, they will place your family in enormous danger.'

CHAPTER NINETEEN

Speaking to Steven Terry in the coffee shop had done nothing to put Charlotte's mind at rest. The man's ability to pinpoint the most important issue was unnerving. He'd got it in one; it was secrets that were causing their problems. But there was no way they could reveal what those secrets were.

Charlotte spent another ten minutes on her own after Steven rushed back to the theatre. He had a soundcheck to work through, once the theatre staff had dismantled the press conference set-up. He'd invited her to the show over the weekend. Charlotte wasn't sure that she could face that; twenty minutes chatting to him had been enough.

She tried to avoid thinking about her fallout with Lucia. She hadn't a clue where her daughter had gone. If only she'd paid more attention to the letter from school. Would Lucia would be counted as a truant if she was challenged on the street by a police officer? This was all uncharted territory, but then her entire life seemed to be like that since Barry McMillan had hanged himself.

It needed positive action, to see Jenna again so she

could ask her about Piper, face to face. It meant another thankless journey on a regional railway line, since it wasn't something her friend could discuss on a prison payphone.

She was beginning to see Jenna through different eyes. Charlotte had despised her for abducting Lucia and attempting a blackmail scam. But the more she learned about her former friend's life since leaving the holiday camp, the more she was beginning to see her as a victim. It looked like the nightmares had continued for Jenna; had she kept Charlotte and her family safe by maintaining her silence?

She booked in her visit at the prison and used a phone app to get her train tickets for early the following week. With her mind distracted from her troubles, she had a sudden flash of inspiration about Fred Walker's death. While she was thinking about other things, her mind had joined up some dots.

Her breakthrough came from a comment that Barry McMillan had made as they were walking back along the promenade on the night he died. It was only a throwaway remark, and it had passed her by completely when he told her. As they walked past a redeveloped arcade on the opposite side of the road, he remarked that he owned a part-share in the building but had never been inside.

At the time it seemed a reasonable enough thing to say. He was, after all, a celebrated author who'd made a good deal of money from his writing; why wouldn't he have invested some of his money in his home town? But the photograph and the manner of Fred Walker's death had given her pause. Were these men connected through property or building deals?

She checked the time on her phone. She was going to pay Jon Rogers a visit at Morecambe Library. If anybody knew who owned what in the town, it would be him. She settled the bill and made her way through the side streets towards the library. She checked in at the reception desk and was delighted to discover that Jon was available to see her.

'Hello Charlotte,' he greeted her. 'I take it we're on first-name terms now?'

'I guess so,' she replied. 'I hope you don't mind me calling in like this, but I want to ask you a couple more questions, if that's all right? It's just that you seem to know everything there is to know about this town.'

'It's nice that you ask,' he said. 'The youngsters probably couldn't care less about the history of the town. I suspect jobs like mine won't exist in the future. Once they pension me off, that will be it. All that local knowledge, gone forever.'

Charlotte thought about Lucia and Olli. He was right. They didn't care about their immediate environment. They were more bothered about the content on their phones and laptops.

'We had a lady enquiring about your place after I saw you last; she was asking about the holiday camp and your guest house. It was the same lady who I mentioned to you last time we spoke. It's funny how Sandy Beaches keeps coming up. Anybody would think there was buried treasure there.'

Jon Rogers didn't know how close he was, but it wasn't treasure that was buried at Sandy Beaches Holiday Camp.

Charlotte knew who the lady was already. She didn't need him to tell her.

'I hope you don't mind. I sent her your way. I gave her your web address and suggested that she stay with you if she was visiting the area. We need to support local businesses as much as we can.'

Under normal circumstances, Charlotte would have been grateful for the referral. But bearing in mind who he'd sent their way, she'd rather have told him to keep his big mouth shut. Instead, she diverted him from his course.

'I wondered if you knew anything about some of the building projects around the town. What sort of things was Fred Walker involved in?'

Jon Rogers looked surprised at her change of subject.

'That's an interesting question to ask, bearing in mind the poor gentleman's recent demise. What a shock that was. And Barry McMillan too. It's interesting that you ask; the thought had crossed my mind too. I was considering mentioning it to the police, but I suspect they'd dismiss me as some local history fantasist.

He'd got Charlotte's attention. She wasn't wide of the mark by the sound of it.

'Fred Walker and Barry McMillan were part of a local building consortium. Fred managed all the projects, of course, but there were a group of them buying up land and putting their money into the local infrastructure. You'll never guess who was in that consortium?'

Charlotte thought it through.

'Not the men in that photograph you copied for me from the microfiche the other day?'

'Bingo!' he replied. 'All but one of them. I don't think Harvey Turnbull was ever one of them; he was just a local copper. But there were four of them; Barry and Fred, as you know, and then Mason Jones, the head teacher of Morecambe's secondary school in those days and Edward Callow, who is now the resort's MP.'

'And they were all sitting around that table in my guest

house,' Charlotte replied. 'What sort of projects were they involved in?'

'Well, the fancy new arcade on the sea front is one of theirs. They pulled together the funding for that massive new academy building too. They also have some contracts at the university. Now you mention it, I've a feeling they may well have bought the land at the holiday camp where you worked. I'm not sure if it's their group who are redeveloping it though. It's funny how so many things are connected in a small town like this.'

He could say that again.

'How could we find out if they're behind the redevelopment of the holiday camp?' Charlotte asked. If she could make that connection, perhaps there might be some sense or reason behind what was happening.

'It's a tricky one. You'd need to check with the planning department, I think. Incidentally, that's where Edward Callow worked when this little consortium came to the fore. He was head of planning by that stage in his career, I think. At the time he was hailed as a hero in Morecambe. The town needed redeveloping, and he and his pals made a lot of ugly areas look very nice. Well, you've read the newspaper article; they were local celebrities then. Edward Callow still is.'

'I don't know anything about him,' Charlotte said, trying to recollect what she knew about the man. They'd been spared an election since their return to Morecambe. She hadn't got to grips yet with whoever represented them in Parliament.

'Between you and me, I reckon he's a nasty man,' Jon replied. 'He's very charming in public, always very obliging and passionate about the town. But I once saw the true man. I'll never forget it.'

'Oh? What happened?'

Jon Rogers was a very even, non-controversial type, but he suddenly looked quite worked up.

'I was once cycling home on my bicycle when Edward Callow roared past me in his car. It was bad enough that he almost sent me flying, but about twenty yards ahead of me, he ran over a cat. A lovely creature it was, jet black, just like a panther. He didn't even slow down for it.'

Jon flushed slightly at the memory. The incident had obviously made a big impact on him.

'What happened next?' Charlotte asked. 'What did he do?'

'He stopped his car, looked in his rear-view mirror, then backed up and reversed over the poor creature without a second thought. What kind of man does a thing like that?'

CHAPTER TWENTY

Charlotte knew Will would accuse her of over-reacting; it was a good reason for moving the furniture around before he got home. She hadn't a clue where Lucia was, Olli had gone into town with his girlfriend, and Will had taken the bus to the university to have a look around, prior to his interview there. The guests wouldn't trouble her for another hour or so, and Isla wasn't due in for some time, so it was the ideal opportunity to re-stage the photograph in the dining room.

She placed the copy of the image that Jon Rogers had made for her onto the small, wooden bar top. It was time to do some rearranging of the furniture, moving the chairs to the edges of the room, and shuffling the tables to the sides, taking care not to disrupt the table settings for the evening meals.

Once the room was cleared, she went through the hallway and into the ground floor cupboard under the stairs. After moving some old boxes and cleaning items, she succeeded in manoeuvring the old circular gate-leg table into the hallway. It was too heavy to lift, so she dragged it, cringing at the noise.

Hot and sweating, she finally succeeded in pushing the heavy, dark wood table into place. She pulled up the rounded edges of the table, placing them on their supports, then moved some chairs to where the men had been sitting. It was the same table, as far as she could tell. The B&B had been sold to them with its fixtures and fittings intact. It was part of the attraction, and although they'd changed the table cloths, upholstery, decoration and tableware, they'd left much of the furniture intact.

Checking that nobody was around, Charlotte placed five cushions where the men had been sitting, with post-it notes attached, on which she'd written their names. She then moved the dining room hat stand into the position where the photographer must have been standing. She reckoned even DCI Summers would have been proud of her reconstruction efforts. It was a feat almost worthy of Crimewatch.

Charlotte picked up the copy of the original photograph from the bar and held it up, making sure everything was in place. It was as close a re-creation as she could have managed, without stripping the wallpaper and tearing down the curtains at either side of the window to change them for the ugly creations that had sat there in 2006. She pulled out her phone and took photographs from different angles. Then she remembered the second photograph that Harvey Turnbull's wife had given them. She had a copy of it upstairs in the family quarters. It was taken from a slightly different angle. She wanted to compare that one too and see if she'd missed any of the details.

She ran up the stairs, stopping on the second landing to catch her breath. Events that week had made her realise how out of condition she was getting. She would need to join a gym.

When she came back into the lounge, Isla was there. She was walking around the lounge, examining the set up.

'Oh, hello,' Charlotte said, 'I wasn't expecting you for another half hour.'

Isla turned away from the round table and looked at Charlotte.

'I wanted to make an early start, since we're a bit busy tonight. I thought it best to get going on the vegetables. I was also hoping I might catch you on your own.'

'Well, I'm here, so what's on your mind?'

'I know George has a soft spot for you,' Isla said, a worried look on her face. 'I feel like a woman who suspects her husband of cheating. Can you believe that I went through his pockets while he was out walking Una this morning? I'm becoming obsessed.'

You and me both, Charlotte thought.

'Are you still worried about him?' she asked.

'We argued about it. That's the real reason I'm here early; I had to get out of the house. It was tense when I left. We shouldn't be having rows at our age; it feels ridiculous.'

'What was the row about? Did you challenge him about being ill?'

'I found an outpatients leaflet in his pocket from three weeks ago. He'd lied to me about where he'd been that day. He said he'd gone to visit an old friend in Lancaster. He told the truth about Lancaster, but he never mentioned the hospital appointment.'

'Perhaps it's something private. He might be embarrassed. He's an older gentleman, from a generation which doesn't tend to speak about private stuff. Had you thought about that?'

'I hadn't,' Isla replied after a short pause. 'He was very defensive when I asked him about it. He told me to mind my business. Can you believe that?'

'It does sound like it might be something embarrassing. Perhaps you need to be a bit gentler with him.'

Charlotte couldn't believe the words were coming out of her mouth. There she was, acting as an agony aunt to a woman almost twenty years her senior. The same agony aunt whose daughter had walked out on her earlier that day.

Isla looked tearful. 'Promise me, if he tells you anything, let me know. I don't want to be kept in the dark if it's something serious. We've only just got to know each other. I'm not ready to lose him so soon.'

Charlotte hadn't even considered the possibility of George dying. He seemed like one of those men who would keep going forever. Maybe it was just that she'd known him as a young man, when he was strong enough to fight a bully like Bruce Craven.

'I will,' Charlotte replied. 'I promise, Isla. If there's anything wrong with George, I'll drive him to the hospital myself. And I'll give him a stern telling off for not sharing what he's going through. That generation of men, they're not used confiding in people where emotions are concerned. At least Olli isn't like that. He seems to be more open about things.'

Isla turned to look at the table again.

'What's this?' she asked, her tone changing.

'Oh, it's just something I'm trying to figure out. Barry McMillan's death has been troubling me.'

'Don't you think that's better left to the police?' Isla asked, her voice harsh. She softened again immediately. 'I didn't mean to challenge you, but it does seem an extreme length to go through. That table is heavy; why do you think it's been kept under the stairs for so many years?'

'You can say that again,' Charlotte replied, keen to keep things friendly. It was her guest house after all; she didn't need to justify to Isla why she was setting up ridiculous scenarios in her own dining area.

'Whatever you're chasing, I'd leave it well alone if I were you. I saw what happened to that local builder, Fred Walker, and with Barry McMillan's suicide, it all feels a bit sinister to me. In your shoes, I'd look after that lovely family of yours and leave the police to do the detective work.'

Charlotte wasn't sure if she'd just received a bit of friendly guidance or a warning. It sounded like advice from a friend, but she sensed Isla was telling her to back off. She wasn't sure how to respond for a moment. Then she had a second breakthrough.

'I'll put it all away in a moment before the new check-ins start to arrive. But will you just indulge me for one moment? Would you stand behind the bar and lean over towards where the photographer would have been?'

Isla looked reluctant, but did it anyway.

'Just move along to your left a little. That's good. Now lean over as if you're working behind the bar and chatting to the men as the photo is taken. That's perfect. Can I take a photo?'

'If you must,' Isla replied. 'I'm not big on all these photos. You're not going to put it on Facebook, are you?'

'No, no, nothing like that,' Charlotte replied. 'Just a couple more. That's great; we're done.'

As Isla stepped out from behind the bar, the sound of the heavy doors opening could be heard along the corridor.

'Must be an early check-in,' Charlotte whispered to Isla. 'They're keen.'

She went to intercept whoever it was who'd shown up before the designated arrival time. It was a mature woman with short, heavily greying hair and a slim build. At her side was a suitcase, indicating this was more than just a weekend stay.

'Good evening, can I help you?' Charlotte asked.

'Yes, you must be Charlotte Grayson. I recognise your voice from the telephone. I'm Daisy Bowker. Remember? I'm looking for my half-brother, Bruce.'

CHAPTER TWENTY-ONE

Daisy Bowker wasn't as Charlotte had imagined her. In her mind, she'd pictured this woman as some kind of monster. She was poor at guessing people's age, but it was even harder in Daisy's case, with her high-quality haircut and her classy and confident look. She even seemed likeable, which came as a shock.

'Welcome to Morecambe,' Charlotte said, slipping into her automatic check-in procedure. She moved to the computer and went through the dual combination of checking for the essential information—such as home address, preferred credit card and email address—alongside issuing keys and running through the mealtimes at the guest house.

Charlotte was consciously stalling Daisy, terrified of engaging in a broader conversation. It was only a matter of time until she started asking for details about Bruce, and Charlotte still hadn't figured out how she was going to deal with the matter when it came up.

'What a lovely little place you have,' Daisy said. 'I was intending to stay at the Midland Hotel, but I thought it would be nice to base myself here. It's amazing that you worked in the same place as my half-brother all those years ago. I feel closer to unearthing his story already.'

'Shall I show you to your room?' Charlotte asked.

Daisy Bowker was the first guest to stay in Barry McMillan's room since he hanged himself. All the guests who'd been staying with them when his body was discovered had now moved on, meaning that she could sneak Daisy in there without some big mouth recounting the story of how he was discovered hanging from the beam.

Charlotte had no intention of telling her guest about the incident. The quicker it was forgotten, the better, as far as she was concerned. Besides, the police were done with it and the professional cleaners had been. It was part of the business, and the room needed to start earning its keep once again.

As Charlotte unlocked the door, she recalled the sight of Barry McMillan's lifeless body hanging there. If anybody had asked her what it looked like, she'd have used the word *heavy*. It was a bizarre way to describe a dead man—there were so many other things she could have said—but the overriding feeling she got was of a dead weight pulling down on the noose, his body entirely unsupported.

Daisy was oblivious to what had gone on in there, and Charlotte did her best not to think about it. She'd taken her guest's case, and she placed it on the carpet, just below where Barry's feet had been, swinging gently above the patterned fabric.

'This looks nice,' Daisy said. 'Thank you for helping me up with my stuff.

So, how did you know Bruce?' she asked.

Charlotte felt her face burning up.

'It feels hot in here; shall I open the window for you?' she asked.

'It's a nice temperature for me,' Daisy replied. 'I like it warm.'

Charlotte cursed herself for not having her responses planned; she'd had enough warning, after all. And now Daisy had caught her off guard. This is how they'd get caught out. What was she even thinking of, believing they could keep a secret like that?

'Well, it's such a long time ago, I can barely remember it, to be honest.'

'You and your husband met at the camp, didn't you?' Daisy asked. She was unpacking one of her bags into the wardrobe, evidently oblivious to the fact that such a simple question sounded like the Spanish Inquisition to her host.

'Yes, we did, we were both students. To be honest with you, it was a bit *us and them* at the camp. The students tended to stick together, and the seasonal workers got to know each other better before we all arrived. I can't remember most of the people I worked with there.'

Daisy was fumbling in her case. There was a large, hardback book sitting among the items of clothing. *Researching Your Family History: How To Investigate Your Past.*

Family history left Charlotte cold. She couldn't care less what her great-grandfather's eldest daughter did one hundred years ago. As far as she was concerned, unless the family tree concealed some long-lost inheritance, it was all water under the bridge. She'd watched the TV programmes featuring celebrities who would begin to get emotional when it was revealed that a woman who was vaguely related to them more than a century ago went to the workhouse because her husband died in a mine and left her massive family destitute. Charlotte didn't get why that mattered. Sure, it was a sad story, but there were a million of those happening every day. She failed to understand what compelled people to research information like that. But Daisy seemed to be taking it seriously, and that meant danger for her family.

Daisy drew out a photograph from between the pages of the book. It was a photo of Bruce, taken at about the same time as she'd known him. He was with a bunch of mates, smiling and looked relaxed. For the first time in many years—and after blaming herself a thousand times for her poor judgement—she saw why she'd been attracted to him as an eighteen-year-old. He was a good-looking guy. Turned out he was also a manipulating, violent psycho.

'Recognise him now?'

Charlotte realised that she'd have to admit to knowing him. That was all she'd confess to though, and Will would have to do the same. She thought about what it would be like if Lucia was in a similar situation. Everything her kids did was recorded on phones and surveillance cameras. When Charlotte was young, photographs were few and far between. Even if she took them, she couldn't always afford to get them developed.

'Yes, he used to work in the kitchen. On the dishwasher, if I remember correctly. It was a big, industrial thing. I didn't know him well, though. We just had snatched exchanges while I was loading up my dirty dishes to put through the washer.'

'Were you and your husband a couple when you arrived at Sandy Beaches?'

It was easier when DCI Summers had been asking the questions earlier in the week.

'Are you sure this room isn't too hot for you?' Charlotte asked.

'No, it's fine. I don't mean to be rude, but if you're going through the menopause, I discovered these patches they have nowadays. They changed my life. I used to suffer from sweats and a red face all the time. Ask your doctor, if you're going through the change. I'm done with all that now, thank God. I can devote myself to more interesting matters, like researching family history. You didn't say if you and your husband were an item back then?'

'No, we came separately and left as a couple,' Charlotte replied. 'I went there with a friend. I met Will on his first day at the camp.'

Daisy was now shuffling papers in a folder packed with handwritten notes and newspaper cuttings.

'I've drawn a complete blank with Bruce,' she said, examining a page of notes. 'We shared a father, but I never knew him. I didn't even realise my parents were on a second marriage until I was at secondary school. My mum never really talked about it until after I left home. There was bad blood there, I think. She'd moved on with her life and didn't want to go back.'

'Did Bruce's father stay in contact with you?'

'No, I think there was violence involved. My mum wanted me well clear of him. In fact, I only found out about Bruce through my aunt. She told me at mum's funeral. She just came out with it out of the blue, like I should have known it all along. *Did you know you have a half-brother out there somewhere?* Just like that, when I told her I was planning to get the family tree written down after mum died. Would you believe it?'

Charlotte would have liked to tell that aunt to keep her mouth shut. This could cause her a lot of trouble. Daisy looked like the kind of woman who not only had time on her hands but also had both the motivation and inclination to worry at this particular knot.

'I honestly can't remember him that well,' Charlotte reiterated. The broken record approach seemed the best option. Keep repeating the same non-committal thing, and hope that Daisy hit a dead-end, tired from a fruitless search.

Daisy put her paperwork down on the quilt and turned to Charlotte. She lowered her voice.

'You know, I'm beginning to suspect that Bruce might have been up to no good. As far as I can tell, my natural father and his mother died in nasty circumstances. It's reported in the newspapers, but it was classed as accidental death. They both died of carbon monoxide poisoning in the family home. It was shortly after Bruce left home to spend his summer at the holiday camp. I know from my aunt that Bruce's father was a violent man. It had crossed my mind that maybe Bruce disappeared for a reason. I just can't figure it all out yet.'

CHAPTER TWENTY-TWO

Charlotte was ready for Friday night when it finally arrived. She'd been unsettled by her conversation with Daisy and was looking forward to an evening out. She'd almost forgotten about it, the week had been so busy. The guests were fed, and Will and the kids were home. Lucia was showing no signs of leaving the house having finally returned from her day's adventures and Olli had agreed to field any guest queries while they were out.

'I can't wait for tonight,' Will said. 'I'm getting a bit stressed out about this job interview next week. I really want it. Imagine working at the university where I got my degree. It feels like things have come full circle.'

Charlotte's mind was elsewhere.

'So we're agreed, we admit to knowing Bruce, but we don't mention Jenna or anything else that happened. She's bound to get fed up at some point. Besides, nobody's missed him in all this time. She'll tire of it eventually.'

'I agree that's the best strategy,' Will confirmed. 'Ready to go?'

Abi Smithson had invited them as her guests to a night

of show songs at the Regent Bay Holiday Park. They'd seen her on and off since their unconventional reunion, and she still credited Will with launching her musical career. She performed every Friday at the holiday park and had been begging Will and Charlotte to come along for some time. They'd put it off for as long as was polite, then decided they had to fix a date.

'I hope she does Mamma Mia,' Charlotte said. 'I'm in the mood for a bit of Abba.'

Charlotte had always had a soft spot for traditional seaside entertainments, ever since their time at Sandy Beaches. As youngsters, they'd frequented the various bars on the site, enjoying the different styles of music on offer in each. A night at Regent Bay was just what she wanted. It was an opportunity to see their old friend sing some great songs, knock a few drinks back and forget everything for one night. Bruce Craven, Jenna Phillips, Daisy Bowker and Barry McMillan could all take a rain check. Charlotte was desperate to park it all for a few hours and give her mind a rest.

'You came!' said Abi, jumping up from her seat where she was applying her make-up for the show.

She welcomed them both with a hug and returned to doing her make-up as she continued the conversation.

'I had a good feeling about tonight,' she said, 'I have another old friend joining me; he's in town, and he should be popping in later. It's like a night of reunions. I might get him up on stage with me if there's time. He's an amazing guy.'

'How's things?' Will asked. 'Sorry it's been so long since we last saw you. Life's been busy.'

They exchanged news, then Abi got the five-minute call that she was next out on the stage.

'If I were you, I'd go and get your drinks in at the bar. It'll start to get busy soon. I'll catch up with you later.'

Will and Charlotte made their exit. The lights were dimmed now, and they had to hunt for two seats and a table.

'I'll get the drinks in,' Will shouted over the amplified voice of the DJ. 'You hang onto my chair.'

'Ladies and gentlemen,' the DJ's voice intervened. 'You've seen her on the TV, she's played the cruise ships and rubbed shoulders with some of the biggest names in the music industry. She started her career right here in Morecambe, and I'm pleased to say that she's here with us every Friday night. Please welcome onto the stage, Miss Abi Smithson!'

The place went crazy. Charlotte thought back to Abi's first tentative performance over three decades ago. Even though she'd never performed in front of a crowd at that time, she'd handled it like a pro; confident, assured and professional.

'I'd like to dedicate this first song to a good friend of mine who's here tonight, the man who gave me the confidence to step up on a stage and perform my very first song. Please put your hands together for Will Grayson. This one's dedicated to you, Will, and thank you from the bottom of my heart.'

As the crowd applauded and Abi began to sing the Shirley Bassey number that she'd debuted at Sandy Beaches Holiday Camp, Charlotte felt a burst of pride in Will. He'd done an amazing thing that day. He'd launched this woman's career. He'd given her the confidence she needed.

Charlotte was almost envious of her performing on that stage. She wondered what her own life amounted to. Would it all unravel now that Daisy Bowker was in the resort?

Will walked up to the table carrying a tray with two drinks.

'Here's your glass of Prosecco, and a large one at that. When the barman realised it was me who Abi was talking about, he gave us those drinks on the house. And he filled your glass to the brim.'

Abi performed an amazing set and Charlotte was blown away by the power of her voice and the way she commanded the stage. For an hour, she was captivated by the songs and the atmosphere, and the Prosecco helped to shift her mind away from the events of the past week. As she cheered and sang along, laughing with Will as he struggled to hit the high notes in the sing-a-longs, it was as if none of it had happened.

As Abi shifted the tempo to a couple of slower songs, it was easier to talk once again as the audience settled. Some just sat and enjoyed the music, while others continued to chat. Charlotte felt light-headed and slightly tipsy. Will had remained a restrained drinker throughout his life, but he'd never given Charlotte a hard time about her own occasional need to get a few drinks down her. She was grateful for that. She needed those drinks, after the week she'd just been through.

Abi finished her song and began to speak to the audience.

'Now I'd like to welcome another great friend of mine onto the stage. When you tour the circuit and play on the cruise ships, you tend to run into the same people time and time again. This man's talent and special gifts never cease to astonish me. He's playing at the Winter Gardens this weekend; in fact, he's just come over here after his first performance this evening. Please welcome an amazing friend, and so much more than a clairvoyant. It's Steven Terry!'

There was a half-hearted ripple of applause as Steven walked onto the stage.

'Isn't that the guy you were telling me about earlier?' Will asked.

'Yes, it is. Funny that he should know Abi.'

'Well, not really,' Will replied. 'These performers must meet each other all the time as they tour the country. Do you want another drink?'

'No thanks,' Charlotte replied. 'I think I've had enough for now. Besides, this chap is interesting. I want to see his act.'

Steven's deep, powerful voice dominated the room, and within two minutes, the couldn't-care-less chatter had turned into silence as the audience turned its attention fully towards the clairvoyant. Steven wore a radio microphone which allowed him to step into the audience. All eyes were on him as he gave his commentary, then began to astound the people around him.

'I get a deep sense that you lost somebody recently. Was their name Phyllis?' he asked a young woman to the side of him.

'She's a plant,' Will said, 'You watch. This stuff is all a big con.'

'She's my mum,' the woman answered.

'Did you lose your mum recently?' Steven asked gently. The eyes of the room were upon him, yet it felt like the only person he was speaking to was this woman in front of him.

'She died two weeks ago,' the woman replied, her voice faltering as she said the words.

'Your mum is with you tonight,' Steven said.

'What a load of bollocks!' Will whispered to Charlotte.

'She says she's pleased to see you out enjoying yourself tonight,' Steven continued. 'She's telling me she was in a lot of pain in the end, and she wanted it to be over. She's in a happy place now. She says she loves you and she thanks you for being with her in her final days. But she wants you to be happy now.'

'I can't believe guys like him are allowed to get away with this nonsense,' Will said. 'Either he's exploiting her vulnerability, or she's a set-up. I don't believe a word of it.'

Charlotte wished he'd shut up and watch; she was enthralled by it. They'd never seen a clairvoyant in action before.

Steven Terry was working his way over to their part of the room now. The lights were still dimmed, but a spotlight followed him as he walked among the tables, chatting to the crowd.

'Does somebody know a man called Norman?'

A woman to Steven's side raised her hand.

'Is he your husband, my darling?' he asked.

The woman nodded.

'He says he loves you and he's sorry for all the snoring!'

Charlotte was close enough to see the tears rolling down the woman's cheeks, but she was laughing.

'He used to snore all night, it would drive me crazy,' she said.

'Norman knows that,' Steven said, 'And he's laughing and crying with you now, my dear.'

'This is nonsense,' Will continued to moan.

'It's not doing any harm, even if it is,' Charlotte replied, annoyed at his attitude. She was warming to Steven.

'I'm getting a very strong sense of a powerful emotion from this part of the room,' Steven continued, as he neared their table. Charlotte wondered if he'd recognise her among the sea of faces in the crowd.

Steven stopped and began to speak in an earnest. The spotlight lit him up, and all eyes were on him.

'Ladies and gentlemen, sometimes this ability I have can be as much a curse as it is a gift. I get a great deal of pleasure from passing on messages from the spirit side, and I know it brings a lot of comfort to people in the rooms I work in. But every now and then, I get a sense of something overwhelming, and I'm getting that right now. I'm not going to put anybody on the spot, or embarrass anybody, but if you want to speak to me in private after Abi finishes her amazing show here tonight, please do so.'

He paused and looked around him before speaking again. 'But I have to say something. I'm getting a strong feeling of darkness from this part of the room. Somebody—more than one person, in fact—somebody is carrying a terrible secret with them. If you do not unburden yourselves of this secret, great suffering will follow. I haven't had such a strong feeling for a long time. Please, if that's you I'm speaking about, come and see me after the show.'

Steven began to move again, and as he did so, the spotlight moved too. It came to rest directly on Will and Charlotte's table. Charlotte saw immediately that Steven recognised her. He looked mortified that he had unknowingly picked her out in the crowd. And the look on Will's face told her he no longer believed Steven Terry was a charlatan.

CHAPTER TWENTY-THREE

'I'm so sorry I put you on the spot like that,' Steven Terry apologised, for the third time. 'If I'd known it was you, I would have moved on.'

'It's all right, honestly,' Charlotte replied. After a few moments of intense embarrassment, she'd quickly rationalised that what he'd said was meaningless to the entire room, apart from her and Will.

Will had been floored momentarily, giving her a guilty look across the table. Then he'd dismissed it with his usual scepticism.

'That's how these people reel you in,' he said, once the spotlight had moved on to another area of the room. 'I'll bet there were people all around us who were thinking about affairs, stuff stolen from work, or lies told to family members. The entire room was probably sweating at that point in the show. I still think it's a load of nonsense.'

Just over an hour later, Will was showing signs of changing his tune. Steven Terry had joined them after his short segment had ended, apologetic for what he'd just put Charlotte through. He insisted on buying a bottle of bubbly, took them to a VIP area to one side of the room, and proceeded to entertain them with gripping stories about the things he'd sensed in the past.

Charlotte had become slowly more inebriated, and although Will had switched to soft drinks, he too was in awe of Steven's ability to enthral his audience. He pushed the clairvoyant about how he did it, repeating his claims about plants in the audience and selecting general topics which applied to half the room, but the things that Steven told them made him seem all the more convincing.

'I don't want to pry or interfere,' Steven said, slurring his words a little from the drink, 'but you must confide in the police if you're in danger or fear for your safety. I know what's going on in this town at the moment; I found one of the bodies, as you know. And you found another, Charlotte. Something links all of this.'

'Can't you see what it is?' Will asked. 'Surely you know what's going on, if you have visions and so on?'

'It doesn't work like that,' Steven explained. 'I get a sense of things. I can feel sadness, tragedy, impending danger. I don't see the specifics. But I feel it very strongly with you two, and it's the same sense I got when I found the body at the Winter Gardens. You need to take action. DCI Summers will give you a sympathetic ear. She's not all rules and procedure.'

'What do you know about Harvey Turnbull?' Charlotte asked, feeling her leg drifting away from her chair as she began to lose full control of it. She knew she needed to stop drinking now, or she'd suffer the next day.

'Nothing,' Steven answered, 'Though it is a name I overheard DCI Summers mention. Should I know who he is?'

'He's connected with whatever is going on at the moment. He committed suicide at Adventure Kingdom several years ago. It was quite macabre by all accounts. His head was taken off by one of the trucks on the big dipper.'

'Is that the leisure park that's closed along the sea front?' Steven asked. 'It looks like a ghost town in there with all the rides closed down.'

'That's the place,' Charlotte said. 'I've heard a rumour that it wasn't suicide. Would you be able to sense that?'

'Only if I could go to the location where it happened, and even then, it's not guaranteed. Do you know where it was?'

'Yes, roughly. There's a bit of the track that extends to the far end of the park, where the customers never went. That's how he managed to attach himself to the tracks without anybody seeing him. That's what his widow told us.'

'Can we get in there?' Steven asked.

'It's all boarded up,' Will replied, killing the idea.

'We could climb over the fence,' Charlotte said.

'You've had too much to drink, Charlotte; you can't go breaking into an old funfair site.'

'Why not?' Steven asked. 'We wouldn't be doing any harm. It might help us figure out what's going on. We could help the police.'

Will shook his head in despair. 'Come on, you two, you've drunk too much bubbly. We're all much too old to do something like this.'

'That's not what you said when we broke through the fence at Sandy Beaches Holiday Camp,' Charlotte reminded him. That stopped him in his tracks. She knew it was the drink speaking, but she was convinced Steven Terry might help, and she had to know. She was annoyed with Will. This was their family they were protecting. He should want to know the truth too.

Within half an hour they'd said their farewells to Abi, taken a taxi to the leisure park and were waiting for the cabbie to drive away so they could climb over the wooden barrier that had been erected around the site. Charlotte staggered a little, struggling to maintain her balance.

'I still can't believe we're doing this,' Will said. 'How are we going to get over the fencing?'

Steven Terry knelt on the pavement, placed his hands open on this right knee and smiled at Charlotte.

'I haven't been caught up in a news story like this since I was last in Blackpool,' he said. 'Up you go, Charlotte; you must have done this as kids, surely?'

It was undignified, ungainly and slow, but between the three of them, they managed to push, shove and pull each other over the flimsy wooden fence.

The rides were in silhouette against the backdrop of a partial moon. The terrifying mouse ride to their right, the wooden ranch directly ahead, a merry-go-round to the side; Charlotte remembered it all. They'd spent many a day off in this place, youngsters in love, enjoying the rides, snuggling up close in the ghost train, and feeling sick after eating too many doughnuts.

She reached out in the darkness for Will's hand and gave it a squeeze, treasuring her years with him. Remembering this place and the fun they'd had there made her appreciate him all the more.

The big dipper was located towards the back of the park. Charlotte remembered standing there with Will, watching the trucks come around, trying to work out if she had enough courage to take a ride. The framework which supported the tracks had been made of wood. That had surprised her; she'd expected it to be constructed out of metal.

'You can see the timber moving as the trucks come round. It doesn't look safe to me,' she'd said to Will, looking at how high it was. By modern standards it was laughable, but in the 80s it had seemed so daring. Will had patiently reassured her that the structure was fine and that it was all about engineering and supporting loads. In the end, she'd gone on the ride once, been terrified and vowed never to go on a big dipper ever again.

They worked their way round to the back of the tracks. Lara Turnbull hadn't been precise about the place where her husband died, but seeing the structure in front of them, even in the darkness, it was clear where it must have been. The tracks went up and down, curving around a circular course, but at the far corner, the metal structure returned to ground level. Harvey Turnbull had to have chosen that as the spot where he would take his life.

As Will put out his arm to steady Charlotte in the darkness, Steven Terry became silent. He stopped as the track took a ninety-degree turn on the furthest corner and began to breathe deeply, as if he'd been struck by a panic attack.

'Are you okay?' Charlotte asked, concerned by the sudden change.

'This is it. This is the place,' he said. Under the influence of drink, his voice had been more informal and relaxed; he was back to his commanding stage presence now.

'My God,' he said. With what little light they'd got, Charlotte could see his eyes were closed. Will shrugged his shoulders at her, and she was annoyed with him; how could he not find this anything but compelling?

'This was no suicide. I sense only fear and horror here.'

'Surely that's how he'd have been feeling before he died?' Will suggested.

'No, I've been to places where people have taken their own lives before. There you feel despair, sadness, loss, helplessness. An act of extreme violence took place here. The man who died in this spot was in a frenzy of terror. Without doubt, he did not take his own life.'

'Is it possible his was not the only suicide to take place here?'

There was silence for a few a moments.

'It is possible,' Steven began. 'These are echoes I'm picking up. I can't attach them to a particular person. It may or not be this man. But something terrible happened here. A poison was spilt in this place that runs deep throughout this whole town. And I'm scared that this is what you're involved in. Please tell me your secret is not connected with these deaths.'

Before Will or Charlotte could reply, they were suddenly dazzled by two bright torch beams.

'Stay where you are, please,' came a voice from behind the lights. 'We're police officers. You do know this is private property?'

CHAPTER TWENTY-FOUR

For a couple who were keen to avoid contact with the police as much as possible, Will and Charlotte were failing miserably. The three of them were sitting in the back of a police car on their way to Morecambe police station when Will's impatience flared up.

'I told you we shouldn't have broken in,' he muttered to Charlotte, who was sitting to his right-hand side.

'You're an adult,' Charlotte whispered back to him. 'You didn't have to come if you didn't want to.'

'I didn't have much choice; I couldn't very well abandon you, not in the state you're in.'

'What state is that?' she snapped. 'I've had a couple too many, but I know exactly what I'm doing.'

Steven Terry intervened.

'You needn't worry about this trip to the police station,' he told them. 'It'll just be a routine matter. I've got past form in this area. We weren't doing anything, we didn't damage anything, and we didn't steal anything. It'll be a storm in a teacup.'

'The problem is, we've got form too,' Will replied.

'Yes, and that's both of us, remember?' Charlotte said, a little louder than she'd intended.

'Everything all right back there?' the police officer who was driving shouted back to them.

'Yes, all's well, Officer,' Steven answered on their behalf.

Charlotte lowered her voice to continue the conversation.

'It was you who got into trouble first, after your scrap in the pub.'

'Yes, but after that, we had your theft of that chap's moped to deal with,' Will added.

'I was trying to rescue our daughter at the time; it hardly counts!'

Charlotte was getting annoyed with her husband now; they'd been through this several times, and she'd had no choice in the matter. Will's run-in with the police had been of his own making.

'Let's focus on what we achieved from the visit,' Steven Terry interjected. 'I'm as certain as I can be that you're right about Harvey Turnbull's death; I don't believe it was suicide.'

'I don't want to insult you, Steven, but there's not a lot of fact to base that theory on. It's just speculation on your part. We might just as well read the tea leaves.'

Charlotte found Will's dismissive attitude of Steven Terry to be grating. She liked the man and believed he had some sort of talent or ability. Will hadn't seen the context in which he'd discovered Fred Walker's body. She couldn't begin to explain what it was that Steven Terry did, or how he did it, but she was certain there was something there. Will's cynicism didn't help.

'I get this all the time. Will, it doesn't trouble me that

you struggle to accept what I'm saying. I would just ask that you keep an open mind. If what I'm saying is correct—and I believe it is—then it could place a number of people in a lot of danger.'

Charlotte didn't want to discuss the details of their own situation in the back of a police car. Steven Terry knew she and Will were hiding something. That was why she was so convinced he was for real. She daren't share their history with him, when they didn't know whether he could be trusted. But she'd seen things that Will hadn't; he'd be less sceptical if he wasn't so preoccupied with his forthcoming job interview.

It took very little time to drive to the police station. The three of them were escorted into the bland, concrete building, which evoked a strong sense of seventies architecture. Inside, it almost smelled of that decade. The decoration was functional and sparse; every surface possible had been scratched or scribbled with graffiti, despite the presence of police officers. There were advisory posters on display in the reception area warning against lax home security or confidence tricksters doing the rounds in the resort, and others seeking information about several local criminals who'd been involved in an array of crimes from burglary to assault. Charlotte felt instantly depressed.

The two officers had ascertained that Charlotte, Will and Steven were far from being criminal masterminds, and didn't even feel the need to supervise them as they left them in the reception area.

'We'll just get a ticking off, maybe a warning,' Steven said. 'It must be a quiet Friday night in town. I'm surprised they even bothered bringing us in.'

'I don't think they would have if we'd had a car,' Will replied. 'I suspect it was easier for everybody. If they could have got a car number plate, it would have helped them to tie us to any other activities that might have taken place. With us being on foot, I think they'll just want to take our details and be sure who we are. It's just an embarrassment. Imagine if this got into the local paper.'

A police officer came out into reception. Charlotte recognised her immediately.

'We'll be on first-name terms with this lot soon,' she whispered. She felt giggly about it, but she didn't want to make things worse with Will; he was prickly enough already.

'I think we've seen you here before, haven't we?' the officer asked.

'I'm afraid so, yes,' Will replied. Charlotte thought he looked like a naughty child summoned to the head teacher's office for a telling off.

Will was taken through the door to the interview rooms first, followed by Charlotte. She knew this drill already; Morecambe police station was more familiar to her than she would care to admit. She thought back to the questions and probing after Lucia's kidnap. They'd all got their stories straight, they'd stuck to them consistently, and everything had gone just as they'd hoped. They'd all had a lot to lose. Jenna was lucky that she got off so lightly; Pat Harris took the biggest hit, due to his use of violence and a previous criminal record.

Charlotte thought about Jenna again; she'd been in a bad way. Had they done the right thing? George had seen her finish Bruce off; she and Will hadn't seriously harmed him, as they'd believed they had for so many years. That had come as a massive relief to both of them. But they'd all kept quiet, and George had hidden the body. And it was

George who covered it all up, by writing Bruce's supposed note of resignation.

No, they'd done the right thing. They'd managed to protect Jenna from the worst of the kidnapping charges and spare her from being jailed as a killer. She had a lot to thank them for, in spite of her present predicament.

Before they'd relocated to Morecambe, if Charlotte had been taken into a police station, she'd have been terrified. Like most people, she'd only ever had positive interactions with the police. Now, sitting in that interview room, she felt calm and in control. They hadn't done anything. They were middle class and trustworthy, and the privilege that it afforded them would have the three of them out of there in no time.

She answered the normal questions—name, address, date of birth, what they'd been doing there—and waited for the information to be corroborated on the police database. The interviewing officer immediately made the connection with Charlotte and the kidnapping, then asked a few questions about how her daughter was recovering. She knew then that she'd receive nothing worse than a warning.

They had agreed between themselves in the back of the car that they wouldn't give the real reason why they were on private land. Another lie. To Charlotte, they were all white lies. But how many could they tell? She worried that they'd slip one day, and the truth would be revealed.

'So, you were re-living your youth at the leisure park site?' the police officer asked, concealing a small smirk.

'Basically, yes,' she answered. 'I'd had a little too much to drink and probably led Steven and Will astray. It's all my fault, really. We didn't mean any harm by it.'

'And what about Mr Terry? He should have seen it coming, shouldn't he?'

Charlotte smiled. If the officer was making clairvoyant jokes, that probably meant the interview was coming to an end.

'Steven Terry has past form in this area,' the officer continued, with a more serious expression. 'He was involved in a serious case in Blackpool. It's not the first time he's broken into a boarded-up premises in search of information. DCI Summers speaks highly of him, however, so we won't be taking this matter any further. However, you do understand that if we get any reports of theft or damage on the site, we may have to interview you again?'

Charlotte nodded.

'You won't,' she said. 'We'd barely been in there for five minutes before your officers apprehended us.'

'About that,' the officer continued. 'The next time you break into private property, you might want to try being a little more inconspicuous. The two officers spotted you clambering over the fence as they drove along the promenade. You were hard to miss, apparently.'

'It wasn't the most dignified break-in in the history of the criminal underworld,' Charlotte admitted with a rueful smile. They'd been ridiculous. At least they'd given the late Friday shift a good laugh to help them through the night. She reckoned it would make a refreshing change from drunkards.

As the officer returned Charlotte to the reception area, she saw that Will was not yet out from his interview, but Steven Terry was deep in conversation with somebody in the seated area. It was DCI Summers. She walked up to them.

'You're working late, DCI Summers,' she said.

'Hello, Charlotte. Steven has just been filling me in on your escapades this evening. Please try to keep out of trouble. We have enough bother with the local ne'er-do-wells on a Friday evening.'

Steven looked at Charlotte. 'I've been telling DCI Summers about my instincts regarding Harvey Turnbull. I hope you don't mind?'

Charlotte wasn't certain if she minded or not. On balance, she thought it was probably safe information to share.

'It couldn't have come at a better time,' DCI Summers continued. 'I've been looking at the old files on Harvey Turnbull's case. That's why I'm here so late. I already suspected foul play, and this tends to confirm it now.'

Will had joined them as they were speaking, but didn't say anything while DCI Summers finished her sentence.

'Surely you take all this clairvoyant nonsense with a pinch of salt?' he said at last.

'Hello Mr Grayson,' DCI Summers said. 'On the contrary, I've worked with Mr Terry before. I was very doubtful about him at first, I admit that. But having worked with him on another case, I take what he says very seriously. And what he's just told me is going to be an invaluable help to us in progressing the murder case involving Fred Walker.'

CHAPTER TWENTY-FIVE

Charlotte had known better days cooking the breakfasts on a Saturday morning. She was regretting her decision to enjoy a couple of glasses of bubbly the night before.

She had finally got to her bed at around one o'clock, after DCI Summers had arranged for them to get a lift back to the guest house. Things had been tense between her and Will, too. He still blamed her for leading him on, unable to believe that somebody like DCI Summers would hold a charlatan like Steven Terry in such high esteem.

'Since when did the police start listening to mystics and fortune-tellers?' he'd muttered to Charlotte, as he removed his trousers to get ready for bed. All Charlotte could think of was sleep.

'They've used people like Steven Terry for years. Sometimes it can give them a breakthrough in a case. Didn't you hear about that case in Blackpool he was involved in? Besides, he just helped to confirm what the DCI was thinking. It's hardly like they've put him in charge of the investigation.'

'I don't know how he does it, but I just can't believe it.

We live in an age of science and evidence. That man belongs with the fortune-tellers and seaside entertainers. I like him, but I can't take him seriously.'

Will had still been complaining about Steven Terry when Charlotte drifted off to sleep. She didn't particularly care to hear Will's thoughts on the matter; they'd just have to agree to disagree on the subject of clairvoyance.

The early morning alarm at six o'clock had come too soon. It felt like her head had barely touched the pillow. Breakfast didn't start until 7.30 on a Saturday, but Isla's working hours meant that she wouldn't be in until eight o'clock that morning, leaving Charlotte to set up the kitchen and be ready for the early risers.

Guests didn't normally begin to surface until eight o'clock, and usually Charlotte enjoyed the silence, busying herself in the kitchen and the dining room, alone with her thoughts while the guests and her family were still tucked up in bed.

However, as she checked the rashers of bacon in the fridge and counted out the eggs, she heard movement out in the corridor. She closed the fridge door and walked over to the dining room. A single female guest was sitting at a table set for two people. Her back was turned to Charlotte, but she was wearing trainers and running gear.

'Good morning,' Charlotte said, still not sure which of the guests had decided to come down so early.

She turned to smile at Charlotte. It was Daisy Bowker.

'You're up early,' Charlotte said. 'Are you an early morning runner?'

'You have a Saturday morning parkrun along the promenade. There's no way I'm missing that while I'm in town. I need to eat early, to give my breakfast a chance to settle before I run.'

At least Daisy was there for leisure too. Charlotte hoped it might distract her from digging too deep for information about her half-brother.

'I've not heard about that,' Charlotte replied.

'It takes place every Saturday along the promenade. It's a lovely location for a run. It doesn't come as far down as your guest house. Maybe that's why you've missed it. Come with me, if you want. It's not just for runners. You can walk it if you like.'

'I think I'm too unfit to do that...' Charlotte began. She stopped half-way through her sentence. She'd cursed her lack of fitness a few times that week. And she wanted to keep Daisy close to her, so she could monitor her progress in finding information about Bruce Craven.

'You can walk it?' she said.

'Yes, honestly. I'm not very fast. I'll walk with you if you want? It'll be nice to have some company. It starts at nine o'clock.'

Charlotte thought about it as she looked out of the lounge window. The weather was calm outside. It could take her breath away when the wind was blowing along the sea front.

'I have some old jogging pants upstairs, and Isla will be here soon to take over. I think I'll take you up on that,' she said with a smile. She'd live to regret it later, she was certain, but her head was foggy from the night before, and a brisk walk along the promenade would help to clear her mind. She'd also use the opportunity to see where Daisy was up to with her family tree research. If she could put her off the scent, even better.

Charlotte took Daisy's order, prepared it in the kitchen and made herself a bacon sandwich. She felt her stomach settling as she demolished the hot food, and she took a couple of aspirin to banish the thudding in her head. Conveniently, Isla was early, entering the kitchen well before eight o'clock.

'Everything all right?' Charlotte asked. Isla looked troubled.

'Nothing I haven't told you already,' she replied. 'Just George again. Last night, he couldn't stop coughing, but he's still insisting there's nothing wrong. He just laughed it off as a chest infection. I know he's lying, Charlotte. Please try and have a word with him. I'm out of my mind with worry.'

'George is a tough one, Isla. He'll be okay, I'm certain.'

Charlotte did her best to reassure Isla, but she could see that she'd failed.

'I promise, next time I get him on his own, I'll ask him. I'm sure it's nothing serious; he'd have told you if it was. I'll mention it to Will too. George might feel more comfortable talking to a man.'

'I'm pleased to be in here cooking this morning,' Isla continued. 'It takes my mind off things. It always has. I don't know what I'd do if I ever had to stop working.'

Charlotte shared Isla's hopes that she'd be able to carry on for years. She wasn't sure they'd ever find somebody to replace her if she left. It didn't bear thinking about; the entire business seemed revolve around her.

Just before nine o'clock, Charlotte and Daisy were nearing the far end of the promenade where the run would start. The promenade was packed with joggers in all types of sports gear: children, adults and pensioners of all shapes and sizes readying themselves for the start.

'I can't believe I didn't know about this,' Charlotte said. 'And it takes place every week?'

'Every Saturday, in different places across the country,' Daisy replied. 'I've been doing it for years. Just take it at your own pace. It's a run, not a race; there's always someone slower than you.'

'I don't know why I agreed to do this,' she said, panting already from their brisk walk. 'I'm usually the last person to volunteer for sports.'

Her heart was pounding in her chest, and she was already sweating.

'It's a nice way to start the weekend,' Daisy replied. 'Besides, I wanted to be up early so I can take a look at the old holiday camp this morning. I hear it's a building site at the moment, but I'm hoping I can get a walk around, perhaps speak to some local people about it. Maybe one of them knew Bruce.'

Charlotte hadn't thought about that. Some of the catering staff were shipped in from Lancaster and Morecambe. Many came from Newcastle, Middlesbrough and Sunderland to work there over the summer. Charlotte knew there were also some local workers at the holiday camp too, people who came in from the surrounding villages. She'd never really got to know any of them. They were older and more mature than the youngsters who worked there. They also went home at night, rather than frequenting the bars and entertainments areas. Their knowledge might be dangerous.

'It's very rural around that area,' she replied, trying to steer Daisy gently away from the idea. 'The camp has been closed down so many years that I doubt many people will remember much about it. And it'll be very difficult without a car.'

'I'm picking up a hire car later,' Daisy continued, barely out of breath. 'I'm determined to find out everything I can about Bruce while I'm in the area. Something doesn't feel right to me.'

They'd arrived at the start line, where there was a pack of runners listening to the briefing. Daisy suggested they work their way to the back, so they wouldn't get in the way of the serious athletes.

Charlotte was grateful for the thinking time. Even Daisy was beginning to get a bad vibe about Bruce already; what did she know? She decided to tackle the issue head-on. They had to stay ahead of Daisy Bowker and prevent her from breaking into their circle of deceit.

'What makes you say that?' Charlotte asked. 'Have you found out something already?'

'It's just a feeling I get. I've been researching my family tree for some time, and none of it has been as difficult as finding out what happened to Bruce. It's almost like he disappeared into thin air. Nobody is talking about him, nobody remembers him. How does somebody just vanish like that? It's almost as if somebody wanted him gone.'

CHAPTER TWENTY-SIX

The start of the run put a stop to the conversation. The crowd surged forward, and Charlotte started to jog alongside Daisy as the faster runners picked up speed and the slower participants hung back, waiting for the way ahead to clear.

'Just go at your own pace,' Daisy said, taking it all in her stride. 'If you want me to slow down, just say.'

Charlotte had barely recovered from the walk along the length of the promenade, and here she was retracing her steps, albeit at an even faster pace. She didn't say anything while she established a steady rhythm alongside Daisy. At least there were a lot of runners behind them. It had been her greatest fear that she might finish in last place, or even worse, not be able to make it to the end.

As she jogged, Charlotte thought about how Daisy had never even met her half-brother, yet already she'd caught the essence of him. Perhaps Steven Terry wasn't the only person who could divine the truth out of thin air.

'How far is it?' she asked, struggling to pace her words with her breathing.

'Five kilometres,' Daisy replied, calm and in control. 'It'll be over in no time. It's not that far.'

They were nearing the Midland Hotel. A snake of runners had forged ahead, and Charlotte could now see the extent of the run. They were circling round by the lighthouse on the stone jetty, then heading further along the promenade to the clock tower. It might be only five kilometres to Daisy, but to Charlotte it looked like a huge challenge. She wondered how she'd got so out of shape; there was a time when she'd have been able to complete a course like that without even thinking about it.

As they ran, volunteers and spectators shouted words of encouragement, and it spurred Charlotte on, inspiring her to push through her tightening chest and shallow breaths. She was pleased she'd followed Daisy's lead by eating breakfast early; a full stomach would have been deadly.

As they passed the lighthouse at the end of the jetty, Charlotte began to understand why so many runners were keen to turn out on a Saturday morning. The bay looked splendid below the light blue sky and the hills across the water in Cumbria were sharp and crisp in the morning sunshine. There was a wonderful sense of camaraderie among the participants, and the mindlessness of it was soothing to her. The small, sea bird sculptures that punctuated the jetty fencing never failed to catch her out; as she neared them, she almost flinched, half expecting them to fly off in front of her. She didn't often get to see Morecambe through the eyes of a tourist, but running along the sea front like that made her grateful to be living there, in spite of everything.

As they circled back along the jetty, something purple caught Charlotte's eye in the distance. She couldn't make out what it was. She wiped her eyes to get rid of the sweat running from her brow and to sharpen her vision. As she neared the road end of the jetty, she figured out what it was. It was a young man, lithe and heavily tattooed, with a bright, purple Mohican haircut.

She thought back to what Olli had told her about his altercation with Lucia. He'd mentioned his sister speaking to somebody who looked like that. Surely there couldn't be anyone else in the resort with such a distinctive hairstyle.

As she neared, she saw that the Mohican was styled in the shape of a dragon. It looked spectacular. This had to be her man.

As she got even closer to him, she considered her options. He was sitting on a wall, draining a high energy drink from a can and talking to a girl who was probably about Lucia's age. Could she break away from the run? Would it matter? She had to remember that Daisy was a guest; she didn't want to offend her. But she might never get to see this man again, and she wanted to ask him some questions. If Lucia wasn't going to be forthcoming, perhaps he might be.

She was almost directly opposite him. It was now or never.

'Run ahead,' she said to Daisy. 'I just have to stop for a few moments.'

'It's okay, I'll wait for you,' Daisy replied, slowing.

'No, I'll catch you up,' Charlotte said, leaving the running route and heading towards the man. He was older than Lucia - much older. She felt her hackles rising. If this was her daughter's boyfriend, he'd be getting the sharp end of her tongue. Lucia was still at school. It wasn't an appropriate relationship; this man looked to be in his mid-twenties.

She slowed down, gasping to steady her breathing.

'Excuse me... do... you... know... Lucia Grayson?'

'Who's asking?' the man replied. She could see from his face that he knew Lucia all right.

'Her mother,' Charlotte began.

She'd barely finished speaking before the man was up on his feet and running off, following the route of the runners.

'Wait!' Charlotte cried after him, 'I need to speak to you.'

The can of energy drink rolled to a stop at her feet; he'd just thrown it away so he could make a fast getaway.

Charlotte was angry. Who was this idiot, thinking he could have a relationship with her daughter and refuse to speak to her? What the hell was he up to?

Without thinking, she turned and began to run after him.

'Whoa, hang on!' came Daisy's voice. 'Wait for me.'

Charlotte gritted her teeth, ignoring Daisy's pleas. She'd hung back for her, waiting for her to continue the run. All Charlotte could focus on was the bright, purple Mohican bobbing up and down straight ahead of her.

The man took a sudden turn at the lifeboat station, jumping off the concrete ramp and onto the shingly beach, stumbling on the stones as he looked behind him to see where his pursuer was.

Charlotte considered following him for a moment, but he'd already realised that he'd made a bad decision heading onto the beach and was running to the edge of the lifeboat station. He'd only have one choice when he got there, and that was to climb back on to the promenade as fast as he could.

'Follow him down the ramp!' Charlotte shouted back to Daisy, who was still on her trail. She pointed, just to be clear. The other runners darted around her, visibly annoyed that she'd stopped dead in their path and had created an unwelcome distraction.

Daisy pushed ahead, ready to cut off the man as he climbed back onto the promenade.

There were no steps down to the beach at that point and, as Charlotte had anticipated, the Mohican guy had run around the lifeboat building and was now pulling himself up with the help of the white fencing which ran the length of the promenade.

'Stop!' she shouted, running towards him as fast as she could. Seeing her, he climbed up and swung over the fence, stepping out into the path of two runners who were deep in conversation and had failed to spot him. They tripped over him, shouting angrily, warning him to look where he was going.

'Got you,' Charlotte said, rushing forward, intent on physically restraining him if she had to. But he was fast. In a moment, he was up on his feet and running around the curve of the promenade. He ducked into the small car park, and Charlotte lost him for a moment.

She scanned the area adjacent to the main road; he hadn't made it that far. He had to be in the car park. She walked wide, so that if he darted out suddenly, she'd be able to get to him before he reached the road. If he got that far, he'd be off down a side street, on the lookout for her. One thing was certain; she had to get Lucia to tell her who this man was. He was up to something, she was sure of it.

As Charlotte approached a white Ford car, she saw his feet through the gap between the chassis and the asphalt.

'Wait, I want to speak to you!' she shouted.

The man was away again, darting towards the promenade and in the direction of the town's famous Eric Morecambe statue. This was a place that attracted the crowds; Charlotte knew that if she couldn't keep up with him, he'd easily shake her off there. She'd lost track of Daisy now. She would just have to hope that she'd run on without her.

If it wasn't for his distinctive hairstyle, she'd have lost him in the crowds of runners and early-to-rise tourists long ago. He was nearing the Eric Morecambe statue, veering towards it as if intent on running through the seated area. He must be planning to cross the road again.

Pushing through the sharp pains in her chest, Charlotte veered off through the parking area and out towards the roadside. As she emerged, he was standing at the edge of the road. He jumped, not expecting her to have anticipated his move.

'Jesus!' he cursed, turning sharply and heading back through the gardens, past the statue and back onto the promenade. Charlotte heard the shouts before she came over the steps and realised what was happening. The fastest runners were now circling back along the promenade and heading back to the start line. The man with the Mohican had run out directly in front of them, sending three of them flying. One of the runners had fallen badly on his arm, another had grazed her knees and the third runner was getting aggressive towards the fool who'd sent them all crashing to the ground. Curses rang out among the other runners.

The man with the Mohican looked up to see Charlotte still pursuing him and dashed off again. Her lungs felt as if they were about to burst, but she was determined to keep up with him if she could. Once past the statue, it was a straight run as far as the second jetty. She'd be able to follow him all the way down; she'd catch him sooner or later.

Desperately snatching small breaths and almost paralysed with pain, Charlotte ran past the children's playground and towards the clock tower. There were people sitting outside at the tables already, enjoying an early morning coffee.

'Stop that man!' she shouted. 'He's stolen my purse.'

She knew she was chancing her luck, but she had to try something to slow him down. He was fast and fit; for some reason, she hadn't expected that.

Two men had stood up from their tables and were looking for the source of the shouting, trying to figure out what was going on. The man with the Mohican suddenly veered off the promenade, cutting across the now steady stream of returning runners, prompting more swearing from those whose path he had crossed. Charlotte knew that she would lose him here if she couldn't follow him across the road.

Not checking her path properly, she darted suddenly across the stream of oncoming runners. There were instant shouts of *Watch what you're doing!* and *Get out of the way you stupid cow!*

Spooked by all the cursing, a collie dog which had been sitting patiently at its owner's feet jumped up and began to bark. Its lead was attached to the foot of one of the metal chairs. As the dog jumped up, the lead tightened, creating a tripwire for Charlotte who had been too slow to react. She crashed into the table, sending the hot teas and coffees splashing over the small party that were sitting there, then watched as the man with the Mohican stopped, turned back, gave her the finger, then crossed calmly to the other side, where he swiftly disappeared down a shady side street.

CHAPTER TWENTY-SEVEN

'Are you sure you're all right?' Daisy asked, helping Charlotte over to one of the spare tables. 'You bolted; what on earth was going on?'

Charlotte felt embarrassed and humiliated by the whole affair. Thanks to Daisy having some money tucked away in a concealed pocket in her jogging pants, she was able to placate the group of people who'd had their table of drinks thrown across the ground when she tripped over the dog's lead and sent everything flying into the air.

Daisy had thrown in some cakes to the group as compensation, and that seemed to settle them down after the shock. She had also apologised profusely to the owner for the disturbance. Charlotte was grateful, since it meant the police wouldn't be summoned. That was all she needed.

'Here, have a coffee and a cake,' said Daisy. 'You look shaken.'

'I'm sorry to wreck your run,' Charlotte said, sipping her drink and giving her leg a rub where it had struck the table. 'That guy with the purple hair is involved with my daughter in some way. At least, I think he is. He matches the description that my son gave. I just wanted to have a word with him, but you saw how fast he ran away. He must have something to hide.'

'Well, he was too fast for either of us to catch. And I'd say you got your morning exercise chasing after him. I'll bet that's the fastest you've run for a long time.'

Charlotte smiled at her. Although it was against every instinct of self-preservation, she liked Daisy. This woman could destroy her family, yet other than being related through blood to Bruce Craven, she couldn't find a single reason to dislike her.

'At least he's easy to spot with that purple dragon shaved into his hair. I'm certain I'll see him in a small town like this. Next time I'll creep up on him, rather than challenging him to a race. That probably wasn't such a good idea for a woman who hasn't been out for a run since leaving school.'

Having finished their drinks, Daisy and Charlotte began the walk back down the promenade towards the guest house. The runners were all gone, and the dog walkers, pram pushers and resort visitors had now reclaimed the space.

'Teenagers can be a struggle; I know all about that,' Daisy said as they walked past the boathouse. 'My daughter was a little devil when she reached sixteen. She's married and got a family of her own now. What goes around comes around. She'll be fighting the same battles with her own daughter soon enough.'

'You didn't mention your husband,' Charlotte began.

'He died of a heart attack two years ago.'

'I'm sorry,' Charlotte replied, by instinct. She worked out how old he must have been. Not that much older than her and Will. They were entering that dangerous zone when the penalties of a carefree life had to be paid.

'It was a classic middle-age scenario. Two years from retirement, too much stress, overweight and not enough exercise, then one day he just dropped dead. Just like that. That's when I started the jogging. It helped me get through it and build a new life. The kids have lives of their own now, so it leaves me free to go on adventures like this, looking up my family tree.'

Charlotte felt an easy comfort with Daisy, but she wanted to resist it; she couldn't afford to let anything slip. This woman had to do whatever she'd come for, then go back home to the north-east and leave them all alone. It was a shame, though; Daisy was a woman who she could happily spend more time with.

Breakfasts were over when they walked through the door of the guest house. Olli was checking out a guest and Isla had all but finished the clearing up.

'That chap from the paper has been trying to get in touch with you,' Isla called from the kitchen.

Daisy made her exit and headed up the stairs back to her room. The room where Barry McMillan's life had ended. At least Daisy hadn't picked up on that. She was oblivious to the dark incident that had taken place there days before.

'Nigel Davies?' Charlotte asked, walking into the kitchen.

'Yes. He said he'd tried your mobile phone. It sounded urgent. It might be a good idea to call him sooner rather than later. He wouldn't say what it was.'

'Unusual for him to call on a Saturday,' Charlotte said. 'I'll get showered, then I'll ring him back. Thanks Isla, and thanks for taking care of breakfasts. I haven't forgotten what you said about George. The next time I see him, I'll pin him down.'

Charlotte showered quickly, eager to find out what Nigel wanted. She was annoyed to discover that Lucia had left the house early, not giving Olli any indication as to where she was heading.

Will seemed equally annoyed with Charlotte for chasing Nigel Davies once again.

'Don't you think it's time to cool things down as far as this wild goose chase is concerned?' he said, looking up from some paperwork. 'We got into enough trouble last night. For somebody who wants to keep a low profile, you're sticking your nose in all over the place.'

Charlotte decided not to tell him about that morning's incident. The man with the purple Mohican would go unmentioned for now.

'I don't even know what he wants,' Charlotte said, more defensively than she intended. The truth was, just like Daisy with her family tree, Charlotte had to begun to pick at a knot and she couldn't stop even if she tried.

Steven Terry might have understood better. She needed to stay ahead of whatever was going on in the resort. The murders, this man with the purple hair, Piper and Daisy; it seemed to her that a storm was brewing, one which could wreak havoc in their lives. She wasn't going to let that happen. Will was happy to lie low in the hope that the turbulence would pass them by, but Charlotte was prepared to run into the eye of the storm and tear out its heart, if that's what it took to keep her family safe.

'Hi Nigel, it's Charlotte. Sorry I couldn't take your call. What's up?'

'Hi Charlotte, are you available today? I've got a bit of

investigative journalism planned, and I thought you might like to be involved.'

'You don't normally work on Saturdays, do you?'

'No, but this can't wait. Edward Callow is back from London for the weekend. He's attending some fundraiser this evening, so he's in his constituency house on the way out to Heysham. He has a police guard on his drive, but I want to try to doorstep him if I can. I could use a decoy if you're up for it.'

Charlotte felt a surge of excitement. She turned away from Will and walked across the hallway towards the sitting room. He wouldn't approve of what Nigel was suggesting, particularly after their run-in with the police. But Edward Callow, the man who rose up from the planning department, seemed to be at the centre of everything.

'That's fine. Can you pick me up outside the guest house? I'll see you in ten minutes.'

'Where are you going now?' Will called to her from the kitchen. 'It's bad enough Lucia sneaking about like she does. Like mother, like daughter.'

That annoyed Charlotte, but she knew better than to pick a fight at that moment. She returned to the kitchen to place the phone back in its cradle.

'I won't be long,' she said. 'Trust me. This is all about our family. I'm just trying to keep us safe.'

Will looked up.

'I know you are,' he said, the confrontational tone now gone. 'I'm sorry, I'm just a bit stressed with this job application. And with the thought of that woman snooping around trying to find out about Bruce Craven... I'm just jittery, that's all. It didn't help having our encounter with the police last night.'

Charlotte gave him a kiss, glad that they'd parted

without tension. If they weren't careful, the stress of keeping their secret would destroy them without it ever coming out.

Within half an hour, she was parked up at the end of Edward Callow's road, sitting in Nigel Davies' car and devising a plan of attack.

'I just want to speak to him,' Nigel said. 'I want to hear what he has to say about these deaths. I've been telephoning his London office all week, and his PA's stonewalled me. As our constituency MP, I'd expect him to make a comment at least.'

Edward Callow's house was on a very expensive cul-de-sac which afforded excellent views across Morecambe Bay. The properties were substantial, each with a drive on which at least three cars were parked. The gardens were well tended, full of shrubs, trees and flowers. This was where the elite of the area gathered: successful business people, those in high office and the lucky ones who'd inherited property through the family. Years ago, Charlotte had home-tutored a child somewhere in this area of the town.

'So what's the plan?' she asked.

'Simple,' Nigel replied. 'Remember when you were a kid, and you'd creep into somebody's garden to pinch their apples?'

'I can't say I ever did that as a child,' Charlotte replied.

'Well, there's a first time for everything. Only this time we've got to creep past a policeman as well.'

CHAPTER TWENTY-EIGHT

'You can tell this is the UK. Look, only one police officer stationed outside his house. That's what counts for protection around here.'

Nigel was peering from behind a large bush which provided them with convenient cover. From their vantage point, they could see a single unarmed police officer standing outside Edward Callow's ornately carved front door. He looked bored out of his mind. It was the most lacklustre protection the local constabulary could have mustered, as far as Charlotte could see.

'As if anybody who wants him dead is going to walk up to the front door and knock,' she said. 'Only in the UK!'

Nigel stooped down to pick up a handful of pebbles from the end of the neighbour's drive.

'I'm going to cross the road so the police officer can't see me. I'll go around to the other side of Edward's house and throw these stones at his garage roof. When the officer goes to investigate, I want you to knock at the door and see if you can raise Edward Callow.'

'What about you?' Charlotte asked.

'Once I've distracted this chap, I'll sneak round the garage and join you at the front door. We'll have to be quick. We won't get long with Callow.'

Nigel crossed the road and tucked himself into the hedge on the opposite side of Edward's house. Charlotte watched as he stealthily moved towards Edward Callow's triple garage, which on its own was bigger than many of the family houses in the resort. She wanted to giggle when she saw Nigel pulling back his arm so he could launch the stones at Edward's garage roof. He wouldn't have looked out of place if he was ten years old and wearing shorts and a school cap.

He threw the first stone. Although Charlotte couldn't see it, she heard it land on the tiled roof on the side that was facing away from her. The police officer heard it too and looked over towards the garage. He scanned the area for a few seconds, then turned away. Charlotte assumed he'd dismissed it as bird movement or something similar.

Nigel threw a second stone. This time it landed just over the ridge of the garage roof on Charlotte's side. It made a loud cracking sound as it struck one of the tiles, then rolled down the roof, flying past the guttering and onto the immaculately kept drive.

The officer was suddenly alert, moving away from the doorway to investigate what had fallen from the roof.

Barely missing a beat, Nigel threw a third, then a fourth stone, this time landing them on his side of the roof. Charlotte wanted to laugh at what they were doing. It was as ridiculous as clambering over fences into the private grounds of abandoned leisure parks.

The officer took the bait and began to move around the far side of the garage. Charlotte made her way up the drive, aware of Nigel to her side, making his way back round. Nigel threw another couple of stones, landing them on the side of the roof where the police officer was now located.

Charlotte rang the doorbell rather than knocking at the door. She hadn't a clue what she'd say to Edward Callow if he answered. Hopefully Nigel would get to her by then.

Now movement could be heard in the hallway, beyond the heavy, wooden door. She glanced around for signs of the police officer. He wouldn't be gone long, Nigel was right about that. As the door began to open, Nigel joined her on the doorstep, perfectly on time, a little out of breath but obviously pleased with himself at having secured his objective.

He threw the last two stones in his hand across the garage roof as the door opened fully to reveal a tall, confident man, wearing expensive glasses which set off his bald head and neatly trimmed beard perfectly. This was a man who paid for his grooming in London, not the local hairdresser in Morecambe. He oozed authority and power. Charlotte shrank back from the door, suddenly feeling stupid and immature. What the hell had she been thinking of?

Nigel engaged him immediately, before he had time to question their presence.

'I'm Nigel Davies from The Bay View Weekly. I've been trying to reach you for a comment on the death of two of your business partners this week...'

'Get off my property, you idiots!' he boomed. 'Where is my police officer? How did you get in here?'

'Mr Callow, you've been involved with Fred Walker, Barry McMillan and Harvey Turnbull as business partners for well over three decades now. Is there any reason why somebody might want to kill you?'

Charlotte watched Edward Callow as he formed a fist with his hand.

'You'd better leave now, before I punch you in the face, Mr Davies. I don't give a shit about your crappy little paper or any half-brained theory you might have about the deaths of my colleagues. Officer! Officer!'

A lady walked by on the pavement above them, her attention drawn by the raised voices.

'Good morning, Mrs Higgins,' Callow shouted, a genial tone in his voice. He waved at her like she was his best friend in the world.

'Now fuck off before I smash your nose in, you silly little man,' he growled.

The officer appeared from the side of the garage, looking flustered and confused.

'How did you get here?' he asked. 'Was it you who—?'

'Escort these fools off my property!' Edward Callow boomed. 'I shall be having a word with the Chief Constable about your incompetence and obvious unsuitability for this task. Get rid of them now!'

The police officer looked like he was about to start crying. Charlotte felt terrible about what they'd just done, landing him in trouble like that. They were no further forward, other than that she now understood why Jon Rogers at the library disliked the man so much. It looked like he was not only happy to run over cats, but he was also equally at ease humiliating young police officers.

'How did you get down the drive? I was only gone a few moments,' the officer said, trying to make sense of what had just happened.

Nigel took out his ID and flashed it at the officer.

'I must admit, I was surprised to see that Edward Callow was not being protected, bearing in mind all that's been going on. But there was nobody to stop us when we arrived, and I just wanted some information for the newspaper.'

'Did you see anybody around the side of the house?' the officer asked.

'Just a couple of kids,' Nigel replied. 'They looked like they were throwing things at houses. I don't think Callow will come to any harm. Besides, with language like that, I reckon he can look after himself, don't you?'

The officer seemed relieved with Nigel's explanation about local children throwing stones. He escorted them to the end of the drive.

'Do you think he'll really report me to the Chief Constable?' the officer asked.

'He's a nasty piece of work, that one. But I doubt he'll trouble the Chief Constable with something so minor. Next time you see him, tell him you had to chase a couple of the local kids out of his garden. If you explain that's why you had to leave your post, it'll blow over, I'm sure.'

Charlotte and Nigel made their way along the pavement, towards the car.

'I feel bad about that,' Charlotte said after a while. 'The poor cop didn't deserve a dressing down like that.'

'Yes, but did you see Callow's face when I challenged him? I'm telling you, if that man isn't in it up to his ears, I'll be very surprised. I think this is about property deals and relationships gone sour. And it's significant that Callow is the one who's still alive.'

'Wasn't there a fifth man in the photograph?' Charlotte asked.

'Yes, and I think I've managed to track him down now. As soon as I can confirm it, I'll arrange a visit.'

It felt like an anti-climax arriving back at the guest

house. Everything was quiet when she walked through the door. Isla was gone for the day, although there were signs that one or two guests were still around. She walked up the stairs to the family accommodation, opening the door that separated them from the rest of the building.

'Anybody at home?' she called as she walked in. She left the door open, remembering that she should have taken out some steaks to defrost from the freezer downstairs.

'Hi Charlotte, I'm in the kitchen.'

Will was home.

She walked in to see him sitting with a worried look on his face.

'What happened?' she asked. 'Are Olli and Lucia around?'

'I haven't seen Lucia since she sneaked out earlier this morning. Olli has gone to Lancaster with his girlfriend. I need to talk to you.'

Will didn't usually speak like this. He obviously had something on his mind.

'What is it?' Charlotte asked.

'I drove that woman—Mrs Bowker—over to the old holiday camp while you were out.'

'Why did you do that?' Charlotte asked, immediately tense.

'She asked me about hiring a car. I told her not to bother. I thought it might put an end to it if I just drove her out there myself and showed her that there's nothing to look at any more. I was thinking about what you said protecting our family. I thought I'd do my bit.'

'What happened?' Charlotte asked. 'Do you think she'll lose interest soon?'

'She was like a dog with a bone,' Will continued. 'All the way over there, she was asking me questions. Did I meet

Bruce? What did he look like? Did he ever mention family? She nearly caught me out. I had to backtrack fast.'

'Damn it, Will, we've got to be careful. What did you say?'

'It's so easy to get tripped up. She was asking me about Jenna. She'd seen the photograph in the paper and noticed that Bruce and Jenna seemed to be an item. She asked me if I knew where Jenna was now. I couldn't lie; you go to visit her in prison, for God's sake. But then I realised that if she talks to Jenna, the whole story might come out. She's not the most reliable of people these days. So I covered my tracks and said we didn't really know Jenna. I'm sure she knew I was lying. We've got to be careful, Charlotte. We've got to keep our stories straight.'

'Hello?'

Daisy walked into the kitchen.

'I hope you don't mind me walking in like that, only your door was wide open. I need an extra towel if you've got one spare.'

Charlotte could see the look of guilt on Will's face. She didn't need a mirror to tell her that she looked just as bad.

Will jumped up from his chair to attend to the towel. As he did so, Daisy began to speak again.

'I hope you don't mind me asking, but that conversation sounded fascinating, whatever it was about. Who has to keep their stories straight?'

CHAPTER TWENTY-NINE

Charlotte hated the person she was becoming. It seemed that every lie she told spawned another, and it was fast getting out of control.

'Kids again,' she replied to Daisy. 'You know how it is. I was just saying to Will that we must to get our stories straight. We need to be consistent with what we're telling Lucia. Sing from the same hymn book, that sort of thing.'

Charlotte knew she was over-explaining, but she had to be sure that the lie had landed well. Daisy didn't seem convinced, but she nodded anyway.

'It was very interesting visiting that old holiday camp with your husband earlier. I hope you don't mind me borrowing him for a while?'

Charlotte didn't think she had much choice in the matter.

'I feel like I've drawn a bit of a blank with Bruce, though. Everything seems to lead nowhere. I'm wondering if I ought to raise it with the police. Do you think they'll have any records?'

Will turned towards Charlotte, with a look of anguish. She tried to compose herself.

'You know how short-staffed the police are these days. They can't even be bothered to solve most of the petty crimes around here, let alone something that might have happened over thirty years ago. Maybe he moved out of the area? That seems the most likely thing to me.'

'Perhaps,' Daisy said, deep in thought. 'I'm going to hire a car anyway, so I can dig a bit deeper. Thanks for driving me earlier Will, but I want my freedom.'

'Do you want me to run you over to the car hire office on the industrial estate?' Will asked.

As Daisy looked at her watch, Will shrugged at Charlotte as if to say *What else can I do?*

Daisy was their friend now, but Charlotte wondered how genial she'd be if she knew what they'd done to her half-brother.

'I don't suppose we could go fairly soon, could we? I'm going to call it a day with the family history research for now, but I would like to take a drive into Lancaster.'

'No problem at all. I'll fetch you that new towel, then I'll be happy to run you over to the car hire place. I'll nip into the cash and carry while we're there.'

Daisy and Will left the family accommodation, and Charlotte listened as they made their way down the stairs and out of the guest house.

She sat at the kitchen table, her eyes scanning Will's notes. She'd barely paid any attention to this new job of his. She knew he wasn't entirely happy in the role he'd taken when they moved to Morecambe and that lecturing at the university would be a move up for him. It did feel a bit parochial, teaching at the same place he'd got his degree.

As she was reading the job description that he'd left out

on the table, she heard a knocking sound. It wasn't unusual to hear guests banging and clattering around the place, but this caught her ear. It sounded like it was on one of the lower floors. She stood up and listened again.

Charlotte walked out onto the landing and shouted down the stairs.

'Will, is that you? Did you forget something?'

She couldn't hear anything from the guests. The entire guest house appeared to be empty. There were no TVs on in the rooms, which was the usual giveaway.

The knocking started again. It seemed to be coming from the ground floor.

Slowly, Charlotte walked down the stairs. They'd had a rat at the back of the property some months previously; she hoped they weren't going to be troubled with vermin again. One rat in the wrong place and they were in deep trouble. Fortunately, it had fallen victim to some poison outside, and the issue had resolved itself since then.

'Is anybody around?' she asked, as she reached the ground floor and stepped into the hallway. 'Isla, is that you?'

There was no response. Charlotte walked into the kitchen and in her state of nervous tension, had a flashback to Isla lying there in a pool of blood after she'd been attacked by Jenna's violent boyfriend, Pat Harris. She shuddered at the thought of it. The noise rang out again, from the direction of the cellar. If they'd got a rat down there, they needed to find out fast and get the thing killed.

She reached out for a kitchen knife from the wooden block that was sitting on the worktop to her side. She had no idea what she was going to do with it, but it seemed like a sensible precaution, in case the rat jumped at her.

Charlotte walked to the back of the hallway, to the white-painted door that led down to the cellar. The door creaked open, and she thrust her hand into the darkness, searching for the light switch. She found it and turned it on. The bulb that hung over the steep, stone staircase came on, then blew immediately. The stairs were dark but the second light, within the cellar, was still on.

Carefully, step-by-step, she walked down the staircase, feeling the coldness from the stone walls creeping over her skin. She held tight to the wooden railing, taking care not to lose her footing.

At the bottom of the steps, she had to take a right turn to get a full view of the cellar. She was beginning to wish she'd left it to Will to investigate. The thought of a rat being down there, or even a mouse, creeped her out.

The bulb was low wattage, so it barely illuminated the boxes and numerous dusty items that were stored in the cellar. Generations of former owners had left out-of-date china, catering equipment and furnishings down there. Will and Charlotte had vowed to clean it out, but as the guest house had got busier, it had swiftly dropped down the list of things to do. The space was cluttered, musty and packed, but narrow pathways had been created between the piles of junk, so at least she could make her way through to check out the noise.

Charlotte jumped as she heard a shuffling noise in the far corner. The light didn't quite reach that far, and she didn't want to move any deeper through the pathways. Discarded furniture had been piled almost as high as the ceiling towards the back of the cellar. Her heart pounded as she imagined a rat appearing at head height.

She felt ridiculous as she held out the kitchen knife in front of her, taking tiny steps closer to the source of the sound. As she stepped around the corner of a pile of tea chests, her eye caught the small basement window which opened out into the back yard where the car was kept. There were a couple of tables out there for the guests who wanted to smoke. They'd tried the window when they first moved in, checked it was closed, then forgot all about it. Where the glass pane had once been was now covered in black-painted wood, allowing no daylight into the cellar. Now, that now seemed a foolish thing to do; Charlotte could have used some natural light.

Beneath the covered window was a box of papers which looked like it had been emptied out over the floor. Had a rat been gnawing at the storage containers down there? Cautious, she moved on, listening for any sounds of scratching.

There was a narrow path running along the far end of the cellar, underneath the window, near where the papers were spread out. She'd have to step over them to check the very far end. She looked down as her feet touched the outer areas of the pile, which seemed to comprise paperwork and photographs. It was hard to see it all, in this shadowy side of the cellar.

Charlotte placed the kitchen knife on the edge of the emptied tea chest so she could put out her hands to steady herself as he stepped over the heaped pile of papers. She couldn't see any signs of gnawing or chewing; perhaps the sound she'd heard was just one of the tea chests falling to the ground?

There was a movement directly ahead of her, and the sound of breathing. Something big was in the corner, much bigger than a mouse or a rat. It moved under the legs of a table.

Charlotte turned quickly in the darkness, holding her breath in terror. She slid on the papers, desperately trying to find her footing, then fell, striking her head on a piece of furniture that jutted out. With a sob of fear, she scrambled to get up. She had to get out of there.

As her hands fumbled to find something to haul herself up with, she sensed movement behind her, then the touch of a cold, human hand. She gasped as she turned around and saw a man grabbing hold of her.

CHAPTER THIRTY

Charlotte remembered the kitchen knife, but it wasn't within reach. She banged at the tea chest next to her head in the hope that it might shake the weapon from where she'd put it down, but instead of dropping to the floor it fell inside the wooden container.

'Leave me alone,' she shouted at the man, who was now trying to place his hands over her mouth to silence her.

'Please be quiet, I'm not here to hurt you,' he told her.

Charlotte struggled on the floor, the man's body looming over her. If he decided to attack her, she'd be helpless.

She rolled to the side, but he reached out, trying to pin her to the ground. A claustrophobic sensation engulfed her, muffling her breath in the confines of the cellar. As she tried to get up, Charlotte struck her head on the side of the cellar wall. The sudden pain stopped her from struggling, and her assailant relaxed his grip.

'I'm not going to hurt you, but please don't shout for help,' he whispered. 'Not until I've explained why I'm here.

If you still don't believe me, call the police. I'll be safer in a cell than I will if I have to go outside.'

Charlotte placed her hand on her forehead to assess the level of damage. No blood; that was a start.

'Who are you?' she shouted at him. 'And how the hell did you get down here?'

'I'm Rex Emery,' he replied. 'I used to own this place.'

Charlotte sat on the cold, damp cellar floor, stunned at his revelation.

'But you're supposed to be in prison, aren't you?'

'Sort of,' he replied. 'I'm due for release very soon; I've been in Haverigg open prison for the past few months. I made a run for it. My life is in danger. I can't stay there.'

'How did you get in here?' Charlotte asked, doing her best to remain calm. His body language wasn't threatening, at least.

'That window has been dodgy for years. I can't believe nobody has mended it. If you give it four or five thumps from the outside, the arm jumps off its retainer, and you can get inside. It's not the sort of thing you'd ever find out unless you'd locked yourself out. You might want to get that sorted, now you know about it.'

'So are you on the run?'

'Yes,' said Rex. 'I'm a wanted man. You can hand me over to the police if you want to, but please listen to what I have to say first.'

'How long were you hoping to hide here? How long have you been down here?'

Charlotte thought about the children being in the guest house on their own, potentially with... What was he, a kidnapper? She shuddered at the thought of exposing her daughter to a man on the run.

'They're trying to silence me,' Rex continued. 'If they

get to me, they'll kill me. I'm a sitting duck in the prison. They have people everywhere.'

Charlotte could just make out his face in the darkness. He looked deadly serious. But didn't all prisoners protest their innocence?

'Who?' Charlotte asked. 'Who's trying to hurt you?'

'You've seen what's happening already. I read it in the newspaper; that's when I finally understood that they're cleaning up their messes. When Barry McMillan died in this place, I knew exactly what was going on. Fred Walker too. They'd already got to Turnbull. He should have known better than to fall out with Edward Callow. I don't know what even happened to Mason Jones. I hope he's dead already. I hope that piece of filth dies of a long, slow and painful cancer. He deserves it.'

'I can't make head or tail of what you're saying,' Charlotte interrupted. 'Slow down. None of this is making sense to me. What about Edward Callow? You didn't mention his name. He's connected with those men too, isn't he?'

'That man is the devil!' Emery shouted. 'I'd like to strangle him with my own bare hands and spit on his dead body. I want to look into his eyes as I take the last seconds of life from him, and I want him to know that it was me that did it. That man wrecked my life.'

'This is all too complicated. Please, start from the beginning,' Charlotte urged. She thought about what she and Nigel Davies had pieced together already. This man didn't seem to be a danger to her. But he did appear to know more than anybody she'd spoken to so far.

'Can I get up now? There are two stools over there; how about we move over towards the light so we can talk better?'

Rex had released his grip on her hands after she'd struck

her head, but he was still towering over her as if he might leap on her at any moment.

'I'm sorry,' he said. 'You frightened the life out of me. I thought I'd be safe down here. I also thought the guest house was empty.'

They both stood up, and Charlotte moved over towards the stools. With their padded, vinyl seats, they looked like they belonged to the seventies. Charlotte handed one to Rex, and they moved over to the bottom of the steps, into an area that was much better lit. He was balding and had heavy bags under his eyes. His dress was plain, but not prison clothing, as she'd expected from her limited experiences of such matters drawn from the TV. He looked tired and weary, but she could see the fear etched into his eyes.

'You know I was jailed for kidnapping Piper Phillips and holding her in the upstairs roof space on this building?'

Charlotte nodded.

'She carved her name up there. I discovered it only the other day.'

'I guess it's true to say I was involved, but I did not kidnap that poor girl, nor was I responsible for holding her like that. My worst crime was a turning a blind eye, but I had no other choice.'

Charlotte could get a better sense of the man now that his face was in the light. Whether it was the truth or a pack of lies, he looked like he believed what he was saying.

'Then who took her?'

'Mason Jones, the head teacher at her school. He was responsible for her welfare at school. He set it up so that she was sent on an errand during school time, and that's when they snatched her. They held her in that loft space. I swear to God, I didn't know she was there. They hired a room from me and told me to look the other way. And when they were finally convinced that man Craven was dead, Turnbull set his officers loose on me, and I got the blame for the whole thing. Those bastards threw me to the lions. The only consolation was that Turnbull got what he deserved. And now the others are getting what's been coming to them too.'

Charlotte's mind could barely keep up with all the information he was giving her. She was still unable to get the full picture; the fragments didn't seem to fit together.

'You mentioned this Craven fellow. What did he have to do with it?'

'That man was a maniac. He once threatened my wife and daughter in the kitchen just above where we are now. The man was an animal. He was like a dog that had got a taste for blood and should have been put down. I sometimes wonder if he was the most dangerous one of all.'

This man had also known Bruce Craven. It seemed incredible.

'Who was Bruce Craven?'

She didn't know if she could trust what Rex was saying. It was best to keep her mouth shut about her own connection.

'Some guy from the north-east who they found to do their dirty work. He used to work at that old holiday camp at Middleton Tower. It closed years ago. It was the perfect cover for him. He was a seasonal worker at the camp, and now and then they'd call him in to carry out a job. They call them sociopaths nowadays; back then we just called them nutters.'

'So, Bruce Craven was working with Edward Callow and his group of investors, or whatever it was they were doing?'

'Yes, he was hired muscle, a nasty piece of work. He was

the reason I turned a blind eye to what was going on in that upstairs room. When you've got a local DCI involved and a man like Bruce Craven is threatening your wife and daughter, believe me, you don't say no.'

This was the Bruce that Charlotte and Will knew, and Jenna too.

'Did you know Jenna Phillips?' Charlotte asked.

Rex nodded.

'That poor woman; they put her through hell over the years. They'd got it into their heads that she somehow knew where Bruce Craven had gone. He just disappeared without a trace one day and nobody ever worked out where he'd gone. It threw them into a state of panic, because they thought some powerful property gangsters were moving in on their pitch. It was all very tense for a while. They used to hold their meetings in the lounge upstairs. This guest house was a popular meeting place once upon a time. They often made me leave the room, but I still got a sense of things through the closed door. They were a bad bunch, and they did a lot of terrible things. They did a terrible thing to me. Now they want me dead, just like all the others.'

Now she was getting closer to the truth. 'Why were they so adamant that Jenna knew something? She was just a student at the holiday camp. She was never involved in anything illegal.'

'They intimidated her within an inch of her life. I'm amazed that she's still alive. But she never said a thing. Even when they took her daughter, she always maintained that she knew nothing. She's a tough woman, I tell you. I'd have caved under less pressure.'

'Why did they target her, though? She was just a bystander in all of this.'

'They were convinced she must have known something

about Bruce Craven's disappearance. They always thought she was protecting somebody, but she never revealed who it was, if she did hold that secret. Whoever it was that got rid of Bruce Craven did the world a favour. But if Edward Callow ever finds out who it was, he'll track them down and torture them. Then he'll toss them out into the sea to rot.'

CHAPTER THIRTY-ONE

Charlotte had to decide what she was going to do with Rex Emery, and fast. Her gut feeling had been right. This was all coming to rest at her doorstep, and goodness knows what would happen if things got out of hand.

But as she sat there listening to Rex, she struggled with an overwhelming sense of guilt and anxiety. Had Jenna Phillips protected her family all this time, even at the expense of her own daughter? If she had, she could hardly blame her former friend for trying to extort money from them. She'd endured a parent's worst nightmare because of what they'd done.

She desperately wanted to jump on the train and see Jenna immediately, to discover the truth about what had gone on and to find out why, after all these years, her friend was still in so much danger. But more than anything, she wanted to flee with her family to somewhere safe, a place where she would never have to give a thought to Bruce Craven ever again.

'What do you want me to do?' she asked Rex Emery.

'I want you to hide me,' he replied. He must have

thought about it already, from the way he didn't beat about the bush with his answer.

'If I hide you here, it puts my family in danger. You of all people should know that. You have a daughter and a wife...'

'I *had* a daughter and a wife,' he interrupted. 'That's something else they took away from me. My wife and daughter refused to believe that I had nothing to do with Piper Phillips' abduction. Harvey Turnbull saw to that. What chance did I have if the cops were happy to set me up as the fall guy? And then leaving that disgusting pornography in the house and saying it was mine. So yes, I know how scary it is when your family are involved. You can say no if you want to, but if they kill me, the truth will never be known. Edward Callow will get away with everything he's ever done.'

Charlotte needed guidance from Nigel Davies. She didn't dare tell Will what she was about to do, even though it involved the two of them and their children.

'There's a room on floor two which is empty until next Thursday,' she said. 'It will have been cleaned and set up for the next guest. If we get any late bookings, I'll have to move you. But you have to stay quiet. You can't go rattling around like you did this afternoon; anybody could have heard you. I'll bring you food when I can, and I'll leave you with some bits and pieces to keep you going in the meantime. But you have to come up with a plan; you can't stay here forever. And if I think for one moment that anybody suspects you're here, you have to go. Is that understood?'

Charlotte couldn't believe she was doing this. But what choice did she have? The safety of her family was at stake. It looked like Jenna had been protecting them all that time. This man was another witness who could tell the story of what Bruce Craven was like and prove why they had to stop him.

But people were being killed. Barry McMillan, Fred Walker and even Harvey Turnbull. Somebody was settling old scores and clearing out their closet. It was getting too close for comfort. Rex Emery—despite the risk—was best where she could see him, safe in her guest house. But she must make sure nobody could know he was there.

'You're absolutely certain that nobody's seen you around the guest house?' she asked.

'I'm not stupid. I stole a cap and sunglasses as a disguise. You can see how I'm dressed now. I had a full head of hair last time I was in this town. Nobody saw me, I swear.'

Ignoring all the doubts screaming in her ears, Charlotte nodded and stood up.

'If there's any chance that my family are in danger, you leave, agreed? Or I'll turn you into the police myself. I will not risk my family to protect you. Do you understand that?'

Rex nodded.

'I get it,' he said. 'And if I'm caught here by the police, I'll tell them I broke in and hid myself in the room. I know how this place works well enough; it used to be my job before it was repossessed after my imprisonment. I won't land you in it, I promise. I know how valuable a family is. I didn't appreciate that fully until I'd lost mine.'

Charlotte was aware of the time. Guests would be arriving back shortly, Isla would be working away in the kitchen, and the place would get steadily busier into the early evening. She let Rex Emery into the vacant room and brought in provisions from the kitchen: milk, fruit, tea, cereals and some pot noodles from the catering pack in their own kitchen that they kept in for the children.

'Put a towel by the door so that nobody sees the light

under the gap and keep your curtains drawn. It's fine to watch the TV on low volume if other guests are making the same sort of noise. Otherwise, not a sound, okay? I'll bring you more food when I can get it to you without anybody spotting me.'

For a moment, Charlotte considered giving Rex the old Nokia phone that had been discarded in a drawer in their family accommodation, along with its charger. Then she thought better of it. If there were records of text messages between them, she couldn't deny knowing he was in the guest house, should the police ever figure out he was there. It would be useful to be able to communicate with him, but she didn't want to create a trail of evidence. She'd seen enough TV detective shows to know how these things worked.

With Rex Emery safely secreted in the room, Charlotte headed back up to the family accommodation to gather her thoughts. Her phone was sitting on the kitchen table where she'd left it before going downstairs to investigate the strange noises. She sat down and checked the screen.

She'd missed several messages: three from Olli, one from Will and a phone call from Nigel Davies. She hated herself for prioritising Nigel over her son—he'd probably only be telling her he was staying out late—but she still called Nigel Davies first. As her finger moved across her phone, she considered telling him about Rex Emery. She shouldn't put herself at risk like that, but she was desperate to tell somebody.

'Hi Nigel, it's Charlotte.'

'Have you heard what's happened?' he replied, not bothering with any pleasantries.

'No, what? I've been pre-occupied since I saw you earlier.'

'Mason Jones is dead. I found him.'

Charlotte's body froze. Had Rex Emery done this? Was she hiding a killer in her home?

'How? What happened?' Charlotte asked.

'After our run-in with Callow, I decided to track down Mason Jones. It took me no time at all. I just called a retired teacher I interviewed a few months back who used to work with him. He lost his marbles a couple of years ago, and he suffers from dementia. He was in a residential home at the far end of the promenade, towards Happy Mount Park; it used to be a huge hotel. The police obviously didn't think he needed any protection, because I just flashed my ID as I walked in, and the staff let me in to see him.'

'What did he say? Was he lucid enough to give you any information?'

'He was dead when I got to his room. They think it was an overdose of medication, but the coroner will have to decide on that one.'

'Were the police there? Who do they think did it?'

'That Rex Emery guy. Do you remember, the one who used to own your guest house?'

'Why do they think he did it?' Charlotte asked, not wanting to hear the answer. She worried about how easily she'd been deceived. Had she learned nothing since she was a teenager, so easily flattered by Bruce Craven's overtures in the holiday camp bar?

'He always claimed Mason Jones was responsible for Piper's abduction. And he's on the run from open prison. Who else would it be?'

'I don't know what to say,' Charlotte began. This was far from irrefutable evidence. At least Rex Emery was safely locked in a room out of harm's way. If she needed to hand him in to the police, she knew exactly where he was.

'There's something else,' Nigel continued. 'Apparently, Jones had very rare moments of lucidity. When I discovered his body, his nurse alerted her supervisor and they started figuring out what had happened to him. They thought he'd just died of old age, but they notified the police because they'd been told to stay alert over his safety. It's the police who reckon foul play is involved. Anyway, there was a torn-up photograph in his bedroom waste bin. At the time I didn't think there was anything suspicious about his death, so I just went ahead and had a look while I was on my own in there. It was an old photograph, very much like the ones taken at your guest house. The wallpaper was the same.'

'How does that help, though? He was probably just reminiscing, wasn't he?'

'It's a different photo, and there's somebody else in it. I had to photograph all the bits on my phone. I need to print them out and piece them together, like a jigsaw puzzle. There must have been another person in your guest house lounge with those men, Charlotte, and looking at the fragments of the photo, once I've managed to reassemble all the torn pieces, I reckon we'll be able to figure out who it was.'

CHAPTER THIRTY-TWO

This was a development Charlotte hadn't anticipated. Who could the extra person be?

'Can I help?' she asked Nigel. She could hear lots of activity going on in the background, it came over loud on her phone.

'I'm still at the home, now. Can you get down here? I'm at the reception desk, trying to piece this photograph together.'

'I can't believe Mason Jones was living along the road from us all this time. It can't be far; probably about a mile away?'

'Yes, it's the Bare area, rather than Morecambe itself. You've probably passed this place a hundred times and never noticed it. It's the Evergreen Retirement Home.'

'I'll see you there,' Charlotte said, and ended the call.

She jumped up from the table and thought about Rex Emery. Was it safe to leave him there? Surely it was; he'd be unlikely to go anywhere. If he'd been responsible for Mason Jones' death, she'd hand him into the police herself.

But there was something that was making her doubt

Nigel's interpretation of events. Rex Emery did not seem like a killer to her; he'd had genuine fear in his eyes. She was convinced that was no act. And he'd said he didn't even know where Mason Jones was living, or if he was alive or dead. He was no threat to her or her family; she had to trust in that assessment.

'Isla? I'm popping out for about half an hour. Are you all right holding the fort here? Give George a call if you need an extra pair of hands; I'll pay him. I won't be long.'

She didn't bother to wait for an answer; she was going whether Isla liked it or not. As she walked along the pathway in front of the guest house, she remembered the missed messages from Will and Olli. As she walked along the path, she examined her phone. Will had messaged her to say that he'd met a colleague whilst calling in at the supermarket on the way home and they'd gone for a coffee. He'd be back later.

Olli had also used Facebook Messenger to try to raise her. She dialled Olli's number, regretting having ignored him for so long.

'Mum, I'm pleased I've got you at last. Lucia is with that guy I told you about. The one with the purple hair. They're in Wetherspoons having a drink. I'm watching them from the other side of the pub. Do you want me to follow them?'

So, the man with the purple Mohican had shown his face again. The cheek of it.

'Are they drinking?' Charlotte asked, realising that her daughter might be committing an offence.

'No, they're both on soft drinks. But they're sharing a plate of nibbles. They seem very comfortable together. Do you want me to say something? I'm worried about her, Mum. That guy must be ten years older than her.'

Charlotte wanted to be in two places at once. It was a

quicker walk up the promenade to the pub than it was towards Happy Mount Park. But she was desperate to know what was in that photo. Lucia was in a public place, she wasn't drinking alcohol and Olli could watch her. It was safe enough for now.

'Look, don't do anything stupid, Olli. Is Willow with you?'

'No, she was feeling unwell, so I took her home. I saw Lucia while I was walking back through the town centre.'

'I've got my phone with me. Promise me you won't do anything stupid, but follow the guy with the purple hair when he leaves the pub. I want to know where he lives, so I can pay him a visit. He's good at staying out of sight, so keep an eye on him; he's a slippery one. But please, Olli, don't intervene. Just get me an address if you can and come straight home. I'll deal with this chap later. He's far too old to be dating a girl as young as Lucia.'

'Okay, mum, I promise, I'll stay out of sight. I've got my grey hoodie on, so I blend in nicely. It's pretty packed in here this afternoon. I doubt I'll get spotted. I'll see you later.'

'You're a good brother to her, Olli. Thank you.'

Charlotte ended the call and began a slow jog, remembering how fast she'd managed to run when chasing that same man earlier in the day. She'd surprised even herself. It wasn't long before she reached the retirement home.

Nigel was right, she must have passed it hundreds of times, but she'd never even registered the place. It wasn't that far from the town's secondary school, where Mason Jones had been head teacher. She wondered how that must have felt for him, in his moments of lucidity, knowing that his brain was gradually fading to nothing. It must have been hard for him, living less than a mile from the place where his younger self used to be so sharp and active.

She could see where she was heading before she arrived, thanks to the police cars parked outside. As she turned into the driveway, her feet crunched the gravel. The pensioners were visible inside, looking out to sea from their armchairs next to the large windows which ran along the entire length of the building. Charlotte blocked out the thought that she might end up there herself within another couple of decades. There had been a time when dementia and old age seemed to belong to another world; now they seemed to be an ever-closer threat.

She saw Nigel Davies the moment she walked into the reception area. He was perched on the edge of a sofa, with scissors, paper and a glue stick on the coffee table in front of him. He had a cup of tea too, delivered in an ornate bone china cup and saucer; he'd made himself at home.

'May I help you?' the lady at the reception desk asked. She sounded flustered.

'I'm here to see Mr Davies, if that's all right? I'm not here to visit anyone.'

For a moment, Charlotte feared she might get a rejection. Fortunately, Nigel looked up and vouched for her.

'It's all right, Sandy, she's my assistant.'

Charlotte joined him at the table.

'It's a devil of a job, piecing all these torn fragments together. I've got almost half of it done, but I'm not quite there yet. The staff here let me use their printer, but it's not very good quality. What do you think? I reckon it's from the same set of pictures as before. Maybe not the same occasion, but it's the same place, with some of the same people.'

Charlotte studied what he'd done. Some of the pictures were blurred, but when they were stuck together, it was easier to see what was going on.

'That's Barry McMillan, I'm sure of it. He's always

wearing light jackets in the photos I've seen. He had one on when he died. And that's definitely the same wallpaper that was in the lounge at the guest house; I'd recognise it anywhere, it's particularly nasty looking.'

She leaned closer to peer at the composite picture. 'I don't know who this fellow is though. It looks like somebody's standing in front of him. We need to find the pieces that fit in this gap. It'll give us a better idea what's going on.'

As she was speaking, Charlotte became aware of two dark figures stepping into the reception area. She looked up. It was a police officer, accompanied by DCI Summers.

'Talk about a couple of bad pennies,' she said with a smile. 'I'm beginning to wonder if I should bring the two of you in for questioning. You both seem to turn up wherever there's trouble.'

'Even I'm beginning to feel the same way,' Nigel replied. 'I've already told one of your officers in there that I disturbed a photograph in Mason Jones' bin before we had any inkling that his death might be suspicious. I'm sorry about that, but it was done in good faith. If you can get those original pieces reassembled as soon as possible, you'll be doing yourself a big favour. I think we might get a clue from this image, but I'm struggling with my copy; it's hard to make it out.'

'Thanks for the heads-up,' DCI Summers acknowledged. 'I take it you've given a formal statement already?'

'Yes, I know the drill. If you need me to answer any more questions, you know where to find me. And I promise we'll do our best not to turn up at any more crime scenes.'

DCI Summers smiled again and headed along the corridor that led to the residents' rooms.

Charlotte had been busying herself with the pieces that Nigel had cut out whilst he'd been chatting to DCI

Summers. It was better to keep her head down; the DCI would sense her guilt from a mile away. She was, after all, giving sanctuary to a fugitive.

The two of them worked quickly, exchanging pieces, trimming edges and applying the glue when they were certain of the positioning.

As they added pieces, bit by bit, Charlotte felt a sickening feeling in her stomach. Once they had built up more of the image, it became clearer what they were looking at. At last, Nigel completed a section and she finally understood exactly what she was looking at. She rushed to the unisex toilet in the corner of the reception area to be sick, and only just made it in time.

It was a horrible scene, taken in the lounge of Charlotte's guest house several years previously. The flock wallpaper, the decor, and the pictures were all the same.

But this photograph hadn't been taken at the same time as the newspaper images. This was a very different set up. It showed Barry McMillan and Mason Jones, both smoking cigars, with whisky tumblers at the table in front of them and smug, entitled smirks across their faces.

Sitting on Mason Jones' knee, half-dressed, blindfolded and looking scared stiff, was a sixteen-year-old Piper Phillips.

CHAPTER THIRTY-THREE

'You look terrible,' said Nigel as she returned. 'Are you okay?'

'I'll be all right; it's just that I don't have much stomach for this sort of thing. You've probably become hardened to it as a reporter. It makes me feel ill, just thinking about it. Poor Piper; no wonder her life is so screwed up. And how did Jenna ever cope with knowing this? It's horrible, just horrible.'

'You never get used to it,' Nigel said, 'But you get better at handling your reaction to it. I had no idea this was going on. I had it all down to property deals. This is something different altogether.'

Charlotte sat down and forced herself to look at the pieced-together image once again.

'Do you think someone was blackmailing Mason Jones with this image? I wonder if that's what made Barry McMillan hang himself. How would you react if the game was up and your secret was out? Photographic evidence like this would be damning to a former head teacher and a world-famous author; you'd never recover from it.'

'Hmm. It's an awful thought, but I have a feeling you may be on the right track.'

Nigel studied the image again, pulling it in close to his eyes.

'I wish we had an original copy, one that's sharper. It's so difficult to make out what's going on. Look, there's the beginnings of the mirror frame there. I think there's a reflection in it. This isn't some professional photograph taken by the newspaper. Let's see if we can complete the image and get a look at who that might be.'

DCI Summers stepped out through the door which led to the residents' bedrooms. She looked preoccupied, as if something was weighing on her mind.

'Take a look at this,' Nigel said to her. 'You need to get your experts to re-assemble that photograph. Look at what we've come up with. I don't know who that man is; he's new.'

At first, DCI Summers seemed reluctant to be distracted from whatever it was she was doing. She walked over to the seating area and picked up the part-image that Nigel and Charlotte had managed to assemble. The way her expression changed showed Charlotte that she knew exactly what she was looking at.

'Do you know who that girl is?' she asked.

'It's Piper Lawrence, Jenna Phillips' daughter,' Nigel began.

Charlotte felt a panic rise in her as she realised this could lead DCI Summers to their secrets, through Jenna. Events were closing in on her. If the police spoke to Jenna about what had happened to her daughter, the trail would eventually lead to the Sandy Beaches Holiday Camp. From there, it would come back to Bruce Craven, and that would bring Daisy Bowker into the situation.

Charlotte struggled to maintain her composure, knowing that what she really wanted to do was run and hide. The past had almost caught up with them, so close that she could hear its heartbeat and smell its breath. She and Will would have to tread carefully. Would she be able to speak to Jenna before DCI Summers got to her? The chances of keeping Piper's kidnapping separate from what happened to Bruce Craven seemed increasingly unlikely.

DCI Summers was frowning. 'Isn't Jenna Phillips...?'

'Yes,' Nigel replied. 'The woman who tried to kidnap Charlotte's daughter. That has to be more than a coincidence, surely?'

'I'm sorry that you keep getting pulled into this,' DCI Summers said, looking at Charlotte. 'You moved here to set up your guest house, and through no fault of your own, you seem to have got caught up with Morecambe's underworld.'

Charlotte could feel her face burning.

'It's strange though,' DCI Summers continued, 'that Jenna Phillips should know you. When I said you were like a bad penny, I meant it in jest, but you do appear to have involved yourself in this fairly deeply. It seems to follow you around.'

Charlotte forced herself to remain casual, thumbing through Nigel's snippets of the photograph, trying to match some more pieces.

'It's just an unhappy coincidence,' Charlotte replied, trying to stop her hands from shaking. 'We knew Jenna when we were students. She saw us as a soft touch for money when she abducted Lucia. We just got unlucky. As for being in the wrong place at the wrong time, what links us to this sad story is the fact that those disgusting men used our hotel for whatever it was they were doing. There aren't that many hotels in Morecambe, and the reason ours was so cheap to buy is that it had a history attached to it. Rex Emery used to own it. But we knew none of this when we bought it. No wonder it was so affordable, and nobody outbid us for it. I think perhaps Will and I just have an ability to make some bad decisions.'

Charlotte knew that she'd over-explained, the sure sign of a liar. She'd seen the TV shows. Too much information and it's obvious you're trying to cover your tracks. DCI Summers could probably smell it a mile off, but her face didn't show it.

'Have you found Barry McMillan's mobile phone yet?' Nigel asked. 'I'll bet he has a copy of that image on it somewhere. I'm not going to try to step into your shoes, DCI Summers, but what do you think? I think this looks like blackmail, with the threat of exposure. If Mason Jones killed himself, or was murdered, wouldn't it confirm that theory? Are you any further forward on Mr Jones, after taking a look in his room?'

'It looks like an overdose. The nursing staff here say he was very lucid this morning and seemed surer of himself than he had done for a long time. They're shocked that he's dead. This is off the record, Nigel—and it's a favour because you've given me a lead with that photograph of Piper—but it looks like Mason Jones has been secreting drugs for some time. Due to his mental state, he may have had to plan his death over a series of lucid episodes; he might not have been able to organise it all at once.'

'How far gone was he?' Charlotte asked.

'Like everybody else with dementia,' DCI Summers continued, 'it was random in its nature. Mason Jones was frequently in sound mind, and the staff say that when he was, he was sharp as a knife. But he could get confused and aggressive at times. He was very volatile. That's why he's a resident here; he was ill enough to be a potential danger to himself.'

Charlotte wondered what degree of plotting must be required if you suffered from memory loss and confusion. If somebody was putting Mason Jones under pressure by sending him that photograph, he'd have rediscovered it several times, realising the risk of exposure every time he was lucid.

He must have planned his death—if indeed it was suicide—over a period of weeks. If what DCI Summers said was correct, he was still sharp enough to figure out how to lay his hands on the drugs he needed to end his life.

'I'm going back to the station. I'll leave my team to finish off here. If you think of anything else, please don't hesitate to call me, even over the weekend. You too Charlotte; if there's anything you need to say to me, I'm always available.'

Charlotte tried to meet DCI Summers' stare, but it was impossible; she had to look away and pretend to be busying herself with the image.

'You know, that only leaves Edward Callow now,' Nigel said, once DCI Summers had left the building. 'He's the only one alive with a link to this group. Other than this new chap, that is, who may just be a client or member of the guest house staff. I've never seen him before. It's a shame Edward isn't in this photograph. If we could place him with these men, the police would be able to take action against him. I hope they'll give him a bit more protection than he had this morning; he was a sitting duck when you and I paid him a visit.'

Charlotte's phone began to ring. That was unusual; her family all tended to message each other unless it was something important. The caller ID showed her it was Olli, so she picked it up.

'Hi Olli, are you okay?'

'I'm being followed, mum. I'm scared.'

'Where are you, Olli? What the hell is going on?'

Nigel Davies looked up at her. She knew she'd been abrupt with Olli, but he sounded scared.

'I followed Lucia and that man into the West End. I don't know this area very well. I was so busy watching them, that I missed what was going on behind me. I'm being followed by some guy. I've never seen him before. I took a few turns to be sure, but he knows the streets better than me. He's always there...'

'Has he threatened you?' Charlotte asked. 'Where are you now?'

Olli's whispers made it sound like he was hiding somewhere.

'I ducked into a side street, but I can still see him. I'm scared, Mum; I'm not sure what to do.'

'Where's Lucia and that man she's with? Whoever he is, he must be safe enough for Lucia to be with. Why don't you find them? You can't come to any harm if you're with them.'

'I lost them, Mum. I was so busy trying to dodge this guy that I lost sight of them. Should I call the police?'

'Where are you in the West End?' Charlotte asked. Olli paused while he figured out which street he was on, then told her.

'Okay, Olli, I want you to go to number 35, which you'll see has a cluster of doorbells outside. Ring the bell that has a Polish name written on it. I can't remember how to spell it, but it should be obvious. The lady's surname was Kowalski, something like that. Ring her doorbell, tell her that Charlotte Grayson and Nigel Davies asked you to wait there, and stay put until I get there. We'll be five minutes, Olli. Wait there and stay safe. We're coming to get you now.'

CHAPTER THIRTY-FOUR

'We have to go,' Charlotte said. 'I'm sorry, but you'll need to drive me, Nigel. I came here on foot.'

Nigel was already clearing away the mess they'd made attempting to assemble the pieces of the photograph.

'There's no time,' she insisted, trying to stay as calm as she could. This felt like Lucia's disappearance all over again. She hated this feeling of her children being in danger.

Nigel looked up, sensing her mood.

'Okay,' he said, leaving the off-cuts spread across the table. He picked up the pieces they needed to complete the photo. 'I'm so sorry,' he said to the lady at the reception desk. 'We need to leave.'

He fumbled in his pocket and took out a five-pound note, held it up to her, then folded it and pushed it into the slot of the charity collection box that was positioned just in front of her.

'That's by way of an apology for not clearing up our mess.'

His gesture seemed to be acceptable to the lady,

because they were out of the residential home and on their way along the promenade within a few minutes.

'You remember where we're heading?' she asked Nigel, willing him to drive faster along the sea front.

'Got it,' Nigel replied. 'Is Olli all right?'

'He was rattled, that's all. I don't think I've ever known him be scared before. He usually has a fairly good idea of what to do.'

'Sorry, Charlotte, the traffic is heavy today; there must be something on in town.'

'I'll see if I can raise Lucia. I'm furious with her. That girl has a row coming her way.'

Charlotte searched through her phone contacts and started to dial Lucia's number; it went to voice mail immediately.

Hi, this is Lucia, please leave a message, and I'll get straight back to you. Unless Made in Chelsea is on TV, in which case I may be gone some time.

'Lucia, call me as soon as you get this. No delays, no excuses. It's serious. Call me or your dad immediately. I mean it. You're not in trouble. It's about Olli.'

'I'm pleased my kids aren't that age yet,' Nigel said. 'I don't envy you having to deal with teenagers.'

'You and me both,' Charlotte said with a grimace. 'Can you not cut around a back street, Nigel? This is taking forever.'

'It's just as slow that way,' Nigel said, nodding towards the side street which was already blocked by cars trying the same thing.

'What the hell is going on today? Why is it so slow?' Charlotte cursed. Her fingers began to move over her phone screen once again, this time calling Will.

Once again, it cut straight to voice mail.

Hi, it's Will Grayson here, I can't take your call right now...

Charlotte ended the call mid-sentence.

'What the hell are my bloody family members up to?' she shouted, thumping the dashboard of the car.

'Steady,' Nigel said, 'You'll fire off the airbag if you carry on like that.'

'Sorry,' Charlotte said, embarrassed. She just wanted to get to Olli and make sure he was safe. She took a few seconds to breathe deeply and steady herself.

'Will it be quicker if I walk?' she asked.

'No, it's clearing now. Look, it was just this lorry blocking the road, it's starting to flow again now.'

Nigel passed the lorry, and Charlotte saw that things were moving again. Soon they were beyond the Midland Hotel and over half-way up the sea front. She tried Olli's phone next, in an attempt to raise at least one member of her family. Once again, it went direct to voice mail.

Hey, it's Olli, you know what to do.

At last they reached the end of the promenade, marked by the boarded-up former pub, The Battery. She and Will had been in there for a drink in the eighties. It had been thriving back then.

Nigel took a left turn into the West End and parked up directly opposite Piper's flat. Charlotte was out of the car before Nigel had even pulled up the hand brake. She rang Agnieszka's bell and banged at the door as if she was the bailiff, come to confiscate her goods.

Charlotte saw Agnieszka looking through her blinds from her living area window before the sound of a door latch being twisted could be heard along the hallway.

The front door opened. Agnieszka looked surprised to see her.

'Is everything all right?' she asked. 'Nothing has happened to Piper, has it?'

Charlotte shook her head. 'Have you seen my son? He's called Olli. I told him to come here fifteen minutes ago.'

'No, I don't know your son. Nobody is here right now.'

'Did anybody knock at the door? Did you hear any shouting?'

'Honestly, I hear nothing. I have never met your son, Olli. Is everything okay, Charlotte? You look very worried.'

'No, things are not okay. My son is in danger. I told him to come to wait with you for safety. Now he's disappeared.'

'I am sorry, Charlotte, I cannot help you. Will you call the police?'

'Soon,' Charlotte replied, thinking back to what had happened to Lucia. Olli was on public streets, in fading daylight. Surely he was safe enough at that time of day? There were people around, so nothing bad could happen to him, could it?

Without even thinking to thank Agnieszka, Charlotte ran across to the car where Nigel had kept the engine running.

'He's not here,' she told him. 'I'm going to run along to the alleyway where he was when he rang me. Will you drive around the block and see if you can spot him?'

'Sure,' Nigel replied, his hand moving directly to the hand brake.

'Meet me back here in ten minutes if I don't see you beforehand.'

Charlotte's phone began to ring. She checked the number and terminated the call once she realised it was an unknown dialler. It didn't matter, unless it was Will, Lucia or Olli. Whoever it was would leave a voice mail.

She ran along the street to where she thought Olli had

been. The way he'd described it, he was opposite a closed hairdressing salon. She tried to picture her son, in a panic, ducking into the alleyway, watching the man from across the road.

This had to be the spot. It was a narrow alley, running between two rows of terraced bedsits. Various items of rubbish were strewn across the cobbled stones, which were fast becoming covered with weeds. Some faded vandalism decorated the whitewashed wall of one of the gable ends; it depressed Charlotte just to see it.

But then, in front of her, something buzzed. She moved to the end of the alley where it joined the pavement. It was Olli's mobile phone, vibrating, notifying him of the call he'd missed. Olli would never lose his phone. He'd never drop it or discard it like that. Somebody must have taken him.

Charlotte took her own phone out of her pocket and dialled 999. The operator answered swiftly.

'Which service do you require?'

'Police,' Charlotte replied. She waited while the connection was made. Her phone sounded while she was waiting; Will was trying to get through. He might have Olli with him. She'd feel ridiculous if she reported Olli missing, only to find he'd taken a taxi home. Why hadn't she thought of that earlier?

She ended the call and spoke to Will. He sounded immediately vague.

'Will, are you okay?' she asked.

'Damn, I've had an accident,' Will said. 'Somebody was upstairs in our family accommodation when I got back. They whacked me on the head. I'm a bit out of it. I don't feel well, Charlotte. Can you come home? I need someone here with me.'

At that moment, Charlotte spotted Nigel's car being

driven slowly along the road as he scoured the streets for Olli. Charlotte ran out in front of him, and he slammed on the brakes.

'Is Olli with you, Will? Or Lucia?'

'I really don't feel well, Charlotte. I've got blood trickling from my head. Please come. I'm going to be sick...'

The line went quiet.

'Will? Will?'

Charlotte ran around to the passenger side of Nigel's car.

'Take me back to the guest house,' she shrieked.

'What about Olli?' Nigel asked. 'Have you heard from him?'

'Just go please, Nigel. I'll tell you while we're driving.'

She slammed the door and Nigel pulled away. Will was no longer at the end of the line. Charlotte ended the call and tried Lucia's number again. Once more, it went to voice mail.

'Shit!' she shouted.

'I'm sure it'll be all right,' Nigel said, in an attempt to reassure her.

'What makes you so sure of that?' she screamed at him. 'Four men have died already, and you think I should be staying calm about my family. You don't know everything, Nigel; in fact, you don't know anything!'

Charlotte stopped as her thoughts spiralled out of control. She hadn't felt as disconnected as this since her breakdown in Bristol. She knew this territory well; she understood how it could break her.

The walls were closing in, and events were about to crush her family. She was damned if she called the police, and damned if she didn't. Yet she still couldn't see the enemy; she still couldn't identify the source of the threat.

Yet there was Will, injured. What the hell had happened? And Olli was missing, having abandoned his phone on the ground, with no clue as to where he'd gone and who the mystery man was. And Lucia, herself the victim of a previous abduction, was wandering around with some strange man who had run away when Charlotte had tried to talk to him.

As Nigel drove her back along the sea front, Charlotte began to sob. Events had suddenly become too overwhelming, and she didn't have a clue what to do about it.

CHAPTER THIRTY-FIVE

'Will... Will! Come on, focus on me.'

'I think he might have a concussion,' Nigel said. 'Have you got a first aid box?'

'Over there, at the side of the tall freezer,' Charlotte told him.

Will seemed to be drifting in and out of consciousness. He'd given her a real panic on the phone, sounding so vague. She lifted the tea towel from the back of his head. The cold water she'd doused it with had washed away most of the blood now. She could see that his wound didn't appear to be too serious, even though the impact had given him such a shock.

'Who did this to you, Will? Did you see them?'

'When are the guests coming?' Will said. 'Hello, Nigel from the paper. What are you doing here?'

'It's like he's drunk,' Charlotte said to Nigel. She checked Will's breath.

'Here, let's patch him up with a bandage,' Nigel said, kneeling down beside him.

Charlotte's phone rang again from the kitchen worktop.

She leapt up and snatched at it, eager to see if it was Olli. It wasn't; it was the same unidentified number that she'd ignored earlier. This time she answered.

'Charlotte Grayson?'

It was a woman's voice, an unfamiliar one.

'Yes?'

She braced herself. Was this news of Olli? Had he been in some kind of accident?

'My name is Rita Cribbins. I'm the governor of Fletcher Prison in Cheshire. Can you talk?'

Charlotte steadied herself with her free hand.

'Yes. Go on.'

'Can I just check some security information with you first, please? Your full name, and your date of birth.'

Charlotte gave the answers.

Nigel appeared to be making good progress with Will. He was properly bandaged now, and Nigel had him sitting upright on a chair.

Charlotte turned her attention back to the prison governor. 'It's in connection with your friend, Jenna Phillips. She has your name down as her only contact, and we know you're the only person who's visited her. So we thought we'd better get in touch with you.'

'Okay, what is it?'

Why couldn't the woman just spit it out? She didn't have time to wait.

'Can I just check that you're not driving or doing anything which might cause an accident?'

Charlotte had heard this before; this was not good news.

'I'm fine, just tell me, please.'

'Jenna tried to hang herself this afternoon...'

'Oh my God. Is she alive?'

'The staff got to her in time, so yes, she's alive, but it was a close call.'

'Don't you monitor your prisoners, for Christ's sake?' Charlotte shouted, furious that nothing had been done to protect her friend. She felt guilty about Piper, and angry at herself for letting Jenna down.

Daisy Bowker had just walked in through the front door of the guest house.

'Is everything all right here?' she asked.

Charlotte motioned towards her phone to indicate that she was busy. Nigel introduced himself and began to explain what had happened in a hushed voice.

'However much we monitor the cells, if an inmate wants to harm herself, there's not much we can do to prevent it. Jenna had complained of anxiety to one of the prison nurses, and she was being treated for that. She managed to get her hands on a length of electrical cable from somewhere. She fastened it to the end of the bunk bed in her room while her cellmate was out.'

'Where is she now?' Charlotte asked.

'She's been transferred to a specialist hospital in Manchester where they can check her for brain and spinal damage. You'll be able to visit her soon, I'm sure, but the hospital can arrange that.'

'Okay, thank you. Send her my love please; I'll visit as soon as I can.'

Charlotte overheard Daisy saying that she needed to speak to her before she went upstairs to her room. Charlotte attempted to end the call, but the prison governor had more to say.

'I need to broach a delicate issue with you, Mrs Grayson. Jenna left a suicide note, and your name was written on the envelope. I understand that this is a personal matter and that you may wish to read the letter in private. However, bearing in mind we'll have to launch an investigation and file a report on this, I wanted your permission to open it now. If Jenna was being bullied or intimidated, it might help us identify the culprit.

Charlotte could see that Daisy was getting impatient to speak to her, so she hurried the conversation with Rita Cribbins. The contents of the note would only make her feel worse about herself. She almost welcomed whatever blame it placed on her shoulders. She'd got Jenna wrong; she'd turned her back on an old friend.

'Open it,' Charlotte instructed.

She heard Rita Cribbins moving her phone under her chin to enable her to tear open the envelope. There was a moment of silence.

'It doesn't say much at all. I'll read it to you.

Charlotte. They know what we did. Be careful. I can't face it any longer. Tell my daughter I love her and that I'm sorry. Her name is Piper. She lives somewhere in Morecambe. Jenna x

'Does that mean anything to you?' Rita asked.

Charlotte felt her body turn stone cold, as if a ghost had walked straight through her.

'No, it's a complete mystery to me,' she lied. 'Thank you for calling. I'll be sure to check in on Jenna.'

Charlotte ended the call and looked over towards Daisy, Nigel and Will. Seeing she was now free, Daisy strode up to her.

'I've got a bone to pick with you,' Daisy said. 'I've just spent the afternoon at Morecambe Library, speaking to a very nice local historian by the name of Jon Rogers. It seems you know him well?'

Charlotte didn't like Daisy's tone. She looked like she was getting ready to lay into her.

'Yes, he's a helpful chap. Why?'

She wanted to call the police about Olli. She had to see if Will needed running to the hospital. And then there was Lucia. Damn, and Rex Emery. Had Rex Emery done this to Will? Had she let a violent man hide in their home after all?

'When I asked Jon about tracing Bruce Craven, he told me you'd already been in several months earlier doing exactly the same thing. So why did you and your husband lie to me? Both of you told me you hardly knew my half-brother, yet now it seems you've been looking for him too.'

Charlotte couldn't think of an answer. Her mind raced, trying to work out who knew what. The lies upon lies were becoming too much. She'd lost track.

'He's recommended I talk to a local singer. A lady called Abi something... Abi Smith or Smithson I think he said. I wrote it down in my notebook. Apparently, she used to work there too, and she knows most people.'

'I have to check something,' Charlotte said. 'I'll explain it all later.'

'Where are you going?' Nigel asked.

'One moment,' Charlotte replied.

She ran down the stairs, taking three steps at a time, fumbling for the master key to open up the guest room in which she'd concealed Rex Emery. The door was damaged; it looked like it had been forced from the outside.

'Rex? Are you in here?'

Charlotte pushed the door open, frantically searching for any sign of his whereabouts. She checked the en suite and even went as far as glancing under the bed, in case he'd taken refuge there. A plain, white mug was resting on the carpet where it had been dropped, its content long since soaked into the pile. Other than that and the door, there was no sign of any struggle. The window was open too, but that seemed normal to her.

Charlotte ran back down the stairs to the kitchen, meeting Daisy on her way.

'I'd really like to speak with you about this,' Daisy insisted. 'I can see that it's not the best time. But you've been lying to me, and I want to know why. My half-brother disappeared off the face of the earth. And you, your husband, and this Abi woman, you've got a connection to him. What's going on, Charlotte? What aren't you telling me about Bruce Craven?'

'Jesus, Daisy, I know you're a guest, but please stop!'

Charlotte knew she was out of control, even as she spat out the words at Daisy, but she was overloaded. She had to ignore the smaller fires that were bursting into flames all around her and focus on the most pressing issues.

Daisy was shocked by the outburst. She backed down.

'I can see you're under a lot of stress, Charlotte, so I'll leave it for now. But I'm not going to let this drop; I want to know what happened.'

'I know you do, and I will explain,' Charlotte said, a little calmer. 'But my son has gone missing, my husband has been attacked in our home, and my daughter has run off with God knows who.'

Daisy nodded and let Charlotte pass on the stairs. She walked up to the family accommodation, taking deep breaths, trying to figure out what to do next. It had to be the police, surely, no matter how exposed that made them.

Nigel was waiting for her when she entered the kitchen.

'I heard what Daisy said to you, and I agree with her,' he began.

'What do you mean?' Charlotte responded, not sure where he was heading with this.

'I've felt it for some time, Charlotte. I agree with your guest. Even DCI Summers suggested it. I think you're hiding something, that you're caught up in what's going on. And I think you're scared of someone.'

CHAPTER THIRTY-SIX

Nigel Davies didn't know how close to the truth he was. But there was no way Charlotte could let him know that. She liked Nigel and was even beginning to trust him. But could she tell him what they'd done? She decided to tell him a partial truth. She needed his help; *they* needed his help, bearing in mind what had just happened to Will.

'Can I trust you?' she said.

'Charlotte, if you don't know that by now, you don't know me very well.'

'I believe we've become accidentally linked to these murders in some way. You already know that Will and I worked at the holiday camp. Jenna did too. Now Daisy is trying to find her half-brother who worked there as well.'

'She seems convinced that you're hiding something from her,' Nigel said.

Charlotte paused. Here came another lie. How many more would they have to tell to hide their secret?

'I am, but only to protect her. Her half-brother worked at the holiday camp. We didn't know him well, but we did know him. I think there must be a connection between all this and the holiday camp. Did Fred Walker get the contract to redevelop the site?'

'That's an excellent question,' said Nigel, picking up his mobile phone to run a search. It didn't take him long to come up with a result.

'Bingo!' he said, after a few minutes of frantic finger movements across the screen of his phone. 'It was their consortium which bought the land, and they're the guys redeveloping the site.'

For once, Charlotte felt like she'd caught a break. This would help her deflect things away from Bruce. It also gave Nigel, Daisy and DCI Summers a reason for her having some loose connection with what was going on. She'd conceal the real connection—Bruce Craven—for as long as possible.

'They seem to have their fingers in every other pie,' Charlotte continued. 'Why not this one?'

Nigel shrugged. 'I don't know why we didn't think of that. Look, what do you want to do about Will? And the kids? It's all right us standing around talking like this, but you need to make some decisions.'

He was right. Will still seemed dazed as he sat quietly on the chair. Charlotte was less concerned about Lucia; she was with an unsuitable person, but in no immediate danger. The panic over Will, the news about Jenna and the conflict with Daisy had caused her to push Olli's situation to the back of her mind. She had to deal with Olli and Will first. Everything else could wait.

'Do you have DCI Summers' direct phone number?' she asked.

'Yes. Do you want me to call her?'

'Do you trust her, Nigel? She strikes me as a straightforward kind of woman. Is she?'

'I'd say so,' Nigel replied. 'I like her. I see her now and again, depending on the severity of the case that the police are dealing with. I think a lot of her work must be deskbound, because she seems to enjoy getting her hands dirty.'

'Good, that's what I thought. I want you to call her and tell her my son is missing.

As Nigel started to call DCI Summers, Charlotte walked over to Will and gave him a gentle kiss on the top of his head. She wanted her husband more than ever now.

'How are you feeling?' she asked.

'It was some blow,' Will replied, still not speaking as he normally would. His speech was slower, not quite engaged. 'I have a headache, but I think I'm okay. I heard what you said about Olli.'

'We need to be careful,' Charlotte whispered, as Nigel began speaking on the phone. 'This is getting too close. I don't know how long we can keep lying about what happened. Olli has disappeared; who knows where he is? I'm scared, Will, really scared.'

'I know, I think we're going to have to come clean soon. We didn't do anything except defend ourselves, Charlotte. We're not killers. We know it was Jenna who finished him off; George was a witness to that.'

'But we all played our part in killing him, Will. That's what I can't shake off. Sure, Jenna ended his life, but she wouldn't have been able to do that if you and I hadn't already hurt him. Didn't all four of us kill Bruce Craven? I think the police would struggle to see it any other way...'

Nigel re-joined them. 'DCI Summers is dispatching some officers to look for Olli. She was pissed to get a call. She was just getting ready to attend Edward Callow's fundraiser at the Midland Hotel.

Charlotte looked at Nigel, having just seen something that they'd all missed.

'We can get to Edward at that fundraiser,' she said. 'He slammed the door on us earlier, but we can ask him what's going on there. As the only man of the five still alive, he must have something to say. At the very least, he's a target; that man is involved in this.'

'You're not suggesting we gate crash the fundraiser?' Nigel replied.

'I am. What else can we do? DCI Summers has officers looking for Olli, yes?'

Nigel nodded.

'She asked me to send over a picture.'

'I'll do that now. I have a lovely picture of him at the kitchen table the other day.'

Charlotte picked up her phone and scrolled through the menus, locating the image. She had his number already, so she texted it over to him. She almost burst into tears when she looked at the image. She prayed that her boy was safe; she had to believe that no harm had come to him.

'What time does this thing start? Can you talk us in using your press pass?'

Nigel looked surprised. Charlotte knew he hadn't seen this side of her before: a mother prepared to do what it took to protect her children.

'It starts at seven o'clock with drinks and canapés. In fact, look at the time: it'll be starting in ten minutes. If Will can lend me a tie and you can get a dress on, I'm sure I can get us in there. Are you sure you want to do this? It might cause a scene.'

'What else can we do?' Charlotte asked. 'I'm out of my mind with worry for Olli, but we have to trust the police to find him. I want to speak to Edward Callow. I'm convinced that man has something to do with all of this. Jon Rogers warned me about him, and we've seen it for ourselves. There's a reason that man is still alive; I think he's killing them all off. He might also be the one who's been threatening my friend Jenna. Either way, I want to speak to him. And this is the best way to do it.'

'What about Will?' Nigel reminded her, looking across at him.

Charlotte picked up her phone again, searching on the web for concussion, checking the various graphics and articles for the symptoms.

'There's a whole list of things here to test whether you've got concussion,' she said. She worked through the list, asking Will if he was suffering from any one of them.

'My head's sore, but you'd expect that,' Will said. 'Look, you know what will happen if I go to A&E. It's a Saturday, so it'll be full of pissheads, and kids with pieces of Lego stuck up their nose. You'll be saddled with me all night before I get seen. The kids are our priority. I'll keep myself dosed up with paracetamol; if I can shake this headache, I'll be fine. I promise I don't feel like anything bad is going to happen.'

'What do you think?' Charlotte asked, turning to Nigel.

'Are you up to a bit of light cutting and gluing?' he asked Will. 'If Will's up to it, he can finish piecing this picture together. There's something else going on in there that I can't make out yet. Are you up to that, Will?'

'I'm not an invalid, you know,' he said, smiling at Nigel.

Charlotte saw a glimpse of the Will she knew and loved. That cheeky sparkle in his eyes was back, if only for a few seconds.

'DCI Summers has the photo of Olli, and she's made it available to officers who are patrolling the town. If he's out there, they'll find him. She did ask if there's anywhere else he might have gone for safety?'

'He has friends in town,' Charlotte replied. 'It's possible, but the fact that I found his phone on the ground is what's worrying me.'

'Okay, we've done as much as we can. I'm going to get the pieces of the photograph from the car so that Will can finish putting together the picture. There may be another clue in there. We might even be able to help DCI Summers solve this case, if we catch a break.'

Charlotte was barely listening. She was already half way out of the family kitchen.

'What are you doing?' Will asked, his voice sounding a little stronger.

'I'm going to put on my best dress. I have a charity fundraiser to attend.'

CHAPTER THIRTY-SEVEN

The last thing Charlotte wanted to be dressed in was a red, formal dress and high heels. Jeans and flats were more her thing, but Edward Callow's charity event was smart attire only, and they were already taking a big chance by turning up without a ticket, and with Nigel dressed in a cobbled-together suit. Charlotte had found him one of Will's jackets, which seemed to fit well enough, and a tie. Will hadn't worn a tie to work for years, but he kept a couple by for emergencies, such as job interviews and funerals.

'You look amazing,' Will said as Charlotte stepped into the family kitchen. 'I can't remember the last time I saw you dressed up like that. I wish I was coming with you.'

'Don't get used to it,' Charlotte replied, adjusting her footwear. 'These shoes were uncomfortable when I bought them, but they're even worse now. I think my feet must have changed. I'd rather be wearing a pair of trainers. I can't believe other women wear these things all the time.'

'We'd best get going,' Nigel said, as he walked in on them. He'd been in the bathroom, trying as best as he could to make himself look presentable.

Charlotte let out a laugh when she saw him.

'I hope you weren't intending to use that tie for your university interview next week,' she said to Will. 'Everybody's wearing narrow ties these days; that one's far too thick at the bottom. And way too flowery too.'

It worried her that Will was still slow to respond. She hoped they were doing the right thing leaving him on his own. He was moving the pieces of Nigel's photographic puzzle around the kitchen table, but didn't appear to be making much progress sticking anything together.

'That's me on my way,' Isla shouted up the stairs.

'Cheerio Isla, thank you!' Charlotte replied. 'Sorry to leave you on your own again.'

Charlotte picked up Olli's phone and searched for somewhere to put it.

'This is why I hate formal wear so much; no pockets,' she said, looking around for somewhere to keep it safe.

'Don't you have a handbag?' Nigel asked.

Charlotte was relieved to see that Will wasn't so out of things that he'd lost his sense of humour. They both chuckled at that comment at the same time.

'I don't do handbags,' Charlotte said. 'I don't think I ever did handbags. I prefer pockets. They're much more practical. But that doesn't solve my phone problem.'

'Do you need to take Olli's phone?' Nigel asked.

'Maybe not,' Charlotte said. 'But he might receive an important call on it, something which could give us a clue where he is. He may even ring it himself to try and work out where he lost it.'

'Hey, I've just remembered about that software on the phones,' Will said. 'I can use that to work out where Lucia is. That's how I found her that time she was going to run away back to Bristol.'

'I forgot about that,' Charlotte replied. 'Give it a try, Will. See if you can figure out where she is. We need to go, Nigel. If we miss the drinks and canapes, we'll never be able to get to Edward Callow when everybody is seated.'

Charlotte checked Will one more time. She still wasn't entirely sure he was clear of all the symptoms of concussion that she'd read about online, but at the same time, she didn't want to get caught in the endless wait at A&E. Olli was the priority; Will was an adult and he could get himself to hospital if he needed to.

In the end, Charlotte took her canvas shoulder bag. It looked great with jeans, but not so appropriate with a formal dress. It would have to do; she needed to put the two phones somewhere.

She was pleased that Nigel was driving the liveried vehicle with the newspaper logos emblazoned all over it. It gave them the credibility that they would need to lie their way through the doors. She'd seen Nigel in action before, so she knew how this worked.

They were early enough to secure parking at the front of the Midland Hotel, meaning they would be easily spotted by the door staff—two men and two women—who were taking tickets and verifying entry. There were banners all over the front of the building and around the car park.

Morecambe and Lonsdale MP Edward Callow welcomes you to the Morecambe Bay Hospice Charity Ball. Please give generously for the benefit of local people!

'Look confident and go with the flow,' Nigel told her. 'I'll bet his consortium has the contract for the new hospice too. It's a huge project, very lucrative for the construction company which landed the deal. Edward is bound to have more than just a charitable finger in that pie.'

'May I see your tickets, sir?'

Charlotte panicked immediately; she was pleased it was Nigel doing the talking.

'We're on the guest list,' Nigel replied, not a trace of trepidation in his voice. 'Nigel Davies, from The Bay View Weekly. And my plus one, Charlotte Grayson.'

'One moment, sir,' the doorman said. He walked over to a small lectern which had been placed just inside the entrance, away from the breeze.

'He's checking the list, and he won't find us on it,' Nigel whispered. 'Stay calm.'

'Did you tell your wife we're here?' Charlotte asked, realising that a lot of local people would spot them at the event. She didn't want it to cause any problems for him.

'It's fine,' he said. 'She's used to me having to leave the house at all hours. News is a 24/7 job. She's very patient about it.'

'I'm sorry sir, we don't appear to have you on the list.'

The doorman was back, his face straight, showing no emotion; it looked like he was used to this kind of thing.

'That's funny,' Nigel said. 'Is Edward around? He specifically wanted the newspaper here tonight, covering the event.'

'Edward, sir?' the doorman replied.

'Edward Callow,' Nigel replied, 'the man who's hosting tonight's event. I don't want to call him away from his guests on such an important night, but I think he'll be very angry if this doesn't get coverage in the local newspaper.'

Then Nigel used what Charlotte thought to be a masterstroke. He sidled up to the doorman and spoke in a confidential tone.

'Personally, I'd rather be at home watching X-Factor, but my boss insisted I come tonight, seeing as the local MP has requested it. If you want to turf me out, I'll be just as happy. I can get home early and tell them the door staff wouldn't let me in.'

The doorman was on the back foot, stuttering and unsure of himself. Perfectly on time, DCI Summers arrived at their side, looking stunning in a glittery ball gown and with her hair loose. Charlotte had never seen it like that before; she always had it hair-clipped to within an inch of its life when she was on the job.

'Well, fancy seeing you two here,' she said. 'You look like you dressed hastily in a charity shop,' she whispered to Nigel. 'Are you coming in?'

'I don't know, are we?' Nigel looked at the doorman.

'I'll add you to the list, it must have been an oversight,' the doorman replied. The arrival of DCI Summers had finally tipped the scales in their favour. Charlotte started breathing again.

They walked through the front doors into the decorated foyer of the hotel. It never ceased to impress Charlotte whenever she saw it, its distinctive cantilevered staircase and contemporary art deco styling creating a unique ambience in the resort. Edward Callow had spared no expense with the decoration; the place oozed wealth and money. The great and the good of the area were all gathered there.

'Why are you here? This doesn't feel like your kind of event,' Nigel asked DCI Summers when they could talk more privately.

'I'm here for work,' she replied. 'Wouldn't you know it? We have security here tonight as well, mixed in among the crowds. Edward Callow is the last man left standing in that photograph. We asked him to call off this event, but he's a pompous, nasty little man, and he wouldn't listen to reason. By the way, that comment is strictly off the record, Nigel.'

He nodded.

'Understood,' he said.

'What about Olli?' Charlotte asked. 'Have any of your officers heard anything yet?'

'You know that we have a set procedure for missing persons,' DCI Summers replied.

'Yes, but you of all people you should know why I'm concerned, after what happened to Lucia.'

Charlotte fumed at DCI Summers' evasiveness. She had children; she should understand.

'Yes, I'm sorry, I do understand why you're so worried. But from a policing point of view, Olli is an adult. There's no suggestion of any wrongdoing here...'

'He telephoned me and told me he was being followed!' Charlotte exclaimed.

'Look, I've pulled some strings for you. All duty officers in the town this evening know to look out for Olli. If he's out there, we'll find him, and as soon as we do, you'll know about it. I promise we're doing what we can.'

'I don't see Edward Callow here yet,' Nigel observed. 'Shouldn't he have arrived by now?'

'Yes, he should,' DCI Summers replied. 'Excuse me, while I check in with my officers. I'd have expected him to show his face.'

'I suggest we mingle,' Nigel said. 'Keep a lookout for Edward. He won't cause a scene in front of all his rich pals. We need to push him on Mason Jones' death this afternoon. I want to know why he's the last man alive.'

Charlotte moved away from him and began to make a circuit of the bar area. She didn't recognise anybody there, and she felt conspicuous, walking warily in her high heels and carrying the canvas bag in which her purse and both the phones were held. She decided to check in on Will, to compensate for the guilt she still felt for leaving him like that.

She walked out of the side door of the bar, where only days previously she'd watched Barry McMillan do the same thing. There were three cars parked at the rear of the hotel, all of them black and very expensive looking. She sat on a nearby wall and opened up her bag to retrieve her phone. As she started to call Will, she saw that somebody was in the far car. She stopped the call. Whoever it was had their head slumped down like they were asleep.

Something about the person's posture made Charlotte stand up to check. As she neared the vehicle, she realised it was Edward Callow. It figured that the host of the event would have his own parking spot away from the guests; but what was he doing? Surely the host of such a high profile Charity Ball shouldn't be napping out in the parking area?

Her heart was beating faster. Something didn't feel right. She tapped on the window. Edward was completely still, the scowl that he'd given when they visited his home now gone.

Charlotte knocked again then placed her hand on the door handle and pulled it so it clicked. As she began to open the door, Edward slumped towards it, his weight pushing against the side. His limp, lifeless body fell out of the driver's seat to the ground before she could do anything to cushion his fall.

She looked around, searching for a witness. Everybody was inside, enjoying the welcome drinks, catching up with their affluent friends.

She knelt down to feel for a pulse, aware of her own heart racing. She fumbled around Edward's neck then felt his wrist, desperate to find some sign of life.

'Help,' she said, half to herself and half to anybody who

might be in the vicinity. There weren't even any smokers about. She was on her own. Then she froze. Even people who liked her—Nigel Davies, Daisy Bowker and DCI Summers—believed she was hiding something from them. As the lies had piled up, it was becoming more and more obvious that she wasn't telling the whole truth. And now here she was, with a motionless and potentially dead MP at her feet, with hers the last set of fingerprints on his vehicle.

CHAPTER THIRTY-EIGHT

Charlotte didn't know what to do. She didn't want to get caught up in the inevitable investigation that would surround the discovery of Edward Callow's body. She still wasn't entirely sure he was dead. She found her phone again and started to dial 999, then stopped on the second digit. Perhaps it made more sense to use Olli's phone. It wouldn't be traced back to her.

She dialled from Olli's phone, constantly looking around to see if anybody had spotted her.

'Ambulance,' she said when the operator answered. 'Yes, there's a man at the rear of the Midland Hotel in Morecambe who's fallen ill. He's not moving. Look, I don't have time to go through all the checks. He isn't moving, so I think he needs an ambulance. Please send one straight away.'

She ended the call, cursing that it took so long to work through the set procedures. What should she do? They weren't getting any information from Edward Callow that night. And it looked like they might have misjudged him;

was this the killer at work, finishing off the last man in the photograph?

Then a thought struck her: the person with the biggest motive in the entire sorry episode was Piper Lawrence. Why hadn't they seen it? Piper was sixteen years old when those men abused her. She hated her mother, and she sure as hell hated those five men. She knew the guest house well—she'd certainly been there as a child—and she would have known Rex Emery too. In fact, she'd said that Rex Emery was innocent.

Charlotte berated herself in her frustration. How had they not made these connections? It had been staring them in the face all this time. Rex Emery must have been the person who struck Will in the guest house. Piper Lawrence must be behind the deaths of the men. She certainly had a motive.

In the distance, she heard the sound of a siren. Hopefully it was the ambulance for Edward. She'd done what she could, and now she had to get out of there. Piper Lawrence lived only ten minutes away just along the road from the end of the promenade. She could be there in no time.

Still conflicted over what to do about Edward Callow, Charlotte leaned over his slumped body, which was half-in and half-out of the car, and switched on the hazard lights. At least that would save the ambulance team precious minutes trying to figure out where he was. She ran along the promenade, seeking a bin. It didn't take her long to find one. She pulled off her high heels and threw them in.

Bloody useless things.

In bare feet and tights, Charlotte could make much better progress. As the chill wind buffeted her along the sea front, she wished she'd brought a cardigan. She would stay off the pavements and stick to the sea side of the path which was flat and smooth all the way along to The Battery at the end. Her feet stood more chance of making it along that route.

She could barely believe that she'd been running the opposite way along that very path eleven hours previously. So much had happened in a ridiculously short time. She'd felt like this once before, after stealing the moped in an attempt to rescue Lucia from the holiday camp. It was a mixture of high-octane adrenaline and stupefying fear and panic. Just like that night, she felt an impending sense of danger, unable to shake the sense that everything was coming to a head. And, just like Lucia's abduction, she still couldn't grasp the whole picture.

Charlotte could hear the sirens in the distance. All hell would have been let loose at the Midland Hotel. She'd face the music later, just as she had previously. She hadn't hurt Edward Callow. In fact, she might even be responsible for saving him. She was innocent, and she had a good reason for fleeing the scene; DCI Summers would understand.

She was out of breath as she reached The Battery. Waiting to cross the road to get to the West End, she lurked in the shadows of the boarded-up pub, in case a police car passed by. It would be the final irony if they spotted her instead of her son.

Convinced that the road was as clear as it was ever likely to be, she darted across. A small shard of broken headlamp, no doubt from some shunt at the junction, stabbed her foot, and she made it across with a mixture of walking and hopping.

It was only a small piece of glass, but the cut felt deep and sore; it was bleeding too.

'Bloody hell!' she shouted out loud, picking the glass out of her foot and looking around for anything that she could use for protection. There was nothing nearby. She'd be at Piper's flat in a few minutes; the sooner she got off the pavement, the better.

She ran through the West End, remembering the streets they'd driven down. It all seemed to take longer on foot. She hesitated at the front door of Piper's flat, wondering if she'd be busy with a client. It was a Saturday evening after all. Charlotte had no idea how that sort of thing worked, but she rang the bell regardless. The safety of her son was at stake. She couldn't care less if a client was there. If Piper was somehow connected with Olli's disappearance, he'd have to pull his trousers up and get lost.

Her phone cheeped; it was Nigel.

Where are you? It's all gone crazy here. We're in a total lockdown. Callow was found outside in the rear car park. Don't know if he's dead.

She hadn't got time to answer, and she didn't want Nigel to know where she was. There was plenty of time to explain everything; Olli was her priority.

There was no answer from Piper's flat, so Charlotte began to bang at the door and press all the bell buttons at the side. She saw Agnieszka peering through the blinds of the front window, in a state of semi-undress. It appeared that Saturday evening was a busy time, after all.

By the time Agnieszka answered the front door to the flats, she'd put a dressing gown on.

'What is it, Charlotte? I tell you already that I have not seen your son...'

Charlotte barged past her and stormed up the stairs.

'I'm not here for you,' she said, taking the stairs two at a time. As she reached the top of the staircase, she could see that the door to Piper's flat was partially open and the lights were on.

'Got you!' she said to herself, as she stormed towards the door, hellbent on giving Piper a piece of her mind.

She stopped dead in her tracks at what greeted her. Piper was lying motionless on the bed, dressed only in her underwear, with a plastic supermarket bag taped securely over her head. She was completely still and did not appear to be breathing.

CHAPTER THIRTY-NINE

'Agnieszka, get up here! Call an ambulance!'

Charlotte rushed over to Piper and began to claw desperately at the plastic bag. Whoever had done this had tied her hands with a length of cable torn from her bedside lamp. Was this a client visit gone terribly wrong, or something more sinister?

She looked around the room for signs that a man had been there recently. No, it wasn't a client; somebody had forced their way into the room. This was an attack, and Piper was the target.

She tore a hole in the bag and ripped the plastic away from Piper's mouth. In her frantic struggle to breathe, Piper had sucked in the plastic, forming a seal against her mouth. Her hair and face were sodden with sweat and her skin was white.

Agnieszka came into the room, followed by a man in boxer shorts and a T-shirt.

'I know how to do CPR,' he said, taking one look at her. 'But please, don't say that I helped her. It'll be the end of my marriage if my wife finds out I'm here.'

Charlotte's instinct was to judge and despise him; but if he could save Piper before the ambulance arrived, it wouldn't matter.

'I don't care about you or your wife,' Charlotte said, 'Just help Piper.'

She had managed to tear the plastic bag from Piper's face and head, but the grey tape holding it fast around her neck was too tough to remove. She needed scissors.

As the man positioned Piper's limp body so he could administer CPR, Charlotte fumbled to undo the tightly knotted cable around her wrists. Agnieszka's client began the process of chest compressions and breathing into Piper's lungs. Charlotte checked that Agnieszka had called the ambulance.

As she finally managed to loosen the cable well enough to undo the knot, she realised that once again, she mustn't be around when the ambulance and police officers arrived. She was making a habit of this, but she simply could not afford to get caught up in the inevitable aftermath and questions.

When they'd apprehended Jenna and Pat, and released Lucia at Sandy Beaches Holiday Camp, it had taken forever to plod through the process of securing the site, gathering evidence, questioning everybody involved, administering first aid, and all the other tasks which allowed the emergency services to perform their jobs so thoroughly. And she'd been relieved to do that, especially with her daughter safe and secure, and being confident that Isla was in safe hands after the assault in the kitchen.

But now? And with Edward Callow possibly dead? Olli could be dead in a ditch before the police even got to the point where they could comprehend the gravity of the situation. She couldn't hang around, but she had to be certain that Piper was safe, despite what she might have done.

Then Charlotte took a second pause; had she been wrong about Piper? This looked like somebody was tidying up loose ends, dealing with Piper, Edward Callow—even Rex Emery. Maybe Rex was responsible. She simply didn't know. It was too much to figure out.

Piper took a sudden gasp of breath, her body reactivating like a toy with new batteries. She breathed fast, gasping for air, her fingers finding the grey tape around her neck and pulling at it to loosen the tension. As she realised that her breathing was no longer restricted, she began to focus on the people around her. As suddenly as she'd begun breathing, she started to scream and thump at the man who'd administered CPR.

'Get off me, leave me alone!' she cried, tears rolling down her face.

The man moved away from her, shocked at the reaction he'd got.

'I suggest you leave now,' Agnieszka said to him. 'The ambulance will be here soon. Thank you. I will make it up to you next time you come to see me.'

The man made his exit, reassuring Agnieszka that he'd close her door before he left the building.

Charlotte moved in to comfort Piper. Sirens could be heard in the distance. Damn, they were fast.

'Piper, it's all right, you're safe now...'

A look of terror washed across Piper's face like she'd just remembered something horrific.

'Charlotte, they have your son, Olli. They took him. That's why they did this to me.'

Charlotte felt the colour drain from her face as fear gripped her body.

'Who's got him? Who took my son? Where is he?'

It was happening all over again. First Lucia, now Olli. She couldn't take it any more. The pressure was becoming unbearable. If she could just find Olli, they'd have to tell the truth. If she lost her son, she'd never forgive herself.

'Two men. He came to the house in a panic. He'd lost his phone, but he said he was being followed. He thought I was Agnieszka, but I saw him at the door, and I took him in because he said your name. He's in terrible danger, Charlotte. These men don't care about the police and they have no sense of right and wrong. I don't know where they've taken him, but you have to find him, Charlotte—he's in terrible danger.'

'Piper, you have to tell me the truth. Was Rex Emery here? Have you seen Rex Emery?'

'Rex is not behind this,' Piper yelled. 'He's innocent, I told you that before. But yes, I've been helping Rex. I know he was at your guest house, and I've seen him this afternoon. We had something important to do, in case Rex gets caught.'

'What were you doing? When did he leave the guest house? He was gone when I looked for him this afternoon.'

'Rex said they came for him and he thinks they hurt your husband. Oh Charlotte, is your husband okay? Rex managed to climb down a drainpipe and make his escape from the guest house. The men wanted a video that he has, did he tell you about that?'

'What video? I don't know anything about a video.'

'He has evidence about what happened to me. It was an old video. We got copies made this afternoon. That's why they want us all dead. And now they have your son...'

There was a loud knock at the main door downstairs, making them all jump.

'Ambulance!' came a voice that carried all the way up the staircase. They'd shouted through the letterbox to get attention.

'Agnieszka, is there a back door? I can't be seen here. I'll talk to the police when I know Olli is safe, but I have to find him now. Okay?'

Agnieszka nodded. Charlotte assumed that as escorts, she and Piper would have a healthy disrespect for the letter of the law. She was in safe hands for a hasty escape.

'Come,' Agnieszka told her. 'Turn left at the bottom of the stairs and open the black-painted door next to the storeroom. It's not locked, it's on a security catch. The gate to the yard is locked, though; if you can climb up on a bin, you will be able to get over the wall.'

Charlotte winced as she began to move; a sharp pain ran through her foot where she'd cut herself on the glass.

The ambulance staff knocked heavily at the door once again. They sounded like they were about to knock it down.

'We have to go,' Agnieszka said. 'Here, take my plimsolls. I have small feet, but they look about your size.'

'Piper, Agnieszka... thank you, thank you so much. I'll be back, I promise. We can make this right.'

She followed Agnieszka down the stairs, and they split off. The last thing Charlotte heard was the sound of the medics rushing in.

The door was exactly as Agnieszka had described. Charlotte closed the latch behind her and surveyed the yard. There were several wheelie bins, each with a badly painted flat number on the side. She chose one with a lid that was closed flat, wheeled it to the far wall and pulled herself up on it, feeling the cut in her foot stretch as she raised herself up. Agnieszka's footwear was tighter than she would have liked, but at least her feet were protected now. Who knew what hazards were lurking in that back alley?

As Charlotte dropped to the ground on the other side, she realised she was no further forward with helping Olli. In fact, things were worse. She knew he was in deadly peril. She saw what they'd done to Piper. And yet she didn't know where he was or what they planned to do with him. She was about to drop to her knees and scream with frustration when she heard a whispered call from the shadows.

'Charlotte, it's me. Don't make a noise. I'm not going to hurt you.'

She recognised the voice immediately: Rex Emery.

CHAPTER FORTY

Charlotte ran at Rex, ready to punch him, so full of anger and helplessness that she could barely contain herself.

'What the hell were you thinking of? Did you hit Will? You've brought the devil to my door...'

'Charlotte, stop, you need to stop,' Rex urged, pulling up his arms to defend himself.

'My son is out there in danger, and you brought this on us, you... you...'

Charlotte could barely speak, like a toddler having a tantrum, so out of control that she couldn't reign herself back in. She knew that she'd implode if she didn't get a grip.

'I'm not to blame,' Rex insisted. 'I promise you, I didn't harm your son, and I had nothing to do with those terrible men, except that they took advantage of me and used my guest house. Do you know who's staying in your home? Do you know what your guests are up to? Barry McMillan hanged himself in your guest house; are you responsible for everything that happens there?'

Charlotte took some deep breaths. Then her phone

vibrated from her canvas bag, still slung over her shoulder. She began to fumble for it in the darkness. Rex moved closer, seeing that she was now much calmer.

'Why are you lurking out here in this alley?' she asked, still not sure of him.

'I was planning on seeing Piper again this evening, but I saw you going into the flats, so I thought I'd better wait for you to come out first. Believe me, I didn't expect to see you here either. When I heard the sirens, I thought I'd been spotted by somebody, so I hid in this alley.'

Charlotte looked at him, unsure what to think.

'They came for me at the guest house earlier on. They were quiet, I didn't even know they were in the building until I heard them whispering outside my room. I had to escape. I'm sorry if they hurt your husband. Is he okay?'

'He was dazed and bruised, but he'll be all right,' Charlotte replied. She'd grabbed Olli's phone in error and was now fumbling for her own while Rex continued his tale.

'I climbed down the drainpipe that runs at the back of the guest house. It's a solid, iron thing; they don't make them like that any more. If they'd found me, they'd have killed me.'

'Why did they hurt Piper?' she asked.

'They hurt Piper?' Rex said, a look of panic washing over his face. 'Is she okay? What did they do to her? I saw the ambulance arriving, but I didn't realise it was Piper's flat they were going to.'

'She's fine. We managed to save her in time. But they've got my son, Olli. He's only eighteen. He was waiting at Piper's flat.'

'Oh my God, when will this end?' Rex gasped, panic now turning to despair.

'Look, Rex, if you know anything, you have to start talking now. Who are these men? What are they protecting?'

'They're Edward Callow's hoodlums...'

'That can't be true,' she interrupted, 'I just left Edward Callow slumped in his car. I don't know if he's dead, but he looked to be in a bad way.'

'He can't be,' Rex said. 'I'm telling you, Edward Callow is behind all this. That bastard used the other four members of the consortium to fuel his business, and now he's too rich to need them, he's finishing them all off.'

'Did you know that Mason Jones is dead?' Charlotte asked.

Rex shook his head in despair. 'Jesus Christ, will that man stop at nothing? That's all four of them gone now, right? He's mopping up his messes, I'm telling you. Whatever you say happened to Edward Callow this evening, I swear, this is his work.'

Charlotte's phone vibrated once again.

'I need to check this,' she said, activating the screen on her phone. Two text messages, both from an unknown number.

We have your son. We need something from you. You help us, you get your son back.

She wanted to scream with relief; at last, some sense was coming of all this. They'd got Olli, but there was a way out. She could get him out alive now.

Rex Emery knows what we want. We know you've been protecting him. Find Rex Emery before 22:32 and reply to this number when you have the package.

Charlotte looked up at Rex.

'What's this package?' she said, her voice cold and

emotionless. There was only one thing standing between her and her son's safety, and that was Rex Emery. If she had to tear his eyes out to get to it, she would. She'd do anything to protect her son.

'It's a video...' he began.

'Is this what Piper was talking about?'

'Yes, probably. Piper must have told them about it if they were threatening her. Poor Piper, she's been through enough. Anyway, that's what Piper and I were doing this afternoon. When I escaped from your guest house, I knew I had to get copies made of the video. It's the only way we can prove what happened back then. I had to make sure they didn't get the only copy. If they found that, I'd go back to prison—maybe even get finished off like everybody else—and Callow would get away with it.'

'You keep blaming Edward Callow, but didn't you hear what I just said? He can't be involved in this. He's on his way to hospital, possibly dead.'

'I can't explain it,' Rex said.

Charlotte could see he seemed genuinely confused.

'Look, I need these videos. I have to save Olli. Where are they?'

Rex Emery shifted uneasily in the darkness. He reached to his coat pocket and pulled something out.

'This is what they want,' he said.

'Is that your only copy?'

'No, we left one copy, and the guy in the shop is making us several more. It's VHS. It takes forever. We stuck around long enough to make sure we got one of the copies, but the master video is still at the shop.'

'You know I have to take that video, don't you?'

'I do,' said Rex.

He handed it to her. It was wrapped in a tatty plastic bag, but she grabbed it from him like it was the cure to a deadly illness.

I have to text them back, let them know I've got it. She glanced at the time on her phone; it was a little after nine o'clock, plenty of time.

I have the package. Give me my son.

Rex Emery watched as she keyed in the letters.

Her phone vibrated almost immediately, as if the people who were holding Olli were waiting for her.

Leave it under the slide at the play area near West End Gardens. Come alone. We'll be watching. Call the police, and your son dies. Text us when you're at the play area.

Charlotte held up the phone so that Rex Emery could read the message.

'I can't go with you,' he said. 'They'll kill me if they see me. You have to go alone.'

'Where will you hide?' Charlotte asked. 'What will you do?'

'I'll sleep rough for a few days, then first thing on Monday morning I'm going to that video store to pick up the copies. There's a boarded-up shop around the corner by the old church, on the sea front. It's not far from where you're heading now. I can hide in there. I promise you I'll walk into Morecambe Police station myself and hand those videos over. You do what you have to do to save your son.'

Charlotte took one last look at him, trying to work out if she trusted him. She had no choice.

'One last thing,' Rex said, before walking away. 'That time they gave you, 22:32. That's a tide time. You don't spend as many years as I did printing out the timetables and hanging them up in the lounge of a guest house and forget that stuff. The time they gave you is high tide, I'll put money on it. They probably have him somewhere near the sea. Take care, Charlotte. Those men are ruthless.'

Charlotte began to run the full length of the alleyway, keen to emerge well away from the ambulance and inevitable police crew. The Battery was not so far. They'd chosen a secluded place, with a play area set in a dip away from the promenade. She'd leave the video where they asked and get Olli back. Then—and only then—would she speak to the police.

Ten minutes later, she was at the play area. She'd have made it faster if her foot wasn't so sore. The tight plimsolls were pinching her toes, and she could feel her skin rubbing raw.

It was quiet and alone there. She placed the bag underneath the play equipment, aware that she was being monitored. She looked around, but could see nobody. It made her shiver to think that the same men who'd taken her son and tried to kill Piper, were probably watching her at that very moment.

Having placed the bag in the exact location, she looked around, not knowing what to do. Her phone vibrated in her hand.

Walk away. Walk towards the Midland Hotel. When we verify the package, you'll get your son.

'You bastards, tell me where my son is!' she shouted into the chill night air.

She began to walk out of the park, up to the promenade, and along the same strip that she'd run with Daisy twelve hours earlier. Exhaustion was setting in; she couldn't take much more of this.

As she neared the Midland Hotel, she could see that there were still police officers on the scene close to where she'd left Edward Callow. She ducked to the side, keen to stay clear of the area. For all she knew, she was a fugitive. Her phone vibrated again.

We have the package. You'll find your son at the end of the stone jetty. Be quick. The tide is rising.

CHAPTER FORTY-ONE

To Charlotte, the tides were just something that came and went. Like the sun and the moon, they punctuated her days, but she took little notice of the details. Now those very tides held the key to her son's life.

She rushed to the fence which ran the entire length of the promenade and stared out into the bay. The light had long gone, but the reflections of the street lamps along the stone jetty showed her all she needed to know. The high tide might be in one hour's time, but the water was already coming in and rising fast.

To reach the stone jetty, she had to pass the Midland Hotel, where the police were active at the side of the rotunda. The alternative was to walk all the way around the hotel and make her approach from the other side. That still took her directly past the rotunda, but she'd have to risk it.

The irony of the lifeboat station being directly opposite the hotel was not lost on her, but there was no way she was leaving Olli while they assembled the crew and launched the boat. She thought quickly. She was committed to the long walk along the stone jetty. She'd been along there already, earlier that morning. Where had they left Olli? Was he near the rocks that marked the end of the jetty, where they'd often watched the waves crashing on their numerous walks along the sea front?

She committed to her plan. While she was running the length of the jetty, she'd call Nigel, then Will. They could alert the police and lifeguard while she was searching for Olli.

Charlotte took out her phone and slung the bag over the edge on a fence post. It would only encumber her. She began to hurry past the Midland Hotel, burying the phone into the right side of her face to conceal herself. She called Nigel, who was eager to hear from her.

'Where did you get to? All hell has broken loose in here. DCI Summers is working overtime, and they've taken Edward Callow...'

'Nigel, I don't care. You need to listen and do what I say. Olli's life depends on it. You have to alert the lifeboat and tell them that Olli is out at the end of the stone jetty somewhere. Do that now. Then, in five minutes time, I need you to speak to DCI Summers and tell her to send her officers to the end of the jetty. She'll get all the explanations she needs if she does that, and she'll find me there.'

'But Charlotte...'

'Just do it, Nigel, we'll speak later.'

She ended the call.

She'd passed the rotunda now. The police officers were too busy to even care about her, assuming that she was just another member of the public out on an evening walk.

The sea breeze rushed over her, making her shiver in her unsuitable clothes. She began to jog, clicking the autodial to get in contact with Will.

'Charlotte, where are you?' he asked.

He sounded brighter, thank goodness.

'Will, I know where Olli is, but he's still in danger. I need you to alert the lifeboat, just in case Nigel doesn't...'

'What the hell is going on?' He appeared sharper over the phone; that was a good sign.

'I don't have time to talk,'

'I need to tell you something...'

'Will, it has to wait! Alert the lifeboat and get over to the stone jetty as soon as you can. Do it now!'

She paused a moment, uncertain whether to say it. She'd seen what these people could do.

'I love you, Will. Whatever happens, remember I love you and the kids.'

'But Charlotte, what are you doing?'

'Call the lifeguard, Will. Now.'

She ended the call and dropped her phone on the ground. If Nigel did as he was told, she had a head start on the police. It would save the endless explanation and delay. The lifeboat crew would get at least one call, if not two, so however this played out now, help was on its way. It was the best she could do in the time that she had.

Fishing boats bobbed about in the sea at her side as she prayed that she would find Olli somewhere safe, perhaps at the rear of the café or tied to the fencing at the jetty's edge. But they could have secured him among the heavy rocks which surrounded the jetty, where local fishermen often set up their equipment when the tide was low.

As she reached the Stone Jetty Café, she called Olli's name. Would they gag him? Probably; the jetty was a public area. They'd have to conceal him somewhere out of view.

She rushed to the rear of the café, calling his name, checking he wasn't hidden in the shadows. There was no sign of him. Growing more desperate, Charlotte began to run as fast as she could towards the end of the jetty, ignoring the pain of the tight shoes and the cut in her foot.

Just before the final section of the jetty was a circular area, much like an asphalt roundabout, from which two concrete platforms ran, suspended over the rocks below and shooting out towards the sea. Had they left Olli at the end of either of these? Charlotte paused a moment, fretting over her three choices at this fork; left, right, or straight ahead?

There were still a few people walking along the jetty. How would a killer think? Where would they have secured Olli? It had to be the head of the jetty, below the platform that reached out into the sea. It had to be.

Charlotte continued to run ahead, aiming straight for the end of the jetty. But as she reached the narrow pathway that would take her there, she realised that the tide was already high. Her only accessible route, without leaping into the water, was to climb over the fence and scramble along the rocks so she could access the space beneath the platform. Olli had to be there. It was the only place that made sense.

She climbed over the fence at the point where the water was now washing over the tops of the rocks.

'Hey, careful luv, it's dangerous out there!'

A middle-aged couple were walking hand in hand just ahead of her.

'When the police come, tell them this is where I am,' she shouted at him.

'Jesus bloody Christ, Hilda, I think she's topping herself!'

Charlotte ignored the man as he ran towards her.

'You can't even swim, Frank! Be careful...' his wife shouted after him.

The wind and the waves were all Charlotte could hear

now, and they seemed even wilder out there. She struggled to find her footing amid the heavy rocks, their hazardous gaps waiting to catch her feet in the dark. She was in the icy cold water already. It was swirling around her knees, making the bottom of her dress heavy and wet.

To her right she could see the flashing lights of the lifeboat being readied for launch. Help would come soon, but would it be too late?

As the stones tapered lower towards the sea, the water came higher up her body, past her waist.

'Olli!' she shouted, straining in the dark to find her son.

A life belt hit the water somewhere nearby, and she looked up at the fencing high above her. She'd quickly moved from the safety of the jetty, with nothing now to support her, blindly making her way across water-covered rocks towards the furthest end of the viewing platform.

'Hang onto that, luv; we've called for help!'

Although Charlotte had heard about the currents of the bay, she'd barely paid any attention, but she could feel the force of the water swirling all around her, tussling with her body as she struggled to stay upright on the rocks. She was at the side of the platform now, the metal supports looming above her. Olli had to be there. If he wasn't, she didn't know what to do next. Then, she saw something; a silhouette moving ahead of her. It was a head, thrashing around in the water, directly in front of her. It had to be him.

'Olli, it's Mum! I'm coming...' she began to shout, but a powerful wave washed across her face, filling her mouth with water and catching her mid breath. In a panic, she slid on the rock that she was standing on, ducking into the water. Now completely immersed, she thrashed her legs around, frantically trying to find a place where she could stand again.

The currents were pulling her one way then another, like spiteful children arguing over who should have a toy. As she found her footing, she snorted seawater out of her nose and mouth, spluttering uncontrollably as she found her breath once again.

Olli didn't have long. Forcing her legs downwards, Charlotte found a rock. She'd been pulled closer to the iron framework which supported the viewing platform at the end of the jetty. With all her might, she thrust her body at one of the heavy posts ahead of her, trying to get a firm grip. She caught it and clung on for dear life.

She could see Olli now in the reflections of moonlight on the water under the platform. He'd seen her too, his eyes terrified and ablaze with fear. His mouth had been taped, and he was fighting to draw breath through his nose as the waves crashed around him.

Charlotte waited for the swell to subside, then forced herself towards her son, reaching out and grasping him.

'I'm here, Olli. I'm so sorry...'

She tore the tape from his mouth. He took a big gasp of air, but a wave washed over him, submerging him.

As the water rolled back, he coughed and spluttered, while Charlotte fought desperately to find the ties that secured him to the bottom of the viewing platform. She found them under the water with her cold, numb fingers. They'd used secure, plastic ties, and there was no way she could release those without a knife or scissors.

'I'm scared Mum, help me. I can't get out of these ties...'

'I can't cut them, Olli. They're too secure...'

A wave crashed over their heads, submerging them both for over twenty seconds. Once the water subsided, they had a moment to fight for their breath, but it returned as quickly as it went. Charlotte could feel herself weakening, the strength wrestled out of her by the sea.

'I don't want to die, Mum... I'm scared.'

As another wave crashed over them, she could feel her son's body shaking uncontrollably, through fear and cold.

'It's okay, Olli. I'm with you... I'll stay with you. I would never leave you on your own.'

CHAPTER FORTY-TWO

'She's back with us.'

Charlotte could barely move her stiff, cold hands and her lungs were burning as if somebody had just poured molten lead down them. She was wrapped in a silver foil blanket and paramedics bustled all around her, focused and intent on their work.

'Take your time, my darling,' the man said. 'You've had one hell of a night out there.'

In the distance, she could hear Will protesting. Even with all that activity around her, she could pick out his voice.

'That's my wife and my son, let me through. It was me who alerted the rescue crew...'

'Where's Olli?' she asked, but her voice felt like it had been shredded, and it was hard to make herself heard.

The medic put his ear close to her face.

'My son. Where is he?'

'It was a close thing, my darling, but you saved him. We found you in there pushing his head up above the water. He was out cold. You did a good thing tonight. You kept him alive until we could get to you.'

Charlotte sobbed with relief. Those final minutes were a blur, apart from the flashing of the orange lights from the lifeboat, and her desperate hope that if she could just keep their heads out of the water for a few more precious minutes, they'd reach them in time. She couldn't remember anything after that.

Where was she? As far as she could tell, she was lying down on a stretcher, but she could still see and hear the sea. She forced her eyes into focus and saw that the jetty was to her right. They must have moved her near the lifeboat building, so the ambulances could get to her. Their flashing blue lights illuminated the entire area, overwhelming her.

'Here, we've got your phone,' a female medic said, tucking it at her side. 'You might need that when you get to hospital. Some guy who'd been walking along the jetty just gave it to one of my colleagues. He said you'd dropped it earlier. It looks like there's been a lot of people trying to contact you. You've a lot of messages waiting.'

A familiar voice rang out. 'I'm her husband. Are they both all right? My son's wrists are red raw; what happened to him?'

Will appeared at her side, reaching for her hand.

'Charlotte, what the hell happened? Are you okay?'

She tried to speak again. This time her voice had a little more power.

'They got Olli. Those bastards nearly killed our son. Is he okay?'

'He's fine. They're taking him to hospital now. I think you'll be next in the ambulance. His wrists are raw where they've been tied. He looks terrible.'

'They wanted to kill him, Will. They won't stop, these people. They just won't stop.'

'I've got to tell you something,' Will began. 'I know it's not the best time to say it, but they're going to take you to hospital, and I won't be able to speak to you for a while.'

'Tell me,' she whispered. 'And check my phone. Lucia might have tried to get in touch.'

She moved her hand to show him where the phone had been tucked away. Will took it, talking as he began scrolling through the messages.

'I was piecing that photograph together while you were gone. It took me some time, but I got there in the end. That's what I want to talk to you about. And something you need to know about George, too.

'Why were you speaking to George?' Charlotte asked, struggling to keep her mind on a single train of thought.

'He came round to collect Isla. While she was setting up the dining room, he sidled up to me and confided in me. Has he spoken to you already? He said you'd been asking lots of questions.'

'No, what is it? I don't know anything about George. Is he okay?'

'No. He's had a cancer diagnosis. He doesn't know how to break the news to Isla. He was asking my advice.'

'Oh no, poor George. I suspected it might be something like that. Poor Isla too, so soon after they found each other. She thought he was hiding something.'

'Don't be so fast with your sympathy for Isla,' Will continued, his eyes darting between Charlotte and the phone screen.

'Why ever not?' she replied, her voice rasping. She just wanted to rest now.

'That photograph, you know the fourth person that you

couldn't identify? The one who was there when that poor girl was being abused or whatever disgusting things they were doing to her? Isla was there. That fourth person is Isla. She knew all about it, Charlotte, and she said nothing.'

Charlotte closed her eyes and her head sunk into the small pillow that she'd been given for support. She couldn't take it in; it was too much information, too soon. She needed to rest.

'There's a voice mail from Lucia,' Will said, turning back to the phone. 'I tried to find her with my tracking app earlier, but her phone must have been switched off. Do you use a code on this thing?'

Charlotte shook her head.

'At least she's okay. Here, I'll play it on speaker so you can hear it before they take you to the hospital. At least you'll know she's safe.

Mum? It's Lucia. I'm sorry, Mum. I should have told you when you asked. I'm in trouble, mum. I need help. Please call me when you get this. I don't know what they're going to do to me.

Find out how the story ends in book 3, Truth Be Told.

AUTHOR NOTES

Phew! What an adventure for poor old Charlotte. There's much more to come too; the story isn't over yet. In the third and final instalment of the trilogy, all the secrets will be revealed and the loose ends tied up. There are a lot of them to sort out too.

When I wrote Left for Dead, I'd intended to leave it as a standalone. My original intention was to turn the Morecambe Bay books into a series, bringing forward characters like Nigel Davies and DCI Kate Summers to have their own adventures.

However, when I began the plotting process, I realised that there was a nice trilogy lurking just below the surface. It only took one person to be looking for Bruce Craven - in this case his half-sister - and for Bruce to be involved in something much more sinister than his bad behaviour at Sandy Beaches Holiday Camp - and you've got all the makings of a deep, dark story.

I have now moved well away from the holiday camp location of the first book to draw from Morecambe's more general landscape. In this book, I make a lot of use of The

Midland Hotel, which you can't miss on any visit to the resort. It sits half-way along the promenade and is an excellent example of art deco styling. Make sure you pop in for afternoon tea if you're in the area.

I have a policy when I write thrillers never to feature murders or terrible events in real-life places; I'm not entirely sure the owners would thank me for it. Instead, I save the gruesome bits for fictional locations, like Charlotte and Will's guest house. Having said that, I did finish off Fred Walker in one of the theatrical boxes at the Winter Gardens. I felt that location, so famous and grand, deserved to have a fictional death based there, I do hope that all theatre lovers will forgive my indulgence.

I decided to incorporate a parkrun in this book at the suggestion of my wife. Just before I wrote this trilogy, while I was researching locations, we stayed in a guest house on Morecambe front, opposite The Battery, another location which features in this story. Not only is Will and Charlotte's guest house based upon our stay in this building—I took lots of research photos while we were there—I also took part in the Morecambe parkrun during our stay.

Being an author is a sedentary lifestyle, so in 2018 I decided to find a way of getting and staying fit. The parkrun is how I chose to do that, and it's worked out very well for me as a writer; it means I can integrate research trips with Saturday morning runs in all sorts of interesting places.

The description of parkrun is as accurate as I can make it; it was a great suggestion from my wife incorporating a chase scene in among the runners at a time when Morecambe Promenade is at its most crowded. By the way, if you're that way inclined, I recommend the free, weekly event in the resort, I hope to run there again sometime soon.

I was delighted to bring in another character from my

Don't Tell Meg trilogy, this time the enigmatic Steven Terry. Steven features heavily in that short series, and I love his character so much, I was keen to give him a cameo in this book. He and DCI Summers know each other as a consequence of the events that take place in Don't Tell Meg and having him touring the country allows him to pop up wherever I need him.

He's based on a guest we used to have in the studios at BBC Radio Humberside when I worked as a journalist there. I can't remember the chap's name now, but I recall a member of staff coming back from speaking to him, shaken by what he'd told her. My wife also used to work with a woman who saw things, and I know that despite her instinctive cynicism, my wife was fascinated by the whole thing and refused to dismiss it as nonsense.

I try not to make a judgement about Steven Terry, instead using him as a catalyst in the story. I also went to see a clairvoyant in my home town to make sure I was depicting him fairly, and I have to say I find the whole thing intriguing.

The tides of Morecambe Bay feature in this story's dramatic conclusion and this storyline is based very much on knowledge that I gained around a national news story which featured the tragic deaths of at least 21 Chinese labourers who were drowned by the tides whilst picking cockles along that coastline.

I have also been aware—through my radio work—of the man who has safely guided walkers across the bay for many years, using his intimate knowledge of the sea's rhythms to keep them safe. Cedric Robinson eventually retired after 56 years of guiding walkers across the bay, and it was a remarkable achievement.

There are also sinking sands across the bay, so it all

makes for a terrifying prospect for Charlotte, who has to brave the incoming tides to try to save her son. Never be deceived by its beauty; the bay is a dangerous place, best navigated by those who are familiar with it.

My apologies to you if you hate cliff-hangers, but this series is billed as a trilogy, and I want to keep you turning the pages as the tension mounts in this story. I have intentionally left lots of loose ends, and I promise that these will all tie up neatly in the final book, Truth Be Told.

These loose ends include George's health bombshell, what really happened to Edward Callow, the storm clouds gathering over Lucia, and the small matter of Daisy Bowker, who refuses to stop looking for her missing half-brother.

Isla is also in the middle of a whirlwind in the final pages of this story. We have the plotline with Rex Emery and Piper to resolve and, of course, you'll want to find out if Charlotte and Will get away with what they did all those years ago at the Sandy Beaches Holiday Camp. Oh, and Jenna, Piper and Abi will make a re-appearance too; I couldn't leave them out of the action.

Truth Be Told will follow the pattern of the first book; it will reveal the secrets of the past alongside the dramatic storyline that is set in the present. I'll reveal the stories of the men who died in this book, and you'll be able to decide for yourself if they got what they deserved. If you want a hint of what's going to happen, the clue is in the title: Truth Be Told. The only question is, who will be left alive and what price will have to be paid for past mistakes?

You'll find several image galleries and links to Morecambe websites over at https://paulteague.co.uk, the home of my thriller books written under Paul J. Teague.

If you liked this story and want to stay in touch, I'll be delighted if you register for my email updates at https://paulteague.net/thrillers, as that's where I share news of what I'm writing and tell you about any reader discounts and freebies that are available.

Thanks so much for reading Circle of Lies and I look forward to connecting with you soon.

All the best,
Paul Teague

ABOUT THE AUTHOR

Hi, I'm Paul Teague, the author of the Don't Tell Meg trilogy as well as several other standalone psychological thrillers such as One Last Chance, Dead of Night and No More Secrets.

I'm a former broadcaster and journalist with the BBC, but I have also worked as a primary school teacher, a disc jockey, a shopkeeper, a waiter and a sales rep.

I've read thrillers all my life, starting with Enid Blyton's Famous Five series as a child, then graduating to James Hadley Chase, Harlan Coben, Linwood Barclay and Mark Edwards.

If you love those authors then you'll like my thrillers too.

Let's get connected!
https://paulteague.co.uk
paul@paulteague.com

This is a work of fiction. Names, characters, businesses, places, events and incidents are either the products of the author's imagination or used in a fictitious manner. Any resemblance to actual persons, living or dead, or actual events is purely coincidental.

All rights reserved. No part of this book may be reproduced or transmitted in any form or by any electronic or mechanical means, including photocopying, recording or by any information storage and retrieval system, without the written permission of the Author, except where permitted by law.

Copyright © 2020 Paul Teague writing as Paul J. Teague

All rights reserved

Printed in Poland
by Amazon Fulfillment
Poland Sp. z o.o., Wrocław